Happy Borthde

DARK
CURRENTS
—

DARK
CURRENTS

———

A NOVEL OF ARUBA INSPIRED BY ACTUAL EVENTS

DANIEL
PUTKOWSKI

HAWSER
PRESS

HAWSER
P R E S S

Although inspired in part by a true incident, the following story is fictional and does not depict any actual person or event. Names, characters, places and incidents are products of the author's imagination or are used fictitiously. Any resemblance to actual events or locales or persons, living or dead, is entirely coincidental.

ISBN 978-0-9815959-3-1

FIRST HAWSER PRESS TRADE PAPERBACK EDITION JUNE 2012
10 9 8 7 6 5 4 3 2 1

facebook.com/DanielPutkowski
DanielPutkowski.com

When justice is done,
it brings joy to the righteous
but terror to evildoers.

———

PROVERBS 21:15

An Island Away

Bonk's Bar

Universal Coverage

Under a Blue Flag

AUTHOR'S NOTE

On a dry August day in 2011, I was sitting in a bar in San Nicolaas, Aruba, making the most of the shade, and taking in the local gossip. A sad rumor was circulating that afternoon about an American tourist—a woman—gone missing while snorkeling with a boyfriend at a spot not three miles from my barstool. By the end of the week, the story was changing, fingers were pointing at the boyfriend, and a police investigation was underway. The tragic and highly publicized 2005 disappearance of Natalee Holloway all but guaranteed another media frenzy. It didn't take long. Within days most major networks were reporting the scattered details of a missing Maryland woman, her questionable male companion, a suspicious life insurance policy, and a snorkel trip gone awry.

As someone who knows the island well—particularly the rugged, less-populated southern end where this drama was unfolding—I assisted NBC's *TODAY* show and even got some facetime on the show's August 31 broadcast. You may have also seen video footage I supplied to CNN and Fox News, including some of the lone suspect's release after four months in Aruban custody. No body, no charges, no answers. We were all left to wonder: was this really a case of accidental drowning or something else?

We may never know what happened in August 2011 in the waters near a secluded strip of Aruban terrain. The following pages are fiction and in no way speculate on the actual case.

1

Kathy Barrow never planned to kill anyone, and she sure as hell never expected to get away with it. But on her way through the airport, returning home to collect one point five million dollars in insurance money, she couldn't help but smile. She never would've done it if he hadn't tried to kill her first. She would have scared him, taught him a lesson, but he would have survived. As it turned out, he had plans of his own, a scenario she never considered because she was used to being in charge of these things.

She'd done it twice before, and the thrill was like winning the lottery. Not exactly because it wasn't money she was after, but rather the kick she got from watching these big, tough guys struggle, nearly drown, and ultimately have to cling to her for their lives. The desperation in their eyes, the complete loss of control, the plea for help, all gave her a sense of power that was as addictive as some of the drugs she metered out as part of her job as a pharmacy technician. She knew what those chemicals did to the human body. She'd gone to school for pharmacology, not all the way because she'd run out of money. Still, she learned enough in college and later during continuing education classes sponsored by the company for which she worked. Then there were the visits by the sales reps from the drug manufacturers. That's when the real information changed hands. The reps knew the off-label effects better than anyone. She swore some of the more kooky reps tested the stuff on themselves. There was one who tried to maintain a four-hour erection with a pill his outfit developed. He claimed to have succeeded and wanted to prove it to her if she was willing. The schmuck had no idea how close he'd come to one of her little games. The problem was, he didn't meet her other requirements.

As far as Kathy knew, Doug, the sales rep, was just a pig. He got off telling lewd jokes to women he knew would blush. Kathy didn't blush no matter how hard he tried. At one point, he asked if she was going to turn him in for sexual harassment. She laughed in his face. She was a lot tougher than he realized, which is another reason why she passed him over. With him it would be too easy.

She searched for bad boys. Not the kind with tattoos and greasy hair or a Ferrari and fifty speeding tickets. Her criteria were specific. The first requirement was a restraining order for physical abuse. One was good; two was better. Three was too many. And they had to be requested by an ex-wife or girlfriend as opposed to co-workers or someone they beat up at a bar for sloshing a drink on a favorite shirt. Second, he had to be handsome, the kind of man who normally wouldn't pay her much attention. In the mirror Kathy saw the twenty pounds she needed to lose and her slightly lopsided right eye that skewed the symmetry of her face. She learned to keep a date on her left as often as possible. From that side, she was better than average with a tall enough frame to give her an athletic appeal that sometimes obscured those extra pounds. Nonetheless, an arrogant guy who tended to his own good looks typically approached women more attractive than her. Therein she found the third criteria, the challenge. If he seemed too eager, she moved on. She didn't like things that were easy, and contrary to what many men said about cavorting with any willing female, it was hard to get somebody handsome and well-built to take her to bed without serious effort.

She'd been working on two men simultaneously when Glenn Hogan's name first came up. She read about him in the paper while eating lunch. *Borough Man Avoids Trial* was the headline. The next few sentences explained that Glenn agreed to a restraining order and a month of community service rather than go to trial on assault charges related to an incident with his soon-to-be ex-wife, with whom he claimed to be trying to reunite. In her follow-up research, Kathy learned her target, recently separately from his wife, Janice, had gone to her house where he forced his way in, shouted at her for fifteen minutes for giving his suits to the Goodwill store, and then socked her in the eye for telling him it was her money that had bought the suits in the first place. Janice had also paid for much of Glenn's night school, where he earned a degree required to gain a promotion at the Pennsylvania Bureau of Licenses and Inspections. He did move up; he was now a building inspector with the authority to declare elevators fit or unfit for service. The problem was his wife found out about Jill, the woman he met while getting that degree. Glenn also made the mistake of not telling Jill about Janice, which left him with a pending divorce, no girlfriend, an empty closet, and plenty of anger to land him in court making a plea deal in order to save his job.

He was perfect for Kathy, not only because he passed all her tests, but because he reminded her so much of her father. Glenn shined his shoes, had friends at local diners, and was the nicest guy to his pals at the microbrewery where he hung out every Sunday afternoon. This was her father, everybody's pal, the first person to buy a round and the one to call if you couldn't get your car started. But if you were his wife or his daughter, you were a pain in the ass. You were expensive and stupid and always in the way of what he wanted to do. When you misread his mood, you got a slap. When you made him the same thing for dinner that he had for lunch, you got a shove. When you asked for something you really needed—this was his favorite—you got a twisted arm and a lecture about what things cost. You learned to ask for nothing because you were too busy giving him what you thought he wanted.

It wasn't until Kathy was a sophomore in high school that she fully realized what a bastard her father was. He would have the occasional cocktail but wasn't a heavy drinker. In fact, she never remembered seeing him drunk. However, on one particular Friday he came in the back door, walked past her grumbling, and gave off a whiff of Scotch. Like all teenagers, she'd experimented with alcohol and knew the aroma. Even before her father broke the news that night, she knew it was going to be bad. Laid off, he said, permanently. It was about time she and her mother did something to support him for a change.

He never worked again. About the only thing he did for them was die conveniently of a heart attack four years later.

The crying at the funeral was remarkable in that it was limited to those not related to him. All his friends, the ones to whom he spent his last years bragging about how his wife supported him, those were the people sad to see him go. Who was going to repair their lawn mowers? Who was going to help them build a deck? Who was going to give them a ride to the airport and save the cab fare? Their old pal was gone and he died so young. What a shame!

Kathy helped clean out her father's things, including his shiny shoes and tailored suits, all of which went into the trash. She almost suggested donating them like Janice had done more recently, but at the last second, she stopped short. Kathy doubled-bagged the garments, carefully stowing them in the cans at the curb to make sure they would travel to the dump unseen. Perhaps the women of this family could find peace if every last remnant of this man were buried.

At first, she thought her father hadn't affected her. Kathy saw herself as smarter than him, wiser. She was above it. More important, she was happy. She lived a good life, in a place of her own, paid for with money she earned through an important job. People liked her. Decent men asked her out on dates. And yet, she was haunted by the reality that she'd never done anything to help her mother. The fun she enjoyed felt like a guilty pleasure, like she was sneaking a candy bar in the middle of the night. Her mother worked as an accounting clerk at Four Star Beverage, wasting her weekend nights watching reruns of *Seinfeld* and *Friends*, while Kathy went to nightclubs or fancy dinners or the theater.

They spent Sunday afternoons together. Sometimes it was a quaint lunch in Philadelphia, other times a movie at a suburban multiplex. These outings went smoothly but her mother always seemed distracted. No doubt she was pleased to be socializing, but there was a consistent lack of joy in her mood and this Kathy blamed on her father. He spoiled the relationship by driving in a wedge where there should have been a bond. He left behind two damaged women who had been forced to put him above everything, rendering them incapable of dealing with each other. His miserable burden had been the lone thing they shared, which left them with little in common once he was gone.

Kathy understood this only after her mother had a debilitating stroke. Instead of the casual Sundays ranging around Philadelphia and the suburbs, their meetings took place in the lounge at Clearwater Lodge, a nursing and rehabilitation home. Sitting with her mother, who was now unable to speak but a few tortured syllables, Kathy grew ever more angry at what both of them had missed. No photos together on prom night. No arguments over provocative attire. No botched cooking experiments in the kitchen. Her father confined their memories to his diatribes, insults, and occasional backhanded compliments.

Worst of all, she blamed herself. She should have intervened, not for herself, but for her mother. Counseling was offered at school for such situations. She never stepped into the office to ask for help. Why not? Embarrassment for one thing. Fear of retribution for another. Her father wasn't afraid to use his hands to make a point now and then. Once he smacked her mother, and Kathy leapt off her seat at the table. The glare he gave her meant she was next. He also had friends who would never believe him to be that kind of man. She grasped this reality implicitly. He was the kid with good grades who framed his dim-witted buddy for a prank. Who tossed a firecracker in the boys' toilet? Not Johnny Barrow. He's the president of the chess club. That was her father. She'd been a coward. She let him get away with it.

Which brought her to Glenn Hogan and the others before him. She wasn't afraid of them. Not one bit. She put the fear into them the way she should have done to her father. Back then she wasn't a pharmacy technician with access to expired yet potent drugs. She wasn't strong enough because she hadn't spent any time in the gym learning self-defense. And she wasn't clever enough to plot out every move so that she could watch the plan unfold like a good movie.

Seeing her mother waste away motivated Kathy to do something about the past. She falsified the records for disposing of those expired drugs, sweated at least part of her ass off at the gym to build some new muscle and to practice Tae Kwon Do moves, and studied a fair number of novels to master the rudiments of getting even.

Revenge wasn't what she wanted, nor was it punishment. Her father was gone; there was nothing she could do to him. These men she selected, she didn't care if they learned a lesson or not. Her motive was simpler, if a bit maniacal. She craved that moment of total control when these scumbags, who were used to lording abusive authority over everyone, suddenly found themselves powerless. Their fate was in her hands. It was life or death and they knew it, too, because Kathy saw the fear in their eyes, the realization that they needed her in order to survive.

She underestimated the thrill of these moments. It was better than anything she'd ever experienced, addictive as well, like those drugs on the top shelf with the warning pamphlets in six languages. When she first pulled it off with Phil Ryan, she rode a wave of joy that lasted a month. Margie, the pharmacist she worked with most often, wanted to know if she'd won the Powerball. Not quite, was the answer Kathy gave, but it had been a win.

Phil earned his restraining orders by punching out two girlfriends with left hooks. He bought his suits at Nordstroms. He fine-tuned his skin with Clinique products. He also begged for salvation when he lost control in the water off Cape May last summer. His muscles cramped, or so he claimed. He went down then popped up like those plastic bobbers fishermen used. Sputtering, he called to Kathy for help. She played like he was making a joke, trying to lure her close for a dunking.

"What's the matter? Can't swim in the deep water with the big kids?" she taunted him.

"H-h-help me," he said.

She circled halfway around him. "Didn't they teach you to doggie paddle in gym class?"

"S-s-stop it! This is real." Phil went under and didn't come up right away.

For a second, Kathy thought she'd given him too much of her special concoction, what used to be called a *mickey,* in his beer earlier.

"Ahhh," he moaned as soon as his head broke the surface. He was angry at this point, struggling against the power of the drugs he didn't know were affecting his normally robust muscles. Seconds later, he panicked.

Kathy surged forward. She got her arm under his then across his chest and eased him on his back. She used a modified side-stroke to swim to shore, just as they had taught her in the life-saving class at her gym. When they arrived in water shallow enough to stand, she dragged Phil up onto the beach where he remained motionless for some time. Checking his eyes, she saw he was conscious, although frightened out of his wits.

"You okay?" she asked.

He didn't answer.

Phil regained his faculties about an hour later, but he felt weak and nauseous and couldn't remember what happened.

"You almost drowned, buddy," Kathy told him as if she were addressing a little boy.

She altered the dose for the next guy, AJ Trent, using a little less but still getting the desired result in the Bahamas, where AJ took her for a weekend mini-vacation. Despite a one-round boxing match with an ex-wife over splitting his 401(k), AJ nearly lost his life in the pool at the Atlantis Resort when his body gave up on him. He was lucky Kathy was there, because it was two o'clock in the morning and no one else was around. Despite these realities, she saw the confusion, frustration, and ultimately the terror in his eyes, illuminated by a full moon.

"Those margaritas pack one hell of a wallop," he told Kathy later.

"You have to be careful, AJ. I could've lost you," she replied.

She lost him a couple weeks later. Rather, she ditched him for Glenn Hogan, her latest mark, the one that she found in the newspaper.

Everything went perfectly with Glenn: The build-up to romance, his assertion as the one in charge of the relationship, a trip to Aruba, ostensibly to show off his gambling skills at the casinos as well as to enjoy some awesome beaches and great weather. She went along for the ride, using the experience gained in her two previous encounters to fine tune her approach. Glenn made it easy, booking a snorkel trip aboard a sailboat named *Consuela*, to prove he was a big spender. It took them to view pristine sea life. She would have pulled her stunt then and there, but the crew supervised their every moment. She bided her time, asking Glenn if they could go snorkeling again, this time entering the water from a nearby beach.

"Sure," Glenn agreed. "Why not?"

Looking back, she should have suspected he was up to something. He agreed without hesitation to a jaunt far from their hotel for nothing more than a glimpse at coral and fish they'd seen before, but she was too engrossed in her own plot to consider the possibility of another one. Furthermore, he bought snorkel gear at the hotel gift shop, paying an outrageous price for equipment likely to be used only once.

"What's a credit card for?" he'd crowed.

After a hotel lunch, they drove their rented car to the southern end of the island, parking on the spit of land they'd seen from the *Consuela*. In the trunk, Glenn had a small cooler loaded with ice and beer, another purchase from the gift shop that morning.

"Have to be prepared to enjoy ourselves," Glenn had said.

Kathy offered to get him one of those beers. Removing a tiny plastic vile hidden and held in place by the elastic of her bathing suit, she spiked Glenn's beer with her knockout pills before handing it over. They sat in the car, windows down, sipping beer, gazing at the waves, soaking up what should have been a romantic moment. Anxious to get in the water before the drugs took effect, Kathy cut it short. She got out, pulled off her dress, and made her way through the rocks toward the shore. Behind her, Glenn fumbled with the snorkels until he finally caught up.

They weren't in the water long before Glenn loomed over her. He wasn't pointing out fish or coral; he was grabbing for her, trying to hold on with a brutal grip. Kathy wiggled away, ducking under the water and pushing off his mid-section with one foot. Suddenly her ankle was locked in his right hand, which squeezed so tight it hurt. Trying to turn over, her head dipped down and water filled her snorkel. This kind of play was rougher than she expected, but she didn't panic. Soon the drugs would have him, and he'd be limp as a dishrag.

Kicking back with her other foot, she struck Glenn squarely in the chest. He released her, but now both his hands were free. She coughed out seawater and backstroked away to no avail. He was on her before she moved a few feet, with his arms around her.

They both sank again, this time he pressed atop her shoulders with those wide palms of his, holding her under the water with the weight of his body. Kathy squirmed back and forth, but he held fast. As her breath ran short, she realized her mistake. In a flash, she recalled every clue signaling his true intentions. Later she would remember more. At the moment, she did what she had to do to survive.

Kathy pushed her hands up at his mask, driving the base of her palm into Glenn's nose. His hands released. As soon as they did, she kicked hard, propelling herself to the surface. Gulping air, she twisted, catching sight of the dive shop not far from where they parked. Between her and it was Glenn, furious and coming for her. Frantic, she used all her strength to stroke arm over arm, pulling herself forward. Then she felt his hand on her foot again, not as strong as before. She broke free with wild kicks and swam as fast as she could.

It might have been a minute or five, she wasn't sure, until she looked for him again. She pulled off her mask and snorkel, letting them drop into the sea, giving her a clear view of the surface. Treading water, she scanned the horizon. Nothing. Then his head appeared twenty yards distant. She turned to swim farther away before checking his progress again. The drugs were slowing him down. Kathy kept an eye on him and the distance to shore. She noticed him dipping under the waves, as if he was trying to touch the bottom. It's getting to him, she thought, he's feeling fatigued. He glanced back at the beach, then pulled up his own mask and looked in her direction.

"Come back!" he called.

No way, Kathy told herself. He wasn't playing around when he held her shoulders down. Both the power of his hands and his crazed eyes behind the mask signaled vicious intentions. He was trying to kill her, and she knew part of the reason why. Instinct drove her in the opposite direction, parallel to shore and far from Glenn. She spotted him moving toward the beach with weak movements, his arms slapping the water. She didn't care if he drowned. All she wanted to do was get away from him. If he didn't make it, that was his problem.

2

Glenn Hogan made it to shore. He clambered amid rocks and broken coral along a narrow path of sand to a spot where he collapsed face down. This much and everything that happened during the previous half hour, he couldn't remember. All he knew was some enormous figure was poking him with the blunt end of a fishing rod.

"Wake up, boy, you gonna be mosquito food."

His head felt heavier than a cement block. Glenn lifted it off the sand, squinting in the direction of the voice.

"You have an accident?"

Unable to prop himself up on his elbows, Glenn rolled onto his side.

"You busted your nose."

He heard some more words that didn't make sense then a bit of rattling. A shadow fell over his face, giving him the first opportunity to focus on whoever was speaking to him.

"Take a drink. I think you need it."

A tubby fellow leaned down to offer him a clear plastic bottle. Glenn took it, guzzling the cool water inside, spilling some over his chin. Exhausted, he couldn't hand it back. He drank again, slowly this time. Wiping his forearm across his mouth, he noticed a red streak had come away from his face.

"Bleeding from your nose."

The taste of blood on his lip brought things into focus. A tackle box and fishing pole sat at the feet of a man twice as wide as Glenn. He wore a shirt that tented over a massive belly. Glenn could lose an eye if the single button holding it closed let go. He had a big, round head, too, framed by about three days of stubble and a crumbling straw hat.

Gaining strength, Glenn sat up, swigged one more time from the bottle, and said, "Thanks for the water."

"*De nada*. What you doing here alone?"

Seconds passed while Glenn struggled to remember where he was. His memory returned all at once, a jumble of images bouncing off each other in his mind. He'd flown to Aruba with a woman. What was her name? Connie? No, Kathy. He and Kathy checked into the Caribbean Club. The first night, he played blackjack at two different places. He lost at the Holiday Inn and then made a comeback with a grand at the Caribbean Club, which comped him dinner at their upscale restaurant. He and Kathy shared a bottle of wine, then a second. Upstairs, they tore up the bed with some hot sex. The girl didn't mind frisky but wouldn't go kinky. The next morning they went on a private snorkel cruise. The crew on the boat served them fruit and sandwiches. Booze, too. Something with rum in it. Back at the casino the second night. Another winner, five thousand this time. Kathy, silly bitch, lost a hundred in the slots. The casino bumped him up to a suite on the top floor. More sex. Did he use his video camera? Glenn thought so, but he wasn't sure. Kathy wanted to go snorkeling again. So did he, and not to look at fish. He bought overpriced masks and snorkels at the gift shop along with a cooler. The cost was nothing; he won plenty at the blackjack table. They took the rental car to the other end of the island. There were a handful of people scattered along a horseshoe-shaped stretch of sand the size of the Eagles stadium back in Philly. Baby Beach it was called. Kathy told him to park nearby. He ignored her; no woman gave him orders. Instead he rolled up to a hodgepodge of buildings featuring a dive shop and an outdoor bar. What a combination, he thought. The rest of the place awaited the wrecking ball.

"Making me worry," the fat man said.

Glenn was worried, too, because there was a hole in his memory. He could see the rental car, a white econo-box with tinted windows. He remembered leaving it there, in the shadow of some scrubby trees. They both had a beer from the cooler then Kathy started whining about getting in the water.

"Let me get the snorkels," he'd said, reaching for the bag from the gift shop.

Then they were in the water, masks over their eyes, snorkels in their mouths. No more talking. He liked it that way. She'd jabbered all through lunch about how she wanted to see the pretty fish. She was going to see the fish all right. They swam to where the boat had taken them the day before.

The hole opened up right there, sucking down everything that happened between the first time he put his face in the water and glanced at her plump ass and now. His thought at the time had been how energetic she was for a chick who needed to drop a few. She wasn't self-conscious, not even a little bit. Didn't mind the lights on during the act. But why couldn't he recall what happened in the water?

"You're talking to yourself," the fat fisherman was saying. "Too much rum maybe?"

"I drink beer," Glenn retorted.

"Ahhh, Balashi."

Yeah, that was it. The light beer in the green bottles. Kathy told him to chug it so they could get in the water. It was getting late, she said.

"The sun goes down quickly near the equator," Glenn heard her say. She liked to show him her smarts every once in a while, as if she had to prove her intelligence. In the three months since he'd met her, Glenn never figured Kathy for a bimbo. She got all his jokes and knew a bit about the Eagles. Like him, she had an associate degree. Even so, she was no Einstein, though she never missed an opportunity to correct him on historical facts, like the year the Gulf War began. Chicks always fuss over the details. As if it mattered.

At the present moment, it did matter because he knew none of the details of the past half hour or however long it had been. He looked at his watch, a waterproof Rolex given to him by a casino manager in Atlantic City three years ago. Twenty past five? Really? What time did they go in the water?

"Getting late for a swim," the fat man said.

"I was snorkeling," Glenn growled.

"Too late for snorkel. Sun low now."

"I'm finished. I was in the water over there."

Gathering up his tackle box and pole he said, "If you okay,

I go home."

"Is Kathy here?"

"Kathy?"

"Yes, a woman," Glenn admonished him. "She was with me in the ocean."

"No woman here."

Did they have a fight? Was she pissed about something and storm off without him? Maybe a slap for grabbing her ass in the water? Is that how he got the bloody nose?

"She must be around here somewhere."

The fat man turned a full circle. "I see people at Baby Beach getting ready to leave. No one here. You say she was in the water with you?"

Rising to his feet, Glenn squinted at the sun in the west. Shielding his eyes, he scanned the water closer to shore. His head began to spin as if he'd been drinking all day. The fisherman dropped his gear just in time to steady him. If not, Glenn would have toppled over.

"Easy, boy. You need some medical attention."

"I'm okay," Glenn muttered as he lowered himself to the ground.

"Help on the way," said the fat man, who somehow managed to dial a cellphone with his thick fingers.

Glenn was too tired to argue. He struggled to think back through the day, but everything was out of focus. They had breakfast at the hotel, on the balcony. Kathy mentioned another snorkel trip. Good idea, he agreed. She nagged him to open the room's safe so she could put away her jewelry. It was cheap stuff, not worth stealing. He didn't want to get up after eating such a big breakfast. She nagged some more. He told her the combination to shut her up. She kissed his cheek and went inside. In a rare burst of suspicion, Glenn peeked in to see if she would help herself to his casino winnings. After pressing the numbers on the keypad, the door popped and she took off her necklace and placed it on top of her passport. She closed the safe and headed for the bathroom.

How could he remember all these details from early this morning and not a single thing from an hour ago? And why did he feel like he'd been hit by a truck? Snorkeling the previous day had been easy. Aruba was supposed to be a windy place, yet the men on the boat complained about not being able to sail. They used the engine to propel the boat. This aggravated Glenn because he'd paid for a private *sailing* cruise. Not only was there no sailing, there was no privacy. He expected a cabin where he could have a romp with Kathy at some point during the day. The captain talked like a tour guide, running on about the island's history, the sea conditions, the short distance to Venezuela. Glenn paid him no attention and stared at the gentle water, which rolled with a two-foot swell.

"This is going to be great," Kathy beamed.

Glenn had smiled but not with the enthusiasm of his companion. For the price of the so-called private sailing cruise, he intended to enjoy her other favors. Given that was impossible, he felt like he was stuck in a high school play. He had to act like the nice guy who gets to kiss the girl on stage, but with a full audience wasn't allowed to put his hand up her dress. Next time, he told himself, waste the day on the beach plowing through a case of beer, and when you get horny, drag her up to the room and have at it. Of course, this was the last trip with Kathy. Too bad for her. She performed better than most in the sack, but in the end he wanted a trophy, a woman who knew less about what time the sun went down near the equator and a whole lot more about how to wear lingerie. With Kathy gone, he would be able to afford a chick who fit the bill.

But was Kathy gone?

Glenn swiveled his head, locking onto the various landmarks: the back of the dilapidated dive shop, the beach, the ocean, the jagged rocks sticking up nearby. The fat man interrupted his search.

"A woman you was with?" he said.

"Yeah," Glenn drawled, surprised by how difficult it was to speak. No sense of urgency pressed him to do more than stare off in the distance. Exhaustion, confusion, like the worst hangover he'd ever had, all weighed him down.

"How far away you go?" the giant fisherman asked.

"Out there," Glenn replied.

"With the woman?"

"Yeah, her name is Kathy."

"Current is not so far out. Pull you away."

Is that what happened? Glenn wondered. He couldn't be sure. He was stuck at the point where they finished their beers, the local stuff, Balashi. After that … nothing.

"Sure you with a woman?"

"Yes, yes, I was with a woman!" barked Glenn. "We went snorkeling right there." Using tremendous effort, he pointed with his right hand.

The fisherman walked in the direction of the rocks. His shadow stretched back over Glenn, who was content to sit there racking his brain. Moments later he returned.

"Ambulance is on the way, but I better call the police, too," he said. "Dark soon and then the woman lost."

The sun seemed to be falling in slow motion, like the time Glenn knocked a ball off the Christmas tree when he was a little boy. It rotated silently through the air, a shiny orb glistening in the sparkling lights, until it shattered on his mother's beautifully polished floor.

"Sir, can you hear me? Can you hear me?"

Glenn snapped his eyes open. He winced at a bitter stink close to his nose.

"Sir, tell me your name."

"Glenn. Glenn Hogan."

"Do you know where you are?"

Do I know where I am? In a rush of white noise and flashing light, Glenn began to made sense of the scene. A man wearing iridescent-green coveralls held smelling salts under his nose. Another person in similar apparel leaned over with a penlight, the beam of which stabbed at his eyes. A group of people stood in a tight knot several feet away, talking among themselves and casting wary glances. An ambulance idled nearby, its pulsing red light marking time. Overhead, the sky loomed purple, orange, and yellow.

"He said he was with a woman. Kathy is her name."

Glenn recognized the sound of the oversized fisherman who had poked him with his rod.

"You were snorkeling?" the ambulance tech asked.

"Yes," Glenn said. He coughed, wiped his face, and tried to stand up. The tech held him down.

"Remain seated, sir. You've had some trouble. You may have a concussion."

"I'm fine," protested Glenn, attempting to rise again. This time a flash interrupted him. It popped once, twice, three times. He put up his forearm to block the strobe and spotted the dried blood.

"Enough with the camera, Romy!"

The flash went off one last time.

"Romy!"

"*Ta bon, ta bon,*" came another nearby voice from a kid dressed in a T-shirt and cargo pants, the two garments bound to his scrawny frame by a sturdy leather belt. An expensive camera was in one hand, a pair of outsized aviator sunglasses in the other, giving him the look of a teenage Hunter Thompson, minus the dangling cigarette. Glenn read Thompson's books in high school.

The ambulance tech got Glenn's attention. "Did the woman you were with come back to shore?"

"I don't know," Glenn said.

"We have been looking. We haven't found her here. Did you have a fight or something? Did she leave with someone else?"

"It was just us."

"No one else? Maybe another man?"

Angry, Glenn replied, "She was with me. We went snorkeling." Now he had the strength to get up and he did, much to the surprise of everyone around him. They backed off, gawking at his burst of energy.

"It will be dark soon. We have to start a search," the ambulance tech said. "Show us where you went in the water."

Checking left then right, Glenn put the scene into perspective. The rental car was back over his right shoulder, Baby Beach was to the left. In the opposite direction, snaked the strip of sand he'd used to get to the water.

"There," he said, indicating with his finger and stepping forward.

The group joined Glenn, including the big fisherman and a swarm of gnats or mosquitoes or some other type of annoying insect. The sound of the camera also followed, a space-age zip, click, whir, but this time there was no flash.

"What time did you enter the sea?" asked the ambulance tech.

"Three? Maybe four?" Glenn suggested.

"More than two hours ago?" pressed the tech.

"What time is it now?" asked Glenn, unable to focus on his watch.

"Quarter past six."

All at once, the group turned away from Glenn and focused their attention on an approaching figure who walked with a sense of determined purpose that caused a collective straightening of spines as if lining up for inspection by their commanding officer. He was San Nicolaas Police Chief Jules Calenda, and he wasted no time taking control of the scene.

Although he couldn't remember what happened in the water, Glenn began to think more clearly than ever. It was like sitting for one of those exams he had to pass for his job. He paid close attention, considered his answers, and said nothing more than the minimum. A cop on the scene meant his words would be scrutinized under the microscope of skeptical people who assumed the worst until something better was proved. Furthermore, his payday was at stake, and Glenn was going to do whatever it took to collect, which meant giving this cop good reasons to believe him.

Time was running out on doing something dramatic. The cop organized the situation with clipped commands.

"Who was the first person here?" Chief Calenda asked.

"I found the man passed out," the fisherman said.

"Good. Who was next?" the cop said.

"We arrived after getting the call from central dispatch," the lead ambulance tech answered. "No one else was here."

"Does this man need further treatment?"

"He's weak but coherent. No serious injuries. He said a woman was with him, snorkeling."

"All of you, wait over there, and Romy, no photos until I instruct you to take them. Understood?"

"Chief, I got here right after the ambulance," Romy put in.

"All right, stay back until I get to you."

The kid appeared ready to argue but had second thoughts. He shuffled away, joining the others who were now muttering back and forth among themselves.

Glenn now stood face to face with the policeman who wore a pale blue shirt over dark blue pants and a shiny-brimmed hat that caught the glint of the fading light. He was clean-shaven with a sharp nose separating dark eyes that were impossible to read.

"You were snorkeling with someone?" he asked.

The words were more challenge than question, causing Glenn to shift on his feet in preparation for a verbal duel. This reaction he checked before stumbling into appearing guilty of something, which is probably what the cop was trying to do, bait him. Having thought this through for the past several months, Glenn was ready for such a trick. The clock is ticking, he reminded himself, and you only get one chance.

"Kathy and I were ..." Glenn spluttered then covered his face with his hands. Shaking his head side to side, he continued, "She asked me to take her snorkeling again." He couldn't work up tears no matter how hard he tried, including a dredged-up memory of his dog, Buddy, who he'd seen die under the tires of a school bus.

"When?" the cop snapped.

"This afternoon. I don't know exactly."

"Where?"

"Right here."

"Why here? Why not over there by Baby Beach?"

If this wasn't a case of landing a fat insurance check, Glenn would have fired a right jab into the cop's face. He would drive it home, all the way to the back of his head, not holding back the way he did when his ex, Janice, wouldn't shut up about the suits. That punch almost cost him his job, but it was worth it, including the restraining order, lawyers' fees, and having to apologize to her in front of a judge. He'd say anything if he had to. What did it matter? "I'm sorry," counted for nothing when compared to *One Million Five Hundred Thousand Dollars* written on a certified insurance company check. In this frame of mind, Glenn let the cop's indignant attitude slide by. He told the truth for a change.

"We took a cruise yesterday and there were all kinds of fish. Kathy wanted to go back to the same place."

"Why didn't you take the boat?" the cop wanted to know.

"Shouldn't we be looking for her?" countered Glenn hoping the sincerity with which he desired the payday came across for Kathy.

"A search is already underway," the cop replied. "Tell me why you didn't take a boat back to the same place."

"Thanks. Thank you for the search," Glenn said. "We should all go out there in case …" He took a step toward the sea before the cop put up his hand like he was directing traffic.

"What happened to your face?"

Instinctively, Glenn touched his nose. He had yet to see himself in a mirror so he couldn't appreciate the damage. Best to play dumb, he reasoned.

"I must have bumped into something, maybe coral."

"You don't remember?"

"I … we …" stammered Glenn before drawing a blank. He rehearsed for this moment. He practiced saying the words in his car driving back and forth to work. Over and over he said them until he had them down. *Relax,* he said to himself. *Take a breath. Act sad. Act worried.*

"You swam ashore without your companion?" the cop was asking.

Inside his brain, Glenn heard himself shouting. *Blurt it out and stick to it!* He hesitated. *Do it!* If they already found her they wouldn't be here asking these stupid questions. And if they find her later, living or dead, don't change the story. At least two hours have passed since pulling on those masks. She has to be gone. And if she isn't, it's soon going to be too dark to find a body in water black as ink.

"I told her we were out too far but she wanted to see the fish. The current was strong and I begged her to go to shore. She wouldn't. I even grabbed her and tried to, you know, pull her in."

As he'd rehearsed, Glenn paused, considered how upset he

should appear, and waited for the cop to prod him. It didn't take but a second.

"Keep going."

"Then she saw how far away we were from the beach. The building looked like a tiny Lego house. She panicked. I tried to calm her down. We both started swimming for shore."

Glenn took another break, adding a wipe of his nose for effect. A grain of sand irritated his eye. He rubbed it hoping some tears would spill.

"I'm listening," the cop said.

"My arms started to cramp, and I was getting scared myself. I thought it wasn't so deep and tried to touch the bottom with my toes. I went under, all the way under, caught a mouthful of water and started gagging. When I could breathe again, Kathy was nowhere in sight."

"Did you call out for her?"

"Loud as I could, but I was scared. I had a ways to go and my muscles were cramping."

"You seem like you're in pretty good shape," commented the cop.

"I am," Glenn said before he could reign in that bit of vanity, "but the currents were strong."

"You lost sight of your companion, called out to her, and then what?"

"I swam farther out, not too far, then headed for shore thinking maybe she got ahead of me. I cramped up again, this time in shallow water, then stumbled up on the beach, where that guy over there found me."

The fisherman stared back at them.

"I'll talk to him in a minute. In the meantime, have a seat

in the ambulance and let them fix you up. Okay?"

"I'd like to help search for Kathy," Glenn said. As if cued by a movie director, a helicopter swooped in over the refinery in the distance. Everyone looked up as its searchlight probed the nearby ocean. Glenn couldn't have been more pleased to see it. To collect on the policy he'd paid for would be much easier if they found Kathy's body. If not, he would still get the money, he'd made sure of that, and it would be a whole lot harder to prove what happened to her.

3

"Here come the ambulance," the cab driver said, the odd lilt to his voice making Kathy smile. She liked the way the Arubans spoke English. They gave the language a sing-song beat by accenting syllables differently than Americans.

"Something bad happen?" she ventured.

"I don't know. Maybe an accident."

Kathy knew, and it was no accident. It was attempted murder. Lucky to be alive, she watched the ambulance rush by and thanked God for watching over her. If nothing else, she learned a lesson today. She'd been playing with fire and getting burned was no fun. It hurt. Specifically, her shoulder where Glenn clamped onto it. *The bastard!* Her ankle, too. He wrenched it hard enough to give her a limp. On top of these injuries, her chest ached, which might've been from coughing up seawater or nearly having a heart attack upon realizing he wasn't fooling around. She wasn't sure which, but every time she took a breath, a burning sensation blossomed through her midsection.

All she wanted to do was get back to the hotel, grab her wallet and passport, and get the hell out of here. She was going to have the cabbie wait until she gathered her stuff and then take her to the airport where she would get on the next flight out. When she was safe, away from that prick, Glenn, she would tell the cops what happened and let them deal with it.

The driver motored up the hill past a large church with well-tended grounds. Kathy remembered seeing it on her way to the snorkel spot.

"Long way from here to the Caribbean Club," he said.

Kathy understood what he wasn't saying. He was worried about her paying the fare. She had two hundred dollars plus twenty florins, the local currency. It was enough to take a cab from the Philadelphia airport to her house in Media and back, twice. Certainly it would suffice to go the length of this small island. She clutched the bills in her hand.

"How much to the hotel?" she asked.

"Forty dollars."

"No problem," she said, surprised at the cheer in her own voice.

"*Danki,* my lady." The driver grinned and stepped on the gas as he made a wicked turn past a big, red ship's anchor standing as a monument of some kind.

It took what felt like an eternity for her to swim back to shore. She picked her way through the rocks, stubbing her toe and aggravating her twisted ankle until she came to an area of smooth sand. There she flopped down, covered her eyes, and wept. The worst she expected from one of these malefactors was a slap or a punch. The thought of them trying to kill her had not crossed her mind. She assumed she was in control, setting the whole thing up, watching it unfold, enjoying the show along the way. She'd had a taste of her own medicine and she didn't like it. No, it wasn't that. She never meant, nor tried, to kill anyone. She gave them a scare, nothing more. Glenn, on the other hand, intended to go all the way.

When she sat up on that patch of warm sand, she stared at the oil refinery for a few minutes. It seemed as bizarre as what had just happened to her, something out of place in an otherwise pristine landscape. A stretch of beach curved away from her, ending at the industrial complex. Kathy had seen a sign naming this beach but couldn't recall what it had been. Some people who apparently didn't mind seeing the smokestacks lounged on folding chairs. They were too far away to make out details other than the square shorts of men and less-covering triangles of fabric on the women.

Reminded that she wore only her bathing suit, Kathy headed for the rental car, where she'd left her things. At first, when she saw Glenn splayed out on the shallow grade tapering up from the water, she was relieved that he hadn't drowned. Then she was livid. He tried to kill her. Too bad if the drugs she'd slipped him had rendered him unable to swim and the sharks had eaten him. He would have deserved what he got. Problem was, he didn't get it. There he was, collapsed on the ground. He was going to live, albeit with a chunk of memory missing.

She needed something to wear back to the hotel, which meant retrieving her dress, money, and room key. For a second, she considered sneaking over to the other beach, waiting for people to go in the water, and stealing a cover-up and just enough money to get a cab. She thought better of the idea. It wasn't necessary when her things were less than fifty yards away and Glenn was unconscious.

Careful not to burden her sore ankle, Kathy staggered to the car, hunched over like a soldier trying to avoid detection. *It's not too far,* she told herself. *Go slow. Take it easy. Don't fall and make it worse.* She fished around the hollow space behind the front bumper and found the car key where Glenn had left it. Once again she was grateful for his diabolical foresight. He hid the key there so as not to risk losing it in the ocean during their struggle.

"Good move," she said aloud.

She pulled on her sundress, slipped her feet into the flip-flops, and grabbed her room key from under the seat. Her sunglasses were tucked in the pocket on the door. Glenn had made fun of them when she put them on at the rental car agency.

"You're going to wear those?" he scolded her. "You look like you escaped from a bad disco movie."

Kathy diverted his insult. "Why don't you buy me a pair that turns you on?" she suggested. What he didn't know about women's fashion was a lot, but she'd let him blow his money on some expensive shades if it made him feel better. He didn't step up to the plate, another clue she'd missed.

All she required was cab fare to take her to the Caribbean Club. When she'd left the hotel after lunch, Kathy didn't expect to need anything other than her bathing suit. They were going snorkeling and then returning for another evening of fine dining and gambling. Therefore, she left her wallet in the room, taking only the local currency to spend on something small if it caught her fancy.

"This winner has plenty of money," Glenn had bragged to her when she asked if she should take anything else.

"Now you have two hundred less," Kathy said, helping herself to four fifties from his wallet under the driver's seat.

It took all her willpower not to throw the car key in the ocean, arc it right over Glenn's head. Instead, she closed the door without a sound then put the key back where she found it. After a last look at him, lying prone and out cold, she returned in the direction she'd come. Thankfully, he hadn't moved since she got there. If he spotted her now, she'd have to deal with him, and she had no idea how that would unfold.

Doing her best to ignore the pain, she stood up straight when an SUV bearing a yellow taxi sign on its roof turned toward a dock sticking out from that other beach, the name of which she couldn't recall. She was astounded that a Mercedes SUV served taxi duty. When it made a full stop, she waited while a man and boy got out then she angled for the vehicle. When the driver turned the wheel in her direction, she was just close enough to get his attention. Forcing herself to hurry, she waved her arms. What a relief when he hit the break and smiled his white teeth through the windshield.

Now he was rolling through the town of San Nicolaas as indicated by the white letters on the blue signs they passed. A stadium went by, a bunch of houses, a traffic circle, and they were on the two-lane highway she remembered from the drive to Baby Beach.

"What's the name of the beach back there?" she asked her driver.

"Two beaches, my lady. Baby Beach and Rodgers Beach."

"Rodgers Beach, that's it."

"Named for Captain Rodgers come from Scotland back in the twenties to survey the harbor. Long way Scotland to Aruba."

Her driver had a firm handle on distances both local and worldwide. Kathy listened to him talk about the island's history before he started with questions for her.

"By yourself down there all day?" he asked.

Not wanting to lie, she answered with a single, "No."

"Having fun with friends?"

"Too much fun," she muttered.

"Aruba easy to have fun."

He was right. The snorkel cruise was a delight as were the meals they enjoyed at the hotel. She cared less about gambling but had to admit to being excited when Glenn's stack of chips rose during the evenings he spent at the blackjack table. A confident player, he never hesitated to split a pair, double down, or wait for his own card. The last trait infuriated his fellow players.

"When you put your money on this spot you can make the decision to take a card or not," he grumbled to one lady displeased at his choice to stand on fifteen.

"Your friends didn't leave you alone, did they?" the cab driver inquired. He kept his eyes on the road, which was to her benefit. Kathy didn't want him to remember her.

"No, they're staying, but I need time to get ready for dinner."

"Ahhh, pretty lady looking good for a night out. Be careful. A handsome island boy come and whisk you away here in paradise."

Almost, she wanted to say. Glenn's plan must have been to

let the current take her to Venezuela or Colombia or wherever it went. She knew why: the travel insurance policy they took out. When he arranged the tickets, he also paid for a policy in case they were injured and needed emergency medical care. Blinded by her own machinations, she wasn't suspicious when he showed up at work with a signature page.

"What's this?" she asked him.

"Insurance," he replied, "in case we get in a car wreck or fall off a balcony. The policy pays for a medical transport back to the States if it comes to that. I always check the box on the computer, but they changed the rules. Now, you have to sign and fax it back to the company or it's not valid."

Kathy scanned the page while Margie stopped counting pills to take in Glenn's physique. His clothes left no secret as to the shape of his body when those custom suits were in the closet and he was lying in his boxers on the bed.

"Here, you have to name a beneficiary, too," he said, tapping his pen at another blank line.

"A beneficiary? For what?"

"There's a payout if you … you know … don't make it back."

"You're kidding, right?" She'd been indignant until he tricked her with another of his ploys.

"I usually name my dad, but I put you in this time."

"Me?"

"Why not?"

Why not, indeed. Kathy mulled it over in the back of the taxi as it hurtled around another traffic circle. Why would he name her as the beneficiary on an insurance policy when they'd been dating only three months? Why would he do that when he could name his dear ol' dad?

"I'd want you to have the cash," he said. "If something happened to me and you collected more than a million, you'd remember me forever. In a good way."

"I would!" Margie called from behind one of the shelves of drugs where she stood, eavesdropping on the conversation.

"Thank you, Glenn," Kathy had said. She felt his warmth at that moment. Maybe he wasn't the wife-beater depicted in the paper. Or, maybe he had changed his ways. It was possible, and Kathy reassessed her entire plan. She decided then that if Glenn proved to be a gentleman she would forget the scare tactic and enjoy the vacation he offered her. It was Aruba they were going to, an island paradise. Why not be civil?

Taking the pen in hand, she saw that the line for beneficiary was already filled in. It was his policy, not hers that he'd given her. KATHY BARROW stood in the space, written in Glenn's own blocky letters. Flustered by this kindness and aroused by the chance of being with a man others found attractive, Kathy took the page and signed her name to acknowledge the policy.

"Maybe you want to put your mom down as beneficiary," Glenn suggested.

It was exactly what she should have done. It would have foiled his plot unless he was simply a woman-hater and not hoping to cash in. Either way, he would not have been in line to become Media's newest millionaire. But instead of writing her mom's name, she put his, Glenn Hogan, which looking back, was precisely what he baited her into doing. She did it with a smile, a giggle, like a child given a treat.

"Tell you what," she said. "Fair's fair. You picked me; I'll pick you."

"No, come on. Your mom's over at Clearwater Lodge, right?

Put her down. She'll need the money to have somebody take care of her."

Fortunately for the cab driver he was on a straight stretch of road. If they had been going around one of those circles, Kathy would've vomited all over his factory-new upholstery. Her stomach gurgled, forcing her to choke back the bile. Generous Glenn didn't give a damn about her mother. He played this out better than a pair of aces at the Caribbean Club Casino.

When his name was inked on the appropriate page, complete with the two n's in Glenn, he asked if it was all right to use the pharmacy's fax machine to send the documents to the insurance company.

"Corporate policy forbids personal use," Kathy had said.

"Okay, I'll do it from work."

Margie stepped out to save the day. "Go ahead," she told them. "It's just two pages. I won't tell anyone."

"You sure?" Glenn confirmed.

"Hurry up."

Kathy wrote out the cover page, dropped them into the machine, and punched in the number. It connected on the first try, sucked through the pages, and spit out a receipt. She handed the collection to Glenn, who leaned over to kiss her cheek.

"Thanks, babe," he said and winked at Margie.

He wasn't ten feet closer to the door when Margie whispered, "He's a keeper."

Glenn turned to say, "I heard that," and left.

"Son of a bitch!"

"Excuse me?" the cabbie's reflection asked from the rearview mirror.

"Sorry," Kathy shrugged. "I just remembered something I was supposed to do at work."

"Don't worry. You're on vacation. You get home, it will be there for you."

Kathy couldn't wait to get home. The ticket change was going to cost her a mint. She would take whatever was available. First class, coach, it didn't matter. Just as she had this thought the light ahead turned green and her driver accelerated, blowing through the intersection at the airport. It seemed busy enough when they arrived. There had to be planes going the other way at regular intervals.

Flexing her ankle, she realized that she'd put on her sundress inside out. The big vivid flower that wrapped the bodice appeared as a ghostly replica. What if the cab driver noticed? For one thing, she'd feel like a fool, even if she blamed it on too many beers at the beach. For another, he might remember her. So what if he did?

It occurred to Kathy that she wasn't handling the situation as she should. *Go straight to the police, explain what happened, have them arrest Glenn,* she thought. Leaning forward, ready to tell the driver to take her to the nearest police station, she reconsidered. It was her word against his. Where was the evidence he tried to kill her? She had a twisted ankle and some bruises, but she was alive and healthy. What if they told her he was woozy and out of it? What if they tested him for drugs? It took twelve hours or more for the concoction she gave him to metabolize and pass out of the body. Even then, there was the possibility of residual traces. Did Aruba have a lab sophisticated enough to screen for these elements? She didn't know.

Slumping back against the seat, she bit her lip to keep from screaming. Glenn could win this one as handily as he'd set her up. All he needed to say was that his companion was a pharmacy tech and she slipped him a dose of something. He was off the hook and she was in the frying pan. How did this happen? How had she been manipulated to such a degree that she was helpless to confront the circumstances? She volunteered, that's how. Like him but in a different way, she'd been arrogant. She let pride lead the way instead of intelligence. Having gotten away with it twice, she assumed she was invincible. Vulnerable to stupidity was the more accurate description.

"Almost there," announced the cab driver as they exited the main commercial strip of Oranjestad where disembarked cruise ship passengers had blocked their way. It was like an invasion in progress. People ignored the crosswalks, darting back and forth across the road like a flock of spooked chickens. There were hundreds of them.

Come on, Kathy, what are you going to do? She asked herself over and over again, until the taxi made the turn off the highway just before the high-rise hotels. If anyone saw her at the Caribbean Club, how would she explain herself? No, she couldn't go there. She needed time, but how much did she have before Glenn woke up, considered her missing, and called the police to set his plan in motion? An hour? Two?

"I'm sorry," she told the driver. "Could you drop me off at the Holiday Inn?"

"Of course, my lady."

The car rolled past the fourteen-story Caribbean Club then another couple of hotels before angling into the circular drive at the Holiday Inn. She handed one of Glenn's fifties between the front seats.

"*Masha danki,*" the driver said, returning her change. "Enjoy your vacation."

Her sunglasses on and her dress gathered up away from her swelling ankle, Kathy entered the open foyer of the hotel. To the right, a group of stores formed a miniature shopping mall. She'd been through here with Glenn on the day they arrived in Aruba when they ducked in out of a rain shower. She hoped to find some elements to patch together a disguise.

The Bamboo Bazaar sold her another dress, this one a black shift made of sturdy fabric suitable for airplane travel, a pair of comfortable sandals, and a straw hat bigger than a trash can lid. Between it and her sunglasses, no one would notice her at the Caribbean Club. The price used up most of her cash, but she wasn't concerned. Glenn's casino winnings remained in the safe in their room. The combination was four easy digits, his birthday in reverse.

Instead of chancing it on her ankle, she went back to the Holiday Inn lobby and used the local currency on a taxi to her hotel. The driver said nothing about the short ride, accepting the twenty florins in payment. Minutes later, she flopped onto the bed in room 1406.

With no time to rest, she set to work. First, she took her knockout pills from her suitcase. Next she opened the safe. There sat the necklace her mother had given her when the acceptance letter came from Temple University. She donned the gold chain and eyed Glenn's casino take, a neat bundle of one-hundred-dollar bills. He had been coy about the amount, so Kathy was surprised to find five thousand dollars after a hasty count. She helped herself to the money, thinking of it as payment for damages. A miniature notebook lay there. Thumbing through the pages, she saw it contained what appeared to be passwords to Glenn's email and other accounts. She pushed it to the side.

The last two items in the box were their passports. If she took hers, there was no denying she'd been in the room, especially if she showed up at the airport with it. Having the passport would reveal she'd also had access to the money. Her case for panicking would be better made if she showed up directly from the beach, hysterical, wanting nothing more than to escape a monster. If it had been some crazy scheme she cooked up, she would have had her passport and skipped off the island before the local authorities could pin her down. No, she decided, it was too late. The passport stays.

But if the passport stays then so does the necklace. She'd asked Glenn for the combination to the safe for the purpose of putting it in there. He knew what it meant to her. It wasn't valuable, hardly worth stealing by the same person who could help themselves to all that cash. Holding back tears, she took off the necklace and draped it within the pages of her passport, and closed the safe.

The suite appeared pretty much the same as they'd left it early in the afternoon. His suitcase was at the foot of the bed. Hers sat on the rack in the closet. His video camera was beside the TV facing the bed. His pants hung over a chair. The blouse she had planned to wear to dinner remained on the bed. She hated leaving it behind. It fit great. Beside the bed was a box of Ambien samples.

"Guilty conscience keeping you awake?" Kathy asked the empty room. She peeked inside the sample box, saw two blister packs and took one of them for spite.

At the risk of disturbing something that may later cause her grief, she searched Glenn's suitcase. He packed neatly, making it easy. Tucked inside a dark sock she found a Ziplock bag filled with oval-shaped pills she recognized as Valium and a small key.

"Son of a bitch," she said for the second time that day. There were enough pills to tranquilize a horse. Did he plan to use them on her if the snorkeling accident didn't work out? She went to the phone, but reaching for it, she pulled back her hand.

The Valium proved nothing. And what if he claimed she had stolen them from work. All the drugs at the pharmacy were counted and recounted. There were cameras everywhere, as many as in a casino. The way she got the drugs she needed to make her knockout cocktail was by pilfering them from the expired lots that were dumped into incinerator boxes. Kathy palmed a few as they were placed into those bright-red biohazard containers that a franchise disposal company came for every week. Certified Incineration was the name. Chris, heavyset with bad skin, drove the truck. He asked her out once. Still, Glenn might make the case that she was stealing pills from work.

Heading for the bathroom to flush the Valium she stopped herself again. *Leave everything as it was. Take only the essentials and get out until you have time to think this through. You can always show up later, claim to have been lost at sea or hit your head, and plead ignorance, which wasn't far from the truth anyway. Don't make it complicated.*

Unable to resist, she took half the Valium to piss him off. In the process of returning the rest of the pills to the sock in the bottom of his suitcase, she felt a soft furry object. She yanked her hand out as if she'd just touched a mouse. Then she remembered that during their late-night escapades, the ones that took place after his casino win, he slid a pair of fur-lined handcuffs from under the pillow. She wasn't that stupid. Nobody, casino big shot or movie star, was cuffing her to the bed. She took them from him, dropped them near the foot of the bed, and then got down to business the way nature intended.

On a hunch, she went back for the miniature key in the bag with the Valium. It fit the cuffs, unlocking them with a full turn. Just to tweak his nose, she took the cuffs, tossing them and the key into the plastic bag from the Bamboo Bazaar. What was he going to do? Tell the cops some burglar made off with his money and kinky accessories? Let him, the weirdo. It was his word against hers, and she didn't want him telling people she was into that kind of thing.

Convinced she was on the right course, Kathy peered out the door, which was difficult given the size of her hat. No one was in the hallway so she slipped out, headed to the elevator and pressed the button. With nonchalance, she scanned the corners of the hall for cameras. She didn't see any but that didn't mean they weren't there. At work, a tiny camera had been made to look like a bolt. It hung directly over the counting table where each pill was tabbed into a tray for pouring into a waiting bottle.

The doors yawned on an empty car. Kathy stepped in, pressed the ground-floor button, and never looked up. Every elevator had a camera. Glenn told her that, and he should know. A bit frightened at what she was doing, Kathy exited the elevator, clutching the plastic bag with her things close to her body. Where she was going, how she was going to get there, and what she was going to do once she arrived escaped her at the moment, but she had five thousand dollars to buy time to decide.

4

___

Unlike the others clustered behind the former Esso Club, Romy Tromp wasted no time waiting for Chief Calenda to get around to talking to him. He attached a big zoom lens to his camera and snapped away, risking a dead battery in pursuit of the perfect shot. There were plenty to get—the helicopter zig-zagging over the water, silhouetted by the setting sun, the guy with the bloody nose painted red by the ambulance lights, and the chief himself, hands on his hips, pointing, giving orders, cocking his head to listen. Romy got all these and more, every one burned onto a compact flash card.

Tromp worked for *Diario,* one of Aruba's three dailies, popular for its political cartoons and sensational, front-page photographs, many of which had been supplied by the eighteen-year-old who dared to taunt San Nicolaas's Police Chief by continuing to take photos. Tromp had been at it since before getting a driver's license. His mother, a part-time taxista, chauffeured him to the scenes of crimes, accidents, and celebrations during his early days. Perhaps riding in the back seat, his camera trained like a sniper, is what nurtured his rock-star attitude. His talent earned him a pass from his editor, who appreciated his dramatic close-ups. Some of them made it into American papers, such as the one he got of a tourist who passed out after winning a progressive slot-machine jackpot for a hundred thousand dollars. She was from Staten Island, and the *New York Post* ran the image on the front page. A framed copy hung on Tromp's bedroom wall.

As much as he lived to take pictures, what Tromp wanted most was to be a hard-news reporter. A running-and-gunning video pro who provided point-of-view reports from war zones and ancient monuments discovered deep in jungles. He would report from outer space if a network would send him there. Although Aruba had two local television stations, there wasn't enough interest in these kinds of stories for them to support his endeavors. Thus, he snapped away for *Diario*, which paid his bills but didn't satisfy his urge for greatness.

On the air was where Romy Tromp longed to be. He practiced in front of a full-length mirror, striving for a voice an octave deeper than the tinny one with which he was born. His mother told him it would get there with time, the way it had for his father, who sang a rich baritone in church every Sunday. He hoped it happened soon.

Every night he waited for his cell to chime with calls to catch a story. This gave him hours to study the big-network correspondents from the States, above all New York's Clive Mitchell, who seemed to be the first on site whenever a revolution broke out, a child went missing, or a psycho murdered his whole family. Mitchell worked for Global News Network, rated number one in hard news thanks to a group of hosts that recycled Mitchell's on-the-scene reportage to their particular bent. The way Tromp saw it, Mitchell either needed some help or some competition, and he was just the person to fill the role. He was fearless, cunning, and didn't pass out at the sight of blood. His technical skills were flawless. Ask *Diario*'s editor. They rarely needed to crop his shots to fit the paper. He spoke unaccented American English, Colombian Spanish, Papiamento, Dutch, and was learning Mandarin Chinese from Old Man Ling who ran a restaurant at the western edge of San Nicolaas. How many under-twenty-year-olds could claim that on their résumés? He also had experience and style, both of which were critical to being an on-air personality.

Tromp ran through a number of scenarios for this drama on the beach. Eavesdropping on the ambulance techs offered a starting point. The tourist's name was Glenn-something and he claimed a woman called Kathy had disappeared in the water. He wasn't torn up enough to have been attacked by a shark or a pirate, neither of which plied the waters of Aruba. It was not unusual for the U.S. Coast Guard and Navy to bust drug smugglers and Venezuelan provocateurs in the area. Or, it might be a case of an Americano getting into a slap-fest with a disgruntled girlfriend who wasn't up to some hanky-panky on a rough stretch of secluded real estate. This made sense given that no one bothered to get in the water behind the old Esso Club when there were more inviting beaches within walking distance. Then again, the helicopter was overhead, searchlight on, and Calenda had been on his phone quite a bit. As if that wasn't enough, the fire department deployed a set of lights that now burned bright out at the water.

If the man with the bloody nose was telling the truth and an American woman was lost, his career was about to bloom. The last time it happened he was too young to count for more than the absentee column at school. He graduated with honors and was prepared to matriculate to the pros. He was ready because no one else had the photos. Arriving just seconds after the ambulance, he nearly slaughtered half a dozen goats when he barreled through what was left of the old Lago Colony on the hill behind him. The word *Exclusive* danced through his head.

If Chief Calenda hadn't asked him to wait, Tromp would have been on the road home to his high-speed Internet lair. The connection cost him a fortune, but if ever he needed to do fast uploads, and now was possibly one of those times, the capacity awaited. He had Global News Network's assignment desk programmed into his smartphone. Once he confirmed the story, he was going to ring them. Clive Mitchell always checked out his own stories. Two independent sources who were reliable eyewitnesses and not second-handers, that was the rule. Tromp had them, the fisherman whom he would talk to when the chief finished, and himself, who heard everyone talking about a woman named Kathy.

"Romy!" called Chief Calenda. "Come with me."

Tromp's collection of photos included dozens of the San Nicolaas Police Chief. The man broke up post-Carnival beer brawls with nothing more than a baton. He was quick with the tool, able to beat back thugs on three sides who should know better than to take on a trained cop who hadn't consumed a single beer all day. Tromp had more civilized photos of Chief Calenda as well. Performing official duties at burial ceremonies or lecturing kids at the elementary schools. In his top-secret file, he had public snaps of him with his girlfriend, Agnes, who worked as an approach controller at the airport. They made a nice couple. Tromp liked to have background material to fill in the blanks if it ever came to that, the way Clive Mitchell would. Mitchell always gave the whole story, sometimes in hour-long retrospectives put on by his network.

"Let's see the photos you took," Calenda said.

"My battery is getting low," Tromp replied.

The chief dismissed this attempted diversion with nothing more than a slow blink. Tromp activated the display on the back of his camera. Using his boney fingers to tap the buttons, he scrolled to the beginning of the set, to the first shot of the subject with the dried blood on his face leaning on the big fisherman. It was a decent, well-lit picture, framed with the two men in the left third, leaving plenty of room to the right for them to move. The next several zoomed in on faces, close-ups, extreme close-ups. Sand and dried blood on the Americano, razor stubble poking beer sweat on the fisherman.

"Doesn't look like his nose is broken," reflected the chief.

The photographer gave a concurring nod to this assessment and went to the next image. Both Tromp and Calenda had seen a variety of facial injuries caused by car wrecks, fights, and household accidents.

"Dennis drank his share of Balashi today," was the chief's next comment, which revealed the fisherman's first name.

"How can you tell?" Romy asked although he already knew the answer. The fisherman's eyes were shattered marbles hovering over a slack jaw.

"Keep going," Calenda said, ignoring the question.

The photos were comprehensive and documented the scene. For this the chief was grateful and he thanked Tromp for doing a professional job. He also requested a copy of every picture.

"I'll burn a disc for you and drop it off in the morning," Tromp agreed.

"Tonight," Calenda told him. "And don't leave anything out."

"You got it, Chief."

Calenda left the photographer and returned to the rear of the ambulance where a tech sat on the rear deck with the man from the beach who had identified himself as Glenn Hogan of Media, Pennsylvania, United States of America.

Calenda reviewed the story as it had been told. According to Mr. Hogan, he went snorkeling at some point in the latter part of the afternoon with his companion, Ms. Kathy Barrow, also of Media, Pennsylvania. The couple are not married, but friends, dating for about three months. During the snorkeling, Ms. Barrow strayed too far from shore. Mr. Hogan encouraged her to return. She panicked as they both struggled against the currents. Mr. Hogan suffered cramps, took in some water, and lost sight of Ms. Barrow. Exhausted, he hauled himself onto the beach. Fisherman Dennis Rosina discovered Mr. Hogan in a semi-conscious state and dialed 911. Of Ms. Barrow there was no trace.

A plausible account of events, Calenda committed it to memory and paper. Every year, someone drowned in this area. Usually it was an over-enthusiastic tourist who swam out from Baby Beach, through the inlet sheltered by a pile of coral courtesy of Hurricane Ivan, and ventured into the sea where they were surprised by difficult conditions. The most recent incident involved two visitors who had been aboard a cruise ship. They both lost their lives in this way. However, to the best of his recollection, Calenda never heard of anyone beginning their adventure from the point behind the old Esso Club. People like Dennis Rosina went fishing there. Young lovers coupled in cars there. Andrés Cortés painted a famous canvas of the moon shining down there. Glenn Hogan and Kathy Barrow were the first to tempt fate from this location, with sadly predictable results.

While Calenda recorded Hogan's statement along with Rosina's, he didn't necessarily believe it. From teenagers to septuagenarians, bums to senior executives, rich, poor, and in between, everyone lied to the police. Calenda considered it an innate human quality, a programmed defect that was linked to the perceived requirement for self-preservation. It began with the proverbial cookie jar. *It wasn't me, Mom!* Where it ended, the chief cared not enough to contemplate. Nefarious reasons or not, he accepted that lies would always be part of the mix. It was his duty to sort through them to prove or disprove criminality. The rest of it was up to God to sort out.

His mandate in mind, Chief Calenda assessed Glenn Hogan and said, "The ambulance will take you to Centro Medico for a full exam."

Hogan's head whipped up with remarkable power. "I'm fine," he said. "I mean, now that I've had a rest, I think I'm all right."

"You should let the doctors check you out," put in the ambulance tech.

"No, I want to get out there and find Kathy," persisted Hogan.

"My team is doing the best they can," Calenda informed him. "More boats are on the way."

"Thank you," Hogan said. "I appreciate everything you're doing to help."

"I'll meet you at Centro Medico then," the chief finished.

"No, I'm fine," Hogan insisted.

"You're refusing further treatment?"

"We're all speaking English here, right?"

"Okay, Mr. Hogan, the next step is we go to your hotel," Calenda informed the American.

"My hotel? Kathy's not there."

"How do you know?"

"We went snorkeling here. We ..."

"Mr. Hogan, I'll escort you to your vehicle where I ask that you retrieve your room key, your shoes, a shirt, and nothing else. Then you will travel with me to your hotel. This is Detective Bakker. He will take possession of your car for a short time and meet us at the hotel."

"I don't understand."

"Neither do I," the chief replied. "That's why I'm going to make sure I have all the facts."

As soon as the chief walked with Hogan to his car then back to the police SUV, Tromp knew he would need to charge his camera's battery. In his car, he always carried a device that converted the 12-volt electricity supplied by the alternator into 120v AC power required by his camera's charger. He connected the wires, double-checked the indicator, and launched after the chief's official vehicle.

If he had to borrow the money from Old Man Ling at

twenty percent interest Tromp was going to buy a video camera. Live footage of this action could pay twice what the camera cost. That is if there was something evil about what happened. It couldn't be a run-of-the-mill drowning, or some drunk falling down after a fight with his girlfriend. If it was, why would Chief Calenda haul out of there with the Americano in the back seat?

Tromp rejiggered the equation. The Americano was spitting mad. He yanked his arm away from the chief, strutted to his car, reached under the bumper for the key, got something, slammed the door, and swaggered to the blue-and-white police SUV where Detective Bakker accepted the key with an open palm. This behavior added up to more than innocent mistakes while on vacation. Someone with nothing to hide would cooperate without a fuss.

Why hadn't he bought a video camera three years ago instead of the Nikon? He could be side by side with Clive Mitchell explaining what he saw, when he saw it, and where he saw it. He would have the man balking at the police, getting into the rear seat, getting out at whatever hotel to which they were taking him. In his mind, Tromp edited the imaginary clips into a tight, 30-second piece.

"Tell us, Mr. Tromp," Clive Mitchell was saying in a medium close-up, "what did you think when you first came upon the scene?"

Obsessed with this fantasy, Tromp lost track of Calenda's vehicle at the Pos Chiquito circle then spotted it again. He gunned his battered four-cylinder, swung out around a lumbering pickup, and jerked back in line. No way was he going to miss this.

Past the airport, through Oranjestad, back on the highway he drove, all the way to the high-rise area where Calenda's cruiser stopped under the portico at the Caribbean Club, one of Aruba's most expensive hotels. Tromp ditched his car in the lot, sprinted across trimmed lawn, and just about bowled over a doorman in the lobby. At the main bank of elevators stood Calenda, the Americano, and Calenda's number two, Eddie Bakker, who must have arrived separately. Bakker, a Dutch transplant, was trained at Holland's national police academy. He brought his considerable technical knowledge to the island along with beach tennis. He organized a popular tournament every year, drawing contestants from all over South America.

No time for beach tennis this week, Tromp thought as he ducked behind a column in the lobby. He spied two patrolmen lingering at the check-in desk. While they chatted-up the receptionist, Tromp took shots of his main targets. The elevator doors opened and the trio stepped in. An older couple tried to enter, but Calenda asked them to please wait for the next car. The doors closed and the digital display counted upward. It didn't stop until it showed fourteen, the top floor.

Romy Tromp, hiding his camera in the crook of his arm, headed for the stairs.

There were ten suites on the top floor of the Caribbean Club. The casino had upgraded Glenn Hogan to 1406, near the west end of the building. It wasn't as nice as 1407 across the hall, which featured unobstructed views of the water, but the balcony on 1406 was spacious enough for a four-person table that overlooked the swimming pool. Inside there was a large bedroom, generous closets, a bathroom with a Jacuzzi

and separate shower, and a salon suitable for an intimate cocktail party.

Glenn entered ahead of the cop he'd first met at the beach,
who had identified himself as Chief of Police. Then came the
other, who was half a head taller than his own six feet. Backer
or Baker or Backler was his name. He toted a big plastic box.
Glenn guessed it was an evidence kit like those he'd seen on
crime shows. *Take all the evidence you want*, he was about to
say. The self-important chief beat him to it.

"Stand over there," he said.

Nonplussed, Glenn folded his arms and leaned against the
wall in the salon. Bakker started with the questions, all asked
over the microphone of a hand-held recorder. Full name, age,
address, and occupation? Then the inquiry became more specific. When did you arrive in Aruba? What did you do after
checking in at the hotel? That night? The next day? The second
night? and so on. What time did you arrive at Baby Beach? Did
you talk to anyone there? How much did you drink? Why did
you park behind the old Esso Club? How long were you in the
water?

Glenn answered with the unmitigated truth to the best of
his ability, which was somewhat hindered by the hole in his
memory. It was carved out right as he put his face down in the
water for the first time. He cleared the snorkel and kicked his
feet, swimming after Kathy, following that round ass of hers.
From there until the big fisherman jabbed him was a blank,
and so he estimated a few things by interpreting what the fisherman had said. He augmented his story with details about
muscle fatigue that he'd learned at the gym.

"You were in the water about an hour, give or take, trying

to find the place where the *Consuela* took you yesterday," the tall cop repeated.

"I didn't look at my watch," Glenn said, giving himself wiggle room.

"Then Kathy panicked."

Calenda jumped on him with, "You said earlier Kathy wanted to swim out farther. Why would she suddenly panic?"

Raising both shoulders, Glenn stepped away from the trap by answering, "I don't know. Maybe it dawned on her where we were. That we were a good distance out."

"How far do you think it was?" Bakker asked with his eyes on the red light of the recorder.

"I'm not too good at estimating distances," Glenn replied to keep things vague. He grasped the dangers of specifics, how they could trip him up.

"What's the name of the pro football team in Philadelphia?" the chief asked next.

This was an off-the-wall question, and Glenn caught himself stuttering the answer as he simultaneously tried to figure out why it was posed. "The, uh, the Eagles," he squeaked.

"Are you an Eagles fan?"

"I watch the games when I have time."

"Would you say you were the length of a football field away from the beach? Put it in relation to the size of the field."

He had to give the cop credit for sneaking that one in there, but Glenn recovered with ease. "Maybe, I really don't know. It's hard to tell when you're that low to the water."

"And you're not good at estimating distances."

"Sorry. Not part of my job."

The chief allowed a moment to draw long before he said,

"My colleague is going to search the room. He will be as careful as possible when he examines your belongings. Do you understand this is a necessary part of our job?"

During his rehearsals, Glenn played at indignation. He anticipated the cops giving him a hard time, but if he went along too easily, he would seem to be prepared as opposed to shocked by what happened to him out of the blue. That's why he got angry at the beach and slammed the car door in a huff. Then he cooled down, played the we're-all-professionals routine, and spooled up a good amount of sincerity. Regardless, this pair pinched hard with the evidence kit and recorder, leaving no doubt they assumed he'd done Kathy in. A man whose girlfriend accidentally drowned couldn't take that lightly. Glenn didn't.

"Mind telling me what you're looking for?" he said, the edge on his voice cutting across the room.

"I don't know," admitted the man in charge.

"Then why aren't we searching for Kathy instead of screwing around here?" argued Glenn, stiffening his back.

"We may have the answer to that when my colleague finishes his search. Detective, you may begin."

"Hold on! You think I'm responsible for Kathy going missing?"

"You went snorkeling with her," returned Calenda. "You lost track of her, this woman you care about."

Before he could catch himself, Glenn took the bait. "Hey, I almost drowned! I did everything I could!" Hearing himself shout snapped him back to the script. It was okay to be bitter at being accused of something he didn't do, but not hysterical. "Go ahead. Tear the place apart," he finished and planted himself in an overstuffed chair.

"Thank you, Mr. Hogan. First, here's your wallet," Bakker said. "I recovered it from under the driver's seat of your rental. I've already documented its contents."

"Swell."

Bakker then worked as professionally as any movie or TV detective Glenn had watched. He rifled through the furniture, the closets, the bathroom. In Kathy's suitcase, among her clothes, he found her wallet. He slowed down when it came to inspecting Glenn's things. He didn't seem to be interested in the Ambien samples, but the loose Valium from deep in his suitcase provoked a reaction. The detective set the pills on the bed.

"I have a prescription for that. Lower-back pain," Glenn put in. "You can call my doctor."

Bakker rocked his head and continued. He finally got to the safe.

"Open it," Calenda said less than politely.

Glenn entered the code and swung the door. Upon seeing his casino winnings missing, he uttered, "What the hell …"

"Something wrong?" said Bakker who was nearest to him.

Luckily, Hogan faced the open box and not the two cops. They missed the rising color flooding his face. He'd been clipped. He won that money at the blackjack table, and he was counting on it to pay some bills, like the lawyer he would have to hire to tidy up the loose ends in Aruba. But did he want to tell these cops somebody finessed the safe and took his cash? No, he did not. It would only send them on another tangent, delving deeper into his behavior. They would find some of that stuff anyway, but the less he gave them, the harder it would be.

"Something wrong, Mr. Hogan?" Bakker repeated.

"No, just not used to strangers searching through my boxers," Glenn replied.

The cop emptied the safe. Out came his little book of passwords and his passport. Kathy's necklace, the one she made a big deal of locking away, slipped from the pages of her passport. The cop caught it before it fell to the floor. For the last time, Glenn returned to the chair as Bakker produced a camera, photographed everything, and then told his boss the search was complete.

"I'll bag the video camera, his smartphone and hers. I didn't find any computers."

"You're taking my phone?" Glenn complained.

"And your video camera," Bakker said.

"That's my personal property."

"It is, and Detective Bakker will give you a receipt," Calenda cut in. "We'll meet again tomorrow, Mr. Hogan. It is not necessary, but you may wish to consult an attorney."

"You're telling me I'm a suspect?"

"Your status has yet to be determined. Please do not attempt to leave the island."

"You think I'm going to run away somewhere? What about Kathy? What about the search?"

"Relax, Mr. Hogan. The search will continue along with my investigation. I appreciate your cooperation. Until tomorrow, I suggest you get some sleep."

Partly camouflaged by the stairwell door on the fourteenth floor, Tromp eliminated several possible rooms when he saw their occupants coming and going. The sound of a door opening at the far end of the west hall got his attention. Out came the chief and Eddie Bakker. At the risk of a night in jail, or worse, he took a photo before ducking as if a machine gunner had stitched the wall. Then he bolted down the stairs. He had what he needed to pursue the story, including the room number of this Americano. Once he had his full name, which was as easy as a fifty-florin note to his relative at the desk downstairs, he'd be on the phone to GNN. His career was ready for takeoff.

5

Aruba's phonebook provided Kathy with plenty of options. As for accommodations, she had the choice of high-end hotels, reasonably priced efficiency apartments, and gorgeous private villas that were displayed on a glossy ad for a real estate company. Transportation was as easy as hiring a car from one of the rental agencies; some had desks at the hotels. Although she might get away with paying cash for a room, she'd have to show a driver's license to rent a vehicle, which prompted her to put on the brakes and rethink her whole scheme. She didn't have her driver's license or any other form of identification. It was all in the room at the Caribbean Club.

She spent ten more of Glenn's dollars on a snack. While she ate the boxed club sandwich, she laid out a plan to spite him in a way he would never forget. If she had kept the passwords to his email, she could've made it look like he set up the whole thing: killing her, collecting the insurance, a trail of evidence for the cops or the FBI or Interpol, whichever agency took the case. After completing that task—the specifics of which eluded her at the moment—she would reappear. A day or two out of sight would be enough time for the authorities to catch on. She thought about going back for the passwords.

Then she asked herself what if the authorities didn't catch on? This question haunted her as she gazed out at the ocean from beneath a vacant palapa hut on the beach by the Hyatt, only a short distance from the Caribbean Club. Behind her, the hotel bustled with guests coming back from dinner, singing karaoke, and holding hands as they walked the promenade that connected all the hotels on Palm Beach. What if the police didn't find the clues she left for them? Or, what if one of those Internet nerds decoded the data and caught her in her own gambit? She'd be the guilty party. They might even charge her with attempted homicide thinking Glenn somehow survived her initial attack. The insurance paid both ways, so that would be a logical conclusion.

The hardest part was accepting that Glenn had been ahead of her, that he nearly got away with killing her. Then again, she asked herself, isn't being alive a victory in itself? Of course she was grateful to be breathing and not shark food, but it was a small consolation when weighed against being outsmarted by a wife-beater turned charmer turned murderer.

But should she push her luck? No. The smart thing to do was camp out for the night, then make her presence known the next morning. There were lots of places along the beach where she could show up, say she'd been lost at sea but managed to paddle in. She did have Glenn's money, which she could hide and come back for another time or just forget about it.

Besides, what was Glenn going to say? Nothing because he couldn't remember what happened. The drugs did that, blanked the tape, erased the data. Kathy knew this from her classes at Temple and online research. The unwitting pharmaceutical reps filled her in on anesthetics as well. The bastard wasn't about to admit trying to kill her. No, he'd win the Academy Award for the grieving boyfriend who found joy when his sweetheart was discovered alive. If she went along, gave him a big hug, shed tears, kissed him like a stoic keeper of the flame, it would all make sense. She guessed Glenn might not even remember his attempt in the ocean, though he would know it had been his plan.

At this point she'd go nowhere with him alone. Not even to the room. Screw him. She would either fake an argument or leave a note for him. Whatever it took, she would get to the airport. Which left her wondering about a place to hide out until dawn.

At last the idea came to her when she saw a sailboat moving parallel to the beach. Glenn booked their snorkel cruise, and *Consuela* sent a minivan to pick them up at the Caribbean Club. They drove halfway down the island to a marina behind the airport. On the way to *Consuela*, Glenn noticed a worn-out wooden boat at the end of the pier. He tried to show off how much he knew by naming the type.

"Old schooner," Glenn said to the minivan driver.

"Belongs to Ernesto. He went to Colombia for special wood to fix her. Coming back on Monday. He's a friend of the captain you'll have for your cruise today."

"Let's take a closer look."

They walked out to the boat, Glenn pretending to be Jack

Kennedy with his head cocked and his hands in his pockets. "It'll be nice when it's finished," Glenn said as if he knew all about such refits.

The van driver had other ideas. "Fiberglass is much better. It doesn't rot like wood."

"Not as pretty," countered Glenn.

Had he been thinking about how he was going to spend his one point five million? Kathy bet he was. *Well, too bad, Glenny-boy. You're not getting a boat to sail off into the sunset.*

It was after ten o'clock when Kathy rode in a taxi from the Hyatt to Marandi, a restaurant only a few hundred yards from the Varadero Marina where that old schooner thumped against the pier. She recalled seeing the blue sign for the restaurant on the way to *Consuela.* She took her time walking along the road, minding her sore ankle with every step. A wide iron gate blocked the road into the marina, but there was no guard. A man twice her width could fit between the bars. She went through peering into the shadows for anyone who might see her. Sticking close to the boats on blocks, she edged toward the pier, conjuring up excuses to use if she were caught. A stray dog ambled over, sniffing at her legs.

"Good puppy," she told him. "No barking, okay?"

He panted expectantly, but when she gave him no food, he trailed off to the other side of the boatyard.

Kathy went down the wrong pier, doubled back, and finally got to the schooner. It took her a full minute to work up the courage to make the short leap onto the deck, which curved like an oversized banana from bow to stern. Had her ankle not been injured it would have been an easy hop. Rocking back and forth, she hurled herself across the narrow span, landing with a thud.

After adding a bruised shoulder to her other minor contusions, she shuffled along the deckhouse to the stern where she recalled seeing a door. It was there, down four steep stairs and held closed with nothing more than a loop of rope tied through the hasp. *Trusting people these boatmen,* Kathy thought.

She pulled open the door with caution, but it didn't so much as squeak. Wishing for a flashlight, Kathy limped forward with her hands feeling along the corridor. Spots of moonlight fell in through oval-shaped portholes. She entered a wider space that transformed into a galley as her eyes adjusted to the darkness. A settee built into the wall or hull or whatever it was called sat behind a table bolted to the floor. She took a seat and listened.

No alarms. No sounds of feet pounding along the dock. Nothing but a quiet creak when the boat pressed against a tire cushioning it from the pier.

From her plastic bag, Kathy removed a bottle of water and took a pull. She raised her legs onto the settee in an effort to relieve her ankle. The pain, the adrenalin flowing from the thought of what had happened, and the possibility of being discovered stowing away was going to make it a long, sleepless night.

She tried breathing exercises and then fantasized about where she might go on vacation when this ordeal was over. Nothing worked. The ankle was pounding away. Wanting relief, she went back into her bag for one of the Ambien samples.

The pill slipped out of the blister pack onto the table. She popped it into her mouth and sent it down behind a gulp of water. *Tomorrow,* she thought, *I'm out of here.*

As powerful as his computer was, Romy Tromp still had to wait twenty minutes for his photos to transfer from his camera to the hard drive and then burn onto a disc for Chief Calenda. It would be Eddie Bakker who opened the images on a computer in his office since Calenda himself was low-tech. In the evenings, the chief walked a beat on the streets of San Nicolaas like a London Bobby, stopping in for a cup of coffee on the balcony above Charlie's Bar now and then. The other cops liked to ride on motorcycles or in air-conditioned SUVs, which didn't seem to bother him because he was marking time until Agnes finished her shift at the airport.

Tromp pressed the disc into a jewel case, and tucked it in his camera bag where he would not forget it. He took out his phone, dialed the Caribbean Club front desk and asked for his cousin's cousin, Reynaldo.

"Reynaldo speaking."

"It's Romy."

"Bon nochi. Pasa bon?"

"*Hopi bon* if you tell me who's checked into 1406."

"You know I can't do that."

"Fifty florins will make you forget you did."

The sound of tapping on a computer keyboard came over the line, then Reynaldo said, "Glenn Hogan."

"Spell that."

"H-O-G-A-N with two n's in Glenn."

"Got it. And where is Mr. Hogan from?"

"A hundred florins?"

"Are you gambling again, Reynaldo? Hundred florins it is."

"Media in Pennsylvania. USA."

"*Danki*. I'll drop the florins off at your mom's because I'm sure you owe her some rent."

"Wait!"

Tromp set the phone on his desk and stared at it, contemplating the risks and rewards of calling GNN. A woman had gone missing before in Aruba, dinging the island's reputation as a carefree tourist destination. Similar to this case, an Aruban was not involved. No matter, when the TV networks got hold of the story, they ran it like a thoroughbred, whipping it all the way to the finish line. Tromp wasn't sure how he might look to his fellow islanders if he was the one who lit the fuse. If big networks came to him afterward, well, he could say he was just doing his job. If he went first, that might be thought of as betrayal.

Startled by his cellphone's old-fashioned ring, which sounded just like the phone that used to hang in his mother's kitchen, he snatched it off the desk and made the connection.

"Tromp," he said.

"You have the photos?" his editor asked without mentioning the subject.

"I'm emailing them to you now."

"What are you waiting for?"

Before he could make an excuse the line went dead. His editor was a decent man, but never agreed to put him on as a salaried employee. In the early days, he was too young. Now, Tromp didn't want to be staff because the photos would belong to the newspaper as work for hire. Being a freelancer meant he got paid for specific images as though they were products on a grocery store shelf, and Tromp picked them himself. More important, if he wanted to peddle them to any other organization, he was free to do so. That didn't mean his regular buyer, *Diario*'s editor, wasn't perturbed when he was passed over, but with flexibility came uncertainty.

Having been taught by his boss what made a solid news story in pictures, Tromp sent five images. A wide shot to set the scene, a medium shot of the Americano with the fisherman and the ambulance tech, two close-ups of the Americano from different angles, and an artistic one with sunset colors and the helicopter. It was the editor's choice which to print. Given the hour, just past eleven, Tromp doubted they'd make the morning edition.

If Clive Mitchell was going to catch the first flight tomorrow, he best not delay any longer to call GNN's assignment desk. Tromp waited four years to make this call. He did a dry run to hone his pitch.

"Hello, Romy Tromp here, calling from Aruba." In his head it sounded too nasal. He cleared his throat, tucked in his chin, and went for a lower tone. "Romy Tromp calling from Aruba." That one was like a boy imitating a man. He wasn't an actor; he was the real thing. He had the pictures to prove it. Say it like you mean it. "Romy Tromp calling." Better that time.

Jumping in with both feet, he pushed send.

Less than one ring later a man came on in rapid-fire, American English. "GNN. Assignment desk. Go!"

"Hi, uh … Romy Tromp …"

"Who?" the man interrupted.

"Romy Tromp from Aruba."

"Row Me Throw who?"

"Romy Tromp. R-O-M-Y. T-R-O-M-P. From Aruba. I have a story."

"From Aruba, yeah, that's good. How's the weather? Snowing yet?"

Tromp double-checked to see if he'd dialed the wrong number. No, it was the right one. This guy was not taking him seriously.

"Listen, a woman's gone missing down here, an American lady."

"Back up, my friend. Spell that name again."

After spelling his name two more times and giving his phone number, the man wanted details.

"American woman. Missing. What happened?"

"They were swimming near Baby Beach …"

"Stop right there. They? Who's they?"

"Glenn Hogan and a woman named Kathy."

"She got a last name?"

"I don't have it yet."

"The story is developing?"

"It is," confirmed Tromp. "I was the first reporter on the scene. I got there with the ambulance."

"Is there a body?"

"She's missing and Hogan had a bloody nose."

"And you're a reporter? Who do you work for?"

"*Diario*, the biggest newspaper on the island."

"Hold on."

Music played for several minutes during which Tromp reviewed his performance. He did well, only stretching the truth a little by saying he was a reporter.

The man came back on the line. "Mr. Tromp," he said. "First

of all, thanks for the call, and I apologize for the hassle at the beginning. We get some crank calls here, and they tend to start this time of night. Another tip came in on this story a while ago."

"From who?" blurted Tromp.

"We don't reveal our sources. Thing is, I'm going to pass your contact info up the ladder, and if men more powerful than me want to know more, we'll be in touch."

"I'm telling you, this is going to break big. It's a story for Clive Mitchell. I can show him …"

"Those men I mentioned a second ago will make that decision. In the meantime, keep your eyes and ears open and give us a call if something new turns up."

"Yeah, but …"

"Thanks again, Mr. Tromp. Stay on it. I got other phones to answer. Have a good night."

His first thought was that Reynaldo beat him to the punch. Upon further consideration, his cousin's cousin palmed twenties to help tourists with their luggage. He wouldn't know how to get GNN's number let alone what to tell them. Besides, he didn't know a woman was missing. Who was it then? One of *Diario's* regular reporters? They were staff and couldn't deal a story without permission. The boss was clever about arranging things that way. A reporter for one of the other papers? Maybe, which meant *Diario's* competition was stepping up to the plate.

"Damn!" Tromp shouted at the ceiling. His big chance and it fizzled in a matter of hours. He hoisted his camera bag onto his shoulder and headed for his car.

Half an hour later he gave the disc with his photos to Bakker. The detective slipped it into the drive on his computer and the full color images filled the screen.

"Good work," commented Bakker.

"If that's all you need, I'm going home." Turning to leave he stood face to face with the chief.

"Everything okay, Romy?"

"Just tired," the photographer replied.

"Thanks for the photos. I'll make a request you get paid for them."

"I'd rather have a get-out-of-jail-free card," groaned Tromp as he sidestepped the chief and headed down the hall.

"Anything we can use?" the chief asked his number two.

"I'm not sure yet, but the video is going to make an impression on you."

"Tromp was taking video?"

"No," Bakker answered. "Glenn Hogan was."

6

Upon seeing the men in blue uniforms, Kathy was sure she was going to jail. She began to cry, holding her head in her hands, as she waited for them to come through the door. Looking up, she watched their black shoes pass by the portholes. Any second now, they would be clomping over the deck, down those few stairs, and entering the cabin where she sat with her swollen ankle up on the settee and her plastic bag filled with things she took from Glenn's room. How was she going to explain what she was doing on someone's boat with a bundle of cash, a pair of fur-lined handcuffs, and a bunch of pills that any pharmacist knew would knock you for a loop?

If she hadn't taken that Ambien, she wouldn't have slept well past dawn. She would have lowered herself into the water and shouted for help. Who was to say she hadn't drifted all the way here? But it was too late. People were out and about, working on their boats, getting ready for a day of fishing. They would see her as would the two policemen.

As she sat there weeping, she wondered if this was somehow part of Glenn's plan. Maybe he was a cop himself, working
undercover, tipped off by one of her old boyfriends. He set her
up. Lured her into a ploy with a trip to Aruba, the insurance,
the whole nine yards to bust her for being a black widow. He
knew she would be able to swim to shore and try to get away.
Others could be working with him, such as the local authorities whom she would never suspect. How stupid could she
have been?

More feet went past the portholes. Eyes darting about the
cabin, she searched for a place to hide the pills. No evidence, no
crime, right? A gap between the boards in the ceiling seemed
like a good place. The first bit of weight on her ankle caused
her to yelp. She fell back on the settee and awaited her fate,
more tears streaming down her cheeks.

Minutes went by as she steeled herself for the inevitable.
She wiped her face on her arm and sat up straight. More time
elapsed and no one came. The urge to pee was overwhelming.

"Let's get this over with," she muttered.

Risking a peek through the nearest porthole, she pulled
herself up with her arms for a better view, taking great care to
avoid any pressure on her ankle. Two officers stood with their
backs to her. They were near the opposite end of the pier talking to a beefy fellow who Kathy thought resembled the captain
from their snorkel cruise.

Dipping down, she reached for a set of binoculars hanging
from a peg on the cabin wall. Using them, she confirmed it was
Captain Hubert. He talked with his hands, bobbed his head,
gestured to his boat, and then shook hands with the policemen

who turned and started in her direction.

Clutching the binoculars, she imagined the conversation. Captain Hubert surely told them about Glenn admiring his pal's schooner, yeah, the one over there by itself. Hubert's crew was no doubt waiting for her to be dragged out of the cabin. What a laugh they'd have watching her being carried away! But nothing happened.

Taking another glance, she watched the cops walk to the parking lot and get into an official-looking SUV. They hadn't come for her. She had another chance. She giggled like a little girl, falling over on the settee with both feet in the air.

Chief Calenda would have arrested Glenn Hogan last night on suspicion of murder, but he didn't have a body. Nor did he have a motive or any of the other evidence needed to bring charges. He had his intuition, which identified Hogan as a liar. Not the typical kind who crashed their car then claimed they had only a beer when it was really a whole case. No, Hogan's deceit was in a different league. Individual circumstances of his account could be true. Any pair of them might be a coincidence. Three or more was pure fabrication. Calenda also had a few clues that experience told him would prove his suspicions accurate.

What gave him pause was the phone call that came while he was driving home.

"Tell me what happened," Aruba's prime minister said into his ear with pure, digital clarity.

Calenda took his time laying out the events as they occurred from the time he got the initial request to the moment he left the station after viewing the footage Bakker copied from Glenn

Hogan's video camera.

"We have to get this exactly right ..." the prime minister sighed. He didn't have to add, "... because of what happened last time."

"I'm meeting with Prosecutor Evert at noon."

"Tell him to call me before doing anything drastic."

"You should know Romy Tromp was there yesterday. He lent us his photographs, but I'm sure they'll be broadcast to the world."

"We've been through it before, Chief."

There ended the call, which gave Calenda good reason to employ restraint. He abhorred the idea of giving a suspect time to prepare, though there was an equal chance Hogan would trip himself by botching the cover-up. In any case, the most important thing was to find Kathy Barrow. To that end, the Dutch Marines, the Fire Department, and several civilian groups were crisscrossing the water off Baby Beach all the way to the refinery. In past drowning incidents in this area, the body always washed ashore within about a mile of where the person was last seen. Calenda expected the same to happen in this case, if, in fact, that part of Hogan's story was true.

Last night, the chief skipped his usual excursion through San Nicolaas. It was normal for him to walk about town before ending his day. Police presence went a long way to foster order, but he left the town to its own devices. He went home to find Agnes waiting up for him with a cup of hot chocolate in her hands.

"A pilot reported flashing red lights at the end of the island," she said. "I take it aliens haven't landed."

A serious man who knew his own personality could be a

heavy burden, Calenda appreciated Agnes's sense of humor. He met her through his friend, Herr Diedrik, a civil lawyer renowned in Aruba and Colombia. Diedrik had been set up on a blind date with Agnes by his sister, who couldn't imagine her brother not being married and expanding the family with children. Diedrik found an excuse to rush off to Colombia, but gentleman that he is, asked Calenda to stand in for him. The lawyer wasn't offended when Agnes and Calenda continued the relationship, he was relieved. It had been his plan all along to slip the marriage noose.

Calenda also had no plans to marry. Nonetheless, her company was a welcome addition to his life. Coming home to another person was an adjustment after thirty years of living alone, but a pot of coffee or a meal on the table or a kiss on the cheek were not to be underestimated. A good laugh now and then didn't hurt either.

Agnes made him a cup of hot chocolate while he gave her the same narrative he shared with the prime minister. By the time he finished, he was sitting beside her on the couch, the two of them sipping from their mugs.

"When this is over," Agnes said, "let's take a vacation to Switzerland. I'd like to see some snow for a change."

He tapped her mug with his and agreed.

Now he was riding in the passenger seat while Detective Bakker drove him to the prosecutor's office. Earlier, they spoke with Captain Hubert who explained everything that happened the day he took Glenn Hogan and Kathy Barrow on a private snorkel cruise. Hubert described them as any other American couple: a little loud, steady drinkers, fair when it came to tips.

"The only thing the man didn't like was we weren't under sail," Hubert said. "I told him this time of year the wind lays down. Hey, I don't want to pay for fuel when the wind is free, but you have to get there somehow."

Other than that, it was a smooth ride. No fights between them, no arguments with the crew. The first mate drove them back to the Caribbean Club, which was part of the package.

"Was he doing reconnaissance?" Bakker postulated as they departed Varadero Marina. "He checked out the conditions so he would know what to expect when he got down there on his own."

"Maybe," Calenda said. "Not that I don't think you did a thorough search, but is it possible you missed the handcuffs?"

"Not a chance," Bakker replied. "On the video, they were bright pink. These eyes would have spotted them."

"Under the mattress? Behind the toilet? Hanging under the sink?"

"No, no, and no."

When Bakker first arrived on the island, the chief took him on because the other jurisdictions didn't want him. They thought the newly minted detective was a European playboy out to use his beach tennis league as a pickup venue. He did have a smash serve and legs long enough to leap over his teammates, but Bakker was a proficient detective and nobody's cousin. He didn't care who he pegged for a crime. He put together evidence piece by piece. Where it led was of no social consequence beyond turning over a provable scenario to the prosecutor's office. That Uncle Jorge was headed to jail wasn't going to ruin his Christmas dinner.

"Do you think the prosecutor will have a report from the

FBI when we get there?" Bakker asked.

"Good question."

Senior Prosecutor Milo Evert handed a sheaf of paper to Bakker even as he continued to speak to Chief Calenda. Evert was a dowdy man of small stature with heavy glasses, tiny hands and thick lips. He held the position for a month more than two years, during which he managed to arrange more plea deals than Calenda would have preferred, but was upfront about his alternatives to prison for non-violent offenders. Calenda admired the man's aspirations, but liked to remind him that even if criminals in prison further spoiled their own kind at least they didn't ply the trade on new recruits.

Today was not the day to argue the justice system. Thanks to Bakker's technological prowess, Evert received a summary report, including a few photos, via email first thing that morning. It didn't take the prime minister's prodding to get Evert to review it at once. He knew what was at stake, the island's image in the eyes of tourists the world over, or as Texans say "the whole kit and caboodle." That was how Agnes put it last night anyway.

"This is from the FBI," Evert said handing over the raft of pages. "Efficient when they want to be. They contacted the local police in Mr. Hogan's district and sent us a copy of his file. I'm impressed."

"Assault of a female," Bakker read aloud from the first sheet. "Pled to a misdemeanor. Restraining order. Community service. A fine paid in cash."

Raising a critical eyebrow at Prosecutor Evert, Calenda allowed Bakker to continue.

"No other criminal history in the past twelve months, but the assault doesn't make him look good."

Evert adjusted his glasses. "In light of the, shall we call it, spotlight that will be shining on us any minute now, I recommend we detain Mr. Hogan while the investigation continues. We don't have to issue charges upon arrest, so he will be our guest, and if things turn out in his favor, then he flies home a vindicated man. If your inquiries provide more evidence, connections if you will, linking him to Ms. Barrow's disappearance, combined with some more data from the FBI up north, I will be happy to provide Mr. Hogan with a list of competent attorneys from which he may choose counsel to argue on his behalf before the judge."

Summarizing, Calenda said, "You're considering a murder charge."

"Difficult without a body," responded Evert. "Let us hope Ms. Barrow returns to us alive. If not, perhaps we talk about criminal neglect. We have plenty of time to mull this over. With today's warrant, I'm asking for a minimum sixty-day detention. Do you think that is sufficient?"

"You never know," Calenda answered.

"Sixty days. Conduct the arrest as discretely as possible before two o'clock this afternoon. I'll brief the prime minister and then make a statement to the press. Anything else?"

Dismissed, Calenda and Bakker went downstairs to find an assortment of reporters waiting just outside the door.

"Want to go the other way?" suggested Bakker.

"Doesn't bother me," Calenda groused, donning his hat and continuing on.

Among the pack, the chief recognized most of the faces.

One he didn't see was Romy Tromp. Between the shouted questions, microphones thrust under his chin, and cameras poked at him, Calenda strained to see if the young man was part of the swarm. He wasn't, and that was cause for concern. Tromp had a habit of sticking his lens in uncomfortable places.

A stack of messages filled the screen of Romy Tromp's cellphone. He scrolled through them, found nothing unexpected, and put the device back on his desk. If it hadn't cost him a thousand florins he would have thrown it across the room. He went through his temper tantrum last night and had now moved on to the more adult expression of sulking.

To maintain a professional air, Tromp called his editor first thing in the morning to say he wouldn't be able to shoot any photos today.

"Sick," he said. "Bad Chinese food."

"How many times do I have to tell you to stay away from that stuff?" his editor admonished him. "Eat your mother's cooking."

Because he lived with his parents, Romy ate nothing but his mother's cooking for dinner. Breakfast and lunch varied from a bag of chips and a can of Coke to something in a Styrofoam container bought from one of Aruba's many snack trucks. His eighteen-year-old stomach and a goat shared the ability to process anything short of broken glass. The only time he got sick was when he once drank half a bottle of Grand Old Parr Scotch Whisky on a dare, and he wouldn't make that mistake again.

"You'll be fine this afternoon," his editor went on. "I want you to get on top of this story. Prosecutor Evert has called a press conference for two o'clock."

"Can't do it," Tromp moaned. "Not today."

"Who's going to get the shots? Miguel? Santo? They can't remember to take off the lens cap."

"They'll get what you need."

"Drink a bottle of Pepto and take a rest. By noon you'll be right as rain. I'll call with the target's location."

His editor liked to use military terms, appropriate given the organization he ran. *Diario's* sources went far beyond a cousin's cousin at a hotel's front desk. Bank employees, flight attendants, waiters, taxi drivers, shipping clerks, any and all trades fed information into the beast. If it happened on the island, it was known to *Diario*. Tromp had a similar list of providers, which he shared with no one.

Beyond someone beating him to the punch with GNN, Tromp was further depressed by the price of video cameras. For two hours he scrolled through retailer websites like Amazon and B&H Photo Video. A decent camera, one with five-star reviews and the moniker *Professional* cost more than three thousand. And that was for a bottom-of-the-barrel pro model with a shorter zoom lens lacking the reach of the ones that cost a couple thousand more. Then there were the accessories: a microphone, tripod, extra batteries, and a light.

He considered trading in his Nikon to raise the cash. Like all electronic equipment it wasn't worth twenty percent what he paid for it three years ago. With that paltry sum and his savings, he was still short of a basic video rig, and if he wanted high quality footage he would need to come up with double what he had.

On a lark he rang his pal, Sandeep Rao, whose father owned

House of Rao, an electronics shop dealing in all things digital.

Sandeep always answered on the first ring because he carried the store's cordless handset in his shirt pocket. "Hey, Romy, saw your photo of the Americano in the paper this morning. Good one!"

Tromp got straight to the point. "Are there any deals on video cameras this week?"

"Don't tell me you're giving up the Nikon."

"No, I'm keeping the Nikon," Tromp said.

"Doubling down. Impressive. Trying to get something on this American dude to sell to the U.S. networks?"

Sandeep got it right, but Tromp didn't want to reveal his intentions so he acted humble by replying with a half-truth.

"They don't have time for me. I want to take video at Disney World next month."

"Disney? Why would you go there when New York City's only two more flying hours away?"

His pal had the bad habit of always having a better idea, which was fine when it came to electronics, but annoying the rest of the time. Tromp inquired again about video cameras.

"Last week, my dad took a trade from a tourist off a cruise ship. I know you're a Nikon guy, but we're talking video now so you have to change horses. The trade-in was a Canon VIXIA. Fits right in your hand. SD cards for storage."

"How's the picture?"

"Good, especially for internet stuff."

"How much?"

"For you, my friend, six hundred."

"Florins?"

"Dollars. That camera sells for twelve hundred new. I'm

offering it half price."

"And used."

"Works perfectly. If not, I'll take it back with no questions asked."

Six hundred dollars was less Tromp's worry than buying a useless camera. What if he recorded something of interest but GNN couldn't use it for lack of quality or compatibility? Then he'd have a six-hundred-dollar paperweight.

Sandeep sweetened the offer. "Free 32-gig SD card," he said. "That's a thirty-dollar value."

"Charge the battery. I'm on my way."

Waking up on a tropical island. Palm trees. Powder-soft beaches. Clear-blue water. Glenn loved it. He pulled back the curtains, took in the view, and ordered breakfast from room service. Stepping onto the balcony, he watched a couple of foxy chicks stake out their territory by the pool. If he wasn't supposed to be in grieving mode, he would have trotted down there, found out where they were from, and asked what they were doing tonight. Unfortunately, his role for the next few days was distraught boyfriend, victim of tragedy. Later, in six months or so, he'd be in playboy heaven, cleaning up at the high-roller tables in the nearest casino and getting plenty of ass. A winner was attractive, but one at a table with a five-hundred-dollar minimum was irresistible.

The hinky look the room-service waiter gave him while waiting for Glenn to sign the bill nearly got him a right hook. Instead, Glenn kept cool, averted his eyes, and wrote in a generous tip. Now was not the time to play cheapskate, not with a mountain of cash on the way. Plus, reporters always interviewed staff for inside dirt. For a second, Glenn wished he thought ahead a little more instead of fantasizing about those pool-side hotties. He could've splashed some water on his face and pretended to be crying.

Through breakfast, he racked his brain in an effort to remember more of what happened yesterday. Nothing came to mind. Not a single memory after they went in the water. In the bathroom mirror, he studied his face. The bruise on the left side wasn't big enough or sufficiently colored to cause a blackout. Not in his judgment anyway. His nose was fine, too. Any tap on the beak can cause a nosebleed. His legs were sore, but otherwise he felt ready for anything. To prove the point, he did a set of push-ups.

Back on the balcony, taking in a fresh medley of beauties sunbathing by the pool, Glenn reassembled his story. Kathy wanted to go snorkeling again, to the same place they'd been on the sailboat. He bought the masks and such at the hotel gift shop. After a late lunch, they drove to the other end of the island. Went in the water behind the dive shop. They got in trouble with the current. He lost track of her. Most of it was true.

For reinforcement he added a warning from one of the crew on the boat, "Stay close." No, not strong enough. "Be careful of the currents." Yeah, that was better. Who told you that? I don't know, one of the deckhands. What were they going to say? That they didn't brief their passengers on the conditions? If that happened in the States, it could spell big trouble, and a whopper of a lawsuit if somebody died.

When the cops returned, he would be ready. They'd either have Kathy's body or not. They were going to play rough. He didn't relish the idea of being a sissy, but a crying fit in their presence would bolster his credibility better than a letter from the Pope. They might not believe him, especially the older one who looked like he swallowed a lemon. It didn't matter. What evidence did they have that he did anything wrong? None. Zero. Nada, as they say in Spanish, which Glenn had heard spoken on the island.

He wasn't oblivious to the material they would dredge up. Of course they would talk to the police in the States, find out about his beef there, the restraining order and so on. Big deal. That was a year ago and long past stale. He did his community service, paid the fine, and even got a commendation at work for hosting a diversity seminar. Oh, you found an insurance policy? Take a closer look and don't forget to talk to the other broad at the pharmacy who faxed it in. She was there when Kathy decided to name a beneficiary. She heard me tell her to put her mom down. She called me a *keeper*.

Chuckling, Glenn continued to survey the pool, thinking he might have a week to go before this mess cleaned itself up. Then he'd request two weeks of family leave to mourn the loss of his *significant other* and recover from the mistreatment he'd suffered at the hands of foreign authorities. Maybe he'd check out the European beaches, a location where this story would never reach. Girls with accents were sexy.

His Euro-jaunt would be a lot more fun if he sued the hotel for the winnings one of their employees stole from his room's safe. They might give him a go-away payment to avoid negative publicity. After all, they knew he won it in their casino. Although he set the combination when he first entered the room, Glenn was certain the hotel had a master number to unlock the box in case some dippy tourist forgot their code.

Seething at the loss, he re-entered the room and headed for the phone but stopped. Quibbling over the five grand was a bad move. It made him seem greedy. The hotel might call the same cops who were investigating him. If they discovered the details of his gambling habits, they may view the insurance policy in a different light. As pissed off as he was, he decided to let it go. Some local clipped him. *Congratulations.* It wasn't one third of one percent of what he had coming.

Glenn wasted the next hours alternately watching TV and the women by the pool. The waiting made him antsy. He wanted to get out, maybe mingle with the chicks, then take a pass through the casino. During the day, low-rollers clogged up the tables, but manipulating them to boost his take was a walk in the park. He showered, pulled on fresh clothes, and counted the bankroll in his wallet. Eight hundred bucks. He thought he had a thousand in there, but then again, he'd been wasting money on Kathy to look like a good sport. Eight hundred, a thousand, what's the difference? He won that much in a single hand.

As for those cops, if they found him at a blackjack table, he'd say something sappy like how he was trying to relive their last day together. Oh, that was good, really good. He put his room key in his pocket and headed for the door.

7

The video camera Sandeep sold him weighed less than a can of Coke. Tromp cupped it in his hand, pointing it at subjects near and far, marveling at how fast the autofocus worked. The start/stop button was convenient to his thumb as was the zoom toggle right under his index finger. He gave it a try, recording some pelicans flying along Palm Beach. They landed on the stern of an empty boat. If he wanted to, he could view the footage on the swing out display.

Satisfied he understood how to operate the new camera, Tromp retreated to his car. He'd parked in the alley between the Hyatt and Occidental hotels, not far from the Caribbean Club. Sitting in the driver's seat with the door open, he worked up the courage to stake out Glenn Hogan's room. No doubt he'd be ejected if he were caught trailing one of the hotel's guests or lingering in the hallway, but he decided to go for it anyway. He needed something to get the attention of GNN.

Leaving his car behind, he walked along the promenade, past all the people having a good time on the beach. He wore a disguise of a loose-fitting Guayabera shirt over a pair of shorts instead of his trademark black T-shirt and cargo pants. The aviator glasses were in place over his eyes. He wasn't giving those up, not in this bright sunshine.

His cellphone rang, catching the attention of a cute girl headed straight for him.

"Not me," she joked.

"Too bad," he returned, pulling the phone out of his pocket. It wasn't *Diario*'s editor calling; it was another number. He made the connection and held the phone to his ear.

"Hey, Romy, it's Reynaldo."

"What's up?"

"They're arresting the Americano. Right now!"

Ahead, Tromp could see the top of the Caribbean Club. He quickened his pace.

Reynaldo babbled on. "There are six cops in the lobby and a van out front. Tons of reporters."

"On my way!"

"Listen! That's a decoy. Calenda and another cop, Dutch-looking, came in the service entrance on the north side where they do load-ins for banquets. They have another van there with two patrolmen."

"Got it!"

"Two hundred florins, Romy. You owe me two hundred for this!"

Tromp stuffed the phone in his shirt and bolted down the promenade. Dodging a family holding hands, he just about tumbled into a heap on the beach. Back on the concrete, he picked up speed, the camera bag flopping against his hip.

The north service entrance to the Caribbean Club was shielded from view by palm trees and a dense hedge. Tromp saw no way through it. His only option was to go out front and come in via the parking lot the way the trucks did. He started for the hotel's main entrance when a flash of orange caught his attention. It was a stray cat lurking out from under the hedge. Tromp dropped to his knees, scaring the cat away and revealing a narrow tunnel of branches.

Stuffing his camera bag through first, Tromp shoved himself into the tiny passage. Popping out on the other side with a number of long scratches on his legs, he wished he'd worn his cargo pants instead of shorts. No matter, he was clear, and being so low to the ground, out of sight. He stayed prone, crawling forward like a sniper getting into position. More cover became available in the form of two trash dumpsters. He got between them, lifted up his video camera, and switched it on.

Nothing much happened. The policemen leaned against the van. A hotel worker came out for a look and went back inside. Tromp zoomed in on the cops then on the stairs leading down from the loading dock. Using his free hand, he yanked out his Nikon. He felt like a Wild West gunfighter with the two cameras ready to fire. If he got video and stills it meant double the money.

At once the two officers by the van straightened up. Tromp tapped the start button on the video camera and the shutter on the Nikon simultaneously. Then he panned right in time for Calenda, Bakker, and Glenn Hogan to enter the frame. Hogan's hands were cuffed in front of his waist. Bakker gripped his arm as they crossed to the van where Hogan was helped into the back. The door slid closed, the other cops got in the front, and off they went at an easy pace. Calenda and Bakker stood in the empty lot for a moment before walking down the driveway.

Tromp's phone rang again. The sound carried across the lot, causing Calenda to stop and turn. In the nick of time Tromp hit the ground. He squashed the phone between his chest and the asphalt, praying for it to stop ringing. It didn't, but Calenda no longer seemed interested. He moved on, nodding for Bakker to join him.

In the clear, Tromp set down his cameras and checked the phone. It was his editor. He returned the call.

"Milo Evert is giving a press conference soon. I'm counting on you to be there."

"I got something better than that," Tromp told him.

Not halfway down the hall to the elevator, Glenn ran into Chief Calenda and Eddie Bakker.

"Let's go back to your room," the chief told him.

"You're in charge," replied Glenn, turning on his heel.

They marched to his room, went inside, and that's when the fun began. Bakker took out a set of those plastic cuffs all the police used these days. Incredulous that they planned to cuff him, Glenn was at a loss for words. He wrestled with something clever then strove for a sympathetic plea worthy of his status as a victim, but came up with nothing but a dumbfounded stare, like a dog left behind at the door.

"You're under arrest," the chief informed him. "Detective Bakker will attach the restraints."

"Attach the restraints?" scoffed Glenn. "You think I'm going to start a fight?"

"Please place your hands together," said the chief.

Glenn obeyed, feeling the plastic loops tighten on his wrists. "I'll cooperate in any way I can," he said.

"Thank you," the chief told him.

Bakker jumped in with a question that rattled him. "Where are the handcuffs?" the detective asked.

At first Glenn didn't know what to think. They were the police; they had the handcuffs. They already put them on. Was this some kind of trick?

"The handcuffs, Mr. Hogan, the pink ones seen in the video you made here in this room. Where are they?"

Later he would wonder why, but for some reason Glenn looked at Chief Calenda and said, "I want a lawyer."

Whenever she thought of sailboats, Kathy imagined a sleek vessel skimming across the water, the wind in her hair, blue skies overhead, and a tan, virile man wearing an open linen shirt at the wheel. She never considered the practical matters of a boat, like how small everything had to be to fit inside a shape without a single right angle.

For example, the bathroom, or head as the crew on the *Consuela* referred to it, was a closet-sized space with a sink not much larger than a soup bowl. Aboard the schooner where she planned to hide out for the night, she found a similar facility. The problem was, she didn't know if the toilet would flush and if she should try it for fear it might make noise and reveal her hiding place. Her bladder demanded relief, leaving her no choice but to use it. Feeling better, she closed the lid and returned to the settee.

Pondering her circumstances, Kathy fidgeted with nervous

energy. Daylight fell into the cabin from the row of portholes on each side, making it easy to see the potential of this boat. The table in front of her, not to mention every other surface, was battered and dusty. Despite this, the wood underneath showed a handsome grain. The cooking space was well-appointed with a stove, sink, and numerous pigeonholes to stash supplies. The owner's current provisions included jars of screws, nuts, and bolts, along with cans of beans and soup. After a thorough cleaning and lots of polish, the galley could become a compact beauty.

The odd thing was the pole standing at the forward end of the room. She figured it was the lower part of the mast that carried the sails above. She guessed it had to be connected to the bottom of the boat for strength. Whatever the case, it got in the way, causing the walkway between the cooking area and the settee to be skewed to one side. Apparently, structural requirements took precedence over interior arrangement.

Kathy ventured around, clutching the many rails and handholds to go easy on her ankle. In back, on either side of the door through which she entered the boat, she found a pair of cramped bunkrooms. Both were cluttered with all types of tools, unfinished lumber, and supplies. Going forward, she came upon another bunkroom with a double bed built into one side and a column of drawers set in the other. The owner must have been sleeping in this room because there were sheets on the mattress and personal articles on a thin shelf.

A bead of sweat rolled down Kathy's cheek. The temperature rose by the minute. She hobbled back to the cabin door and risked opening it a crack. Although the weak breeze sent in fresh air, it was hardly enough to make the space habitable. In the galley, she went to the portholes opposite the settee. They faced the water instead of the pier. Four latches secured each one. She twisted them free, swung back the heavy glass, and figured out how to use the latches to prop them open. Immediately, more air and the sound of voices flowed into the cabin.

Frightened of being discovered through the portholes, Kathy limped to the forward bunk where she sprawled on the bed. People outside laughed and spoke in a language she didn't know. It sounded vaguely like Spanish salted with English and a smattering of guttural tones. On the plane ride to the island she'd read in a free magazine that Aruba's local dialect was Papiamento, which she assumed was the language the people outside were using.

Staring up at the ceiling she noticed a crank handle at the end of a wide pipe. Curious, she stood up and peered into the tube. Another vent, she determined, and gave the crank a try. Ten complete turns later, the warm air stuck close to the ceiling rose out through the pipe like a chimney.

Soon the interior of the schooner settled into a comfortable range, warmer in the bow, cooler at the stern. Kathy stole glances through the portholes, keeping an eye on the comings and goings of the people on the pier. After a while, she seemed to be alone. The spaces where fishing boats had been parked were empty as was the spot *Consuela* had occupied.

Taking up the binoculars, she scanned the building at the end of the pier. A bar faced her, a line of empty stools standing guard and a single bartender whose attention was focused on a television mounted on the wall. A window behind him must have opened into a kitchen because a set of hands passed a platter through and he took it to the counter, sat down, and began to eat.

Kathy's stomach rumbled at the sight of the man munching through his lunch. She hadn't eaten since the previous day. After hanging the binoculars in their place, she rummaged through the galley. It was clear the owner wasn't making his meals on board. Other than the cans of beans and soup, she found nothing more edible than a bottle of ketchup, two jars of peas, and a tin of uncooked rice. A case of bottled water sat in the bottom of the biggest cabinet, 24 one-liter bottles coated with dust like everything else. She'd always wanted to lose some weight, but this was a hell of a way to get started.

A bottle of water in hand, Kathy propped herself up in the bed, flexing her ankle to improve the range of motion. While the boat's owner may not be back until Monday, she vowed to stick to her plan. The last thing she wanted was to put the Arubans through the trouble of a pointless search. Then there was her mother. With her mental impairment, would she understand her daughter had gone missing? The stress might cause her to have another stroke. And why? Because her daughter had fun evening the score for something her father had done years ago.

Stupid, Kathy, stupid and vain. Consequences for you and others might be more than you bargained for.

Talking to herself brought on a sense of calm. Kathy managed to relax and review how she intended to regain control. A full day's rest would do wonders for her ankle. Stronger and with a clear head, she would walk down to that restaurant and call a taxi. She'd pay the driver to take her to the airport. Then, she'd have another taxi drive her to a house near the shore, where a nonexistent friend had invited her to stay for the week. She believed the two cabs were necessary so there would be no direct link to where she'd come from. That's how spies did it in the movies, wasn't it? A *cutout* they called it. Once the cab was out of sight, she'd work her way to the water. From then on, it would be a matter of staying awake until dawn, at which time she would call out to the first person she saw.

What about the bag of stuff from the Bamboo Bazaar? What about the money you stole? What about those stupid handcuffs that creep wanted to clamp on your wrists? If the cops found any of it a week later, or a month later, her story would be blown.

The money was the easiest part. Leaving it under a rock for some lucky soul might earn her points with Saint Peter at the pearly gates. Her sundress with the flower and the new dress she bought at the Bamboo Bazaar? They could be torn up and thrown in the trash somewhere near the beach and hopefully the police would never find them.

The last problem was the handcuffs. Beneath the faux fur they were metal. To the bottom they would sink if she dropped them over the side. But how deep was the water at the pier? What if a fisherman saw the vivid pink color through the clear water and thought it was an expensive lure someone had lost? Maybe she could rip off the fur then ditch the pieces separately.

Satisfied that she had most of the plan worked out, Kathy set the water down and took a deep breath. Her stomach pined for more than water, but she forced herself to think on the bright side. If losing a few pounds was the worst thing that came from this predicament, she would consider herself fortunate. On that happy note, she allowed the gentle rocking of the boat to lull her to sleep.

The unposted speed limit on Aruba's main roads was 80 kilometers per hour. Romy Tromp doubled it on his way home. To avoid any distractions, he tossed his cellphone over his shoulder to the back seat and kept both hands on the wheel. The phone's incessant ring annoyed him to no end, but he didn't allow it to affect his driving.

His parents' house was in San Fuego, just about the center of the island. There were several routes from the Caribbean Club to it, all of them jammed at this time of day. He knew there were two cruise ships docked in Oranjestad, rendering the 1A a linear parking lot. And the schools were about to let out putting extra cars and buses on the 2A leading to and from Santa Cruz.

As a result, he ran on the 3A into Ponton, whipped around the traffic circle, exiting toward Oranjestad. There he decelerated through the back streets, away from the schools, and popped out on Vondellan, a wide avenue that connected at another circle with the 1A. Then it was full speed past the airport, past the turn off for Parkietenbos and the sea beyond. That's where the Varadero Marina was. He photographed a fishing championship at the place every year in November.

"Romy Tromp reporting live from Aruba," he said loud enough to be heard over his car's roaring engine.

Hurtling for the traffic light at Balashi, he swung into the passing lane, sped past a delivery van, and dodged in just in time to avoid an on-coming Mercedes. The light ahead turned red. He let off the throttle, coasting in anticipation of the change.

Upon seeing green, he jammed the pedal down again.

"Today I obtained *exclusive* footage of the arrest of Glenn Hogan."

The shortest route was to make a left at the Balashi light, go up the hill to Santa Cruz then a right in the direction of Urataka and San Fuego. Knowing the school children would be milling about the area, he plunged ahead instead, making it to Pos Chiquito in less than thirty seconds. There he turned inland, racing up through Frenchmen's Pass and skirting the clogged areas by coming into San Fuego from the south.

"With continuing coverage live from Aruba," he said, "this is Romy Tromp. Back to you, Clive."

He slid to a stop in his family's driveway followed by a cloud of gritty dust that billowed over the house. To protect his equipment, he waited inside the car until the air cleared. His phone rang again. Taking it in hand, he saw his editor had called him twelve times. He stuffed the phone in his shirt, and grabbed his photo bag. Correction, it was now his video bag because that compact wonder he bought this morning was nestled in beside his Nikon.

His room had originally been a maid's quarters built at the rear of his parents' property. Romy moved in when the maid moved out. His parents could no longer afford her, not since his father had been laid off at the refinery and took a job as an air conditioning repairman. He had three small rooms and a bath, all to himself. A closet served as a darkroom until he went digital. Now it stored his favorite prints and copies of his best *Diario* front-page stories.

In the tiny living room, he installed an office in the manner of big-time news agencies. He'd seen photos online of Reuters,

The New York Times, and most important, GNN. A wide desk sat not against a wall, but in the middle where it bisected the room. His computer squatted on a rolling cart to the right, cables running over to the monitor on his desk. This way, the area both above and below the desk was free of clutter. The only thing occupying the blotter was a docking station to plug in his camera's memory cards.

While his computer spooled up, he eased his video and still cameras from the bag and set them on the desk. He wanted to see the live footage first, but as a professional he knew the most important task was to back up everything to avoid a digital disaster. The process took several minutes, during which he paced back and forth while the bar on the screen tracked from left to right. With the files secure on his spare hard drive, Tromp launched the video player program and stared at the screen.

The footage started crooked, with the van too high on the left side of the frame. Then it leveled as he panned right. There was Chief Calenda, then Eddie Bakker holding Glenn Hogan's arm. As they crossed to the van, he began a slow zoom that ended with a medium shot of Hogan ducking through the open door. Tromp didn't remember making the zoom; he must have done it by instinct. The van pulled out and that was the end.

He watched it a second time.

And a third.

His ticket to GNN was there on the desk, a ten-minute upload away from greatness.

For fun, he looked at the still images. They were all canted to the right but in focus. Some cropping and his editor would be thrilled. Tromp rubbed his hands together at the double dip. GNN on video. *Diario* in print.

It took him only a few minutes to clean up the photos, cue them in an email, and call his editor.

"Since when don't you answer the phone for me?" his editor barked. "Evert's doing the press conference this minute and you better hope Santo gets something useful."

"I got the arrest," Tromp replied.

"Nobody got the arrest because there was no arrest," his editor said. "It was a ruse put on by that wily Chief of Police from San Nicolaas."

"I got it." Tromp tapped the send button, forwarding the photos through cyberspace to his editor five miles away.

"Don't make up stories to cover your ass."

"Check your email."

After a long silence, his editor gulped, "*¡Por dios!* Excellent work Tromp."

"Going to cost double the usual price," Tromp teased. "I'm freelance, remember?"

"It's time you go on contract."

"Too late."

"I'll make a good deal with you."

Tromp disconnected. His money from *Diario* was as good as in the bank. The bonus from sales to worldwide news agencies like Associated Press and Reuters would recharge his savings, too. Combined it wouldn't be worth what the video might get him, but he wasn't thinking about money. He was thinking about his face on TV.

He shoved away from his desk and stood in front of the full-length mirror hanging on the wall. He had to get hold of himself if he was going to call the GNN assignment desk again to pitch his footage, and there was no better way than to act like who he wanted to be, an on-site reporter.

First he squared his shoulders, then placed one foot slightly ahead of the other. Not satisfied, he shifted, angling his body to the camera that wasn't there. He raised his chin, held up an imaginary microphone, and squinted his right eye.

"Romy Tromp reporting live," he said, listening to his voice bounce back. "Today in Aruba, an arrest."

His ringing phone interrupted his presentation. He started again.

"Tonight on GNN," he began, imitating the faceless man who introduced the evening programs. "We go to Romy Tromp with an update on the Aruba case."

The phone continued to ring.

"*Masha danki* ... I mean, thank you ..." His phone distracted him, but if Clive Mitchell could do this with bullets flying in Afghanistan, Tromp believed he could do it against an annoying cellphone.

"I'm standing here in front of the Caribbean Club, on Aruba's famous Palm Beach. This afternoon, police arrested an Americano ..." *Not an Americano, an American!*

He went to his desk, grabbed the phone, and just before he switched if off, saw a number on the screen he didn't recognize. The ten digits hinted at a number from the United States.

"Tromp," he answered.

"Hi there, Romy. Clive Mitchell calling."

8

——

Like Aruba's hotels, the island's prison overlooked the sea. It stood on a bluff near the southern tip, where guards in the corner towers watched kite surfers at Boca Grandi. Unlike those beautiful hotels, the prison lacked the dramatic grandeur of a building designed to impress guests with its luxury. It was a square fortress painted a single color with no balconies, corporate logos, or bellmen to handle luggage.

Chief Calenda and Detective Bakker escorted Glenn Hogan through a steel door into a drab room where he was relieved of the plastic bag containing his one change of clothes. A guard searched everything, filled out the official paperwork naming Hogan a prisoner, then showed the man to his cell. Hogan said nothing, not even acknowledging the time of his meeting the next day with Calenda, Bakker, and members of the prosecution. He stared at the walls, lips pressed shut, breathing through his nose like the wheezing steam iron at his favorite laundromat.

Returning to the police station, Calenda questioned Bakker about his examination of Glenn Hogan's vehicle.

"Let's talk about the car," the chief began. "Explain what you found."

"It's what I didn't find," Bakker replied. "We're supposed to believe this woman went snorkeling. So, I think about my beloved Hilda and myself when we go to swim with the fish. Hilda has a nice bikini …"

"You didn't find what?" interrupted Calenda.

"Kathy Barrow's clothing. No dress. No shorts. No pants. Nothing. Same with shoes. None. I don't gamble, but if you want to take a bet, I'll wager a hundred florins Ms. Barrow was not in the water wearing her clothes."

Agreeing, Calenda turned onto the road leading to Esso Heights, the last neighborhood Hogan and Barrow would have driven through before reaching what was left of the old Lago Colony.

"The next one is less certain, but still, I'd risk my money on it. You know, some people have those watertight pouches or boxes for their room keys, a few dollars, perhaps a credit card. They go into the ocean with this thing hanging around their neck or tied to a wrist. This way, no chance of losing the important stuff."

"Or having it stolen," Calenda put in.

"As you say. Did Ms. Barrow do this?" Bakker answered his own question. "I don't think so."

"Why not?"

"Her passport was in the room safe, her wallet in her luggage. The most she took with her for this excursion was some money, maybe one credit card, maybe a room key."

"If that's true then it doesn't point to Hogan as disposing of her personal items."

Releasing a big smile, Bakker said, "The room key, Chief. Where's her room key?"

"You're certain it was not in the car?"

"It was not under the carpet, over the visor, under the spare tire, tucked in the seat, or in the glove box. Not even in the pages of the owner's manual, where I always hide mine when I'm on vacation. And, more important, it was not in the room."

"The front desk confirms two keys were given out?"

"The Caribbean Club uses magnetic cards like the other hotels for guest rooms on every level except for the top floor, which is all suites, reserved for celebrities and other high-profile visitors. Old time metal keys are issued. Mr. Hogan was upgraded to Suite 1406 because the hotel wanted him to be comfortable after winning six thousand dollars over two nights at their casino. He requested two keys. The desk clerk provided them and marked the log where he was advised that a lost key would incur a five-hundred-dollar fee to change the locks."

"Expensive."

"I don't know why they haven't switched to the swipe cards that cost next to nothing and can be reprogrammed at the touch of a button. Something about giving VIP guests the feeling of a home away from home. Also, out of respect for privacy, there are no security cameras on the top floor."

"Naturally," Calenda acknowledged. "Therefore, her clothes and room key are missing, things that should have been in the car or nearby, and we have no video of them coming and going from the room."

"Correct. Using Romy Tromp's photos and a careful search of the area as far as the parking lot in front of the old Esso Club, we have no trace of the personal items. Already we dumped the trashcans at Baby Beach, Rodgers Beach, and checked a dumpster filled with debris at a house being remodeled in the Colony. The clothing should have been in the car or maybe under a rock near the water."

Thinking back to last night when he escorted Hogan to his rental to dress before heading to the hotel, Calenda recalled the man's footwear had been on the floor and his shirt was draped over the driver's seat.

"His clothes were in the car," the chief said to Bakker.

"They were. Are we to believe they disrobed for snorkeling in separate locations?"

"These facts have me speculating," the chief said, "about whether or not Kathy Barrow ever went in the water."

Bakker watched the smoke pouring out of a stack at the refinery. He cautioned his boss by saying, "It's always dangerous to speculate in police work."

"Let's hear your theory."

"I don't have one yet."

"There goes your trophy for Detective of the Year," chided Calenda.

"The facts tell us a woman is missing. No one saw her go in the water. Not fisherman Dennis, nor anyone else we interviewed. That doesn't mean she didn't go in the water. It means no one saw her."

"What about the dive shop?"

"They were busy inside, refilling tanks and cleaning equipment that came in from a dive earlier in the day. They finished work around four-thirty and went home."

"And didn't see anything?"

"They park in front of the building. They had no reason to look out back."

Calenda doubted that a more perfect place to cast someone adrift existed in Aruba. He stopped himself from further speculation with a reminder that jumping to conclusions on partial information often led to complete embarrassment.

"What else did you find in the car?"

"Nothing but the receipt from the rental company. No blood stains, weapons, or signs of struggle. The car has roughly 2,000 kilometers on it. Smells like new. No handcuffs and no key for the handcuffs, either."

Yes, the cuffs were on the video, and when he got to the station, the chief intended to review it again in preparation for discussing it with the prosecutor, which was going to be uncomfortable for everyone.

His bed wasn't half the size of the one at the Caribbean Club. The stainless steel toilet built into the wall lacked a cushioned seat. At least he had the cell to himself, which Glenn took as a sign indicating this thing was going the way he planned. They hadn't stuck him in with a giant thug to ratchet up the fear factor, or with a sniveling snitch who asked a million times why he was there in the hopes of getting him to admit something.

He stretched out on the bed, folded his hands behind his neck, and took stock of his position. The handcuffs had been a mistake. Even so, he knew they were playing him with that one. Of course, they must have taken them from under the socks in the bottom of his rolling carry-on. The cop with the sandy hair and blue eyes who searched his room probably tucked them into his pocket. It was their hole card to draw him into admitting something. In reality, it was a bluff because he knew he put the cuffs back. And no, they weren't stolen with the five grand, because his suitcase had been untouched. The thief that grabbed the money wasn't interested in trinkets or he would've taken Kathy's necklace, ripped apart her bag for more, and done the same to Glenn's suitcase in the off chance a watch had been left behind. Whoever pulled that little caper was likely a casino employee who knew about his wins. Cash and carry was his modus operandi. Untraceable.

The best way to handle the issue was to deny the cuffs were missing. Say they had to be in the suitcase. Say you put them back in there. When they hammer the table, telling you they're gone, just shrug.

"You guys took them because you lost your own," he said aloud to the overhead light.

The next thing he considered was his financial position. Before he left the States, he'd built up some cash in his checking account and whittled down the credit card bills. He still owed the casino in Atlantic City twenty-five large, but that was a recent blunder, a bad streak. It didn't matter because he'd enrolled in Gamblers Anonymous last month. The weekly meetings were the biggest pain in the ass but also the best cover he could find. Anticipating the questions about playing blackjack in Aruba, Glenn would whine like a whipped dog and say he fell off the wagon. He'd only started in the program; he hadn't built up the strength to resist. Better yet, blame it on Kathy. She insisted on dumping money in the slots. She dragged him into the lion's den. Then again, maybe it wasn't a good idea to paint her as the temptress. Stick to the weakness angle. You tried; you failed. Enough already.

It was also convenient that Glenn's bookie wasn't required to report to the credit rating agencies or the IRS the way the casinos were. When Calenda hit him with that question about the Eagles, he almost blundered into a buzzsaw because he'd lost a bundle last football season, close to a hundred grand and the interest hurt worse than tugging on his short hairs. In an attempt to dig out of the hole, he bet on hockey, which didn't go any better, although he did make a score on basketball. The only person keeping him walking on two legs was his bookie's friend, a slumlord who owned some buildings in Philadelphia with elevators. Glenn faked the certificates for him, and he told the bookie to forget the interest once in a while. Otherwise, it would have been a baseball bat across the knees and wheelchair service at the airport.

All this made it easy to firewall the insurance-money angle. If they wanted to accuse him of dunking Kathy for an Atlantic City marker so small it wouldn't even buy a decent sports car, let them go for it. No one would believe that, not when there were sharp lawyers willing to challenge the casinos as dens of iniquity that preyed on weak people. Glenn had proved himself to be just such a person by joining a program and making it to every meeting.

Which brought him to the need for a local lawyer. Had he the money from the safe, he could have plunked it into some counselor's hand and told him to get to work, pronto. Out of this blockhouse on bail. Back to the Caribbean Club to wait out the storm. Kathy doesn't show up or she does in a body bag, then a weeping press conference and a ride to the airport.

Adios, or whatever they say on this rock.

Since he didn't have the cash, Glenn hoped his freedom could be granted via MasterCard.

Cargo pants. Black T-shirt. Belt. Aviator glasses. Romy Tromp donned a clean version of his uniform, hauled his camera bag to his car, and headed for the Renaissance Hotel in downtown Oranjestad. He told only his mother about the call from Clive Mitchell. She started bawling and thanking Jesus. Her boy was going to be a star.

"Not yet," he cautioned, not wanting to jinx his luck.

She waved him out of the driveway, mouthing, "Be careful," as he headed for town.

He stuck to the speed limits, used his turn signals, and reviewed Mitchell's call in his head.

"The assignment desk gave me your number," Mitchell began. "Tell me about yourself."

The voice! Mitchell had pipes like a Mack Truck, even deeper and smoother than Tromp's own father who could rattle glass.

"I'm a photographer here in Aruba," he answered. "Going on five years now."

"Print, web?"

"Both," Tromp answered because *Diario* had a website.

"What do you know about this case?" Mitchell went one.

"American tourist, Glenn Hogan, went snorkeling with his companion, a woman named Kathy. He came back. She didn't. He was arrested a few hours ago."

Mitchell grunted like an angry bear. "Tell me something I don't know."

"I have footage of the arrest."

Tromp heard Mitchell repeat in the background, "He's got footage of the arrest." Another person's reply was garbled.

Back in full power, Mitchell asked, "Know the Renaissance Hotel?"

"Of course. Central location. Close to the courthouse. As close as you can get to the scene and still have full service. Free parking. A nice pool …"

"Meet me in the lobby in thirty minutes or less."

"On my way."

"Bring the footage."

Tromp brought his video on the original memory card from the camera. He arrived at the hotel in short order because the traffic was leaving Oranjestad as the workday ended, clearing a path for inbound cars. An escalator carried him from ground level up to the lobby, where leaning against the bar he saw the man he'd wanted to meet since he was old enough to change the channels. Mitchell wore cargo pants, a safari shirt with two pockets on the chest, and a pair of battered hiking boots loosely tied.

"Romy Tromp," he introduced himself with his hand out.

Mitchell took in his outfit, clapped him on the shoulder, and said, "Let's go, young man. We have a deadline."

The voice in person was like nothing Tromp could have imagined. How was he ever going to match that? He'd have to take hormones or steroids to get into that range. And the walk Mitchell had, it was deliberate, fearless.

They went down the escalator and crossed the street to where the Renaissance operated a timeshare facility. It was all suites, some with two bedrooms, glassed-in bathrooms, views of the cruise ship terminal, and a private beach. Mitchell said nothing the whole way. No one recognized him, except for maybe one lady who started to say something then changed her mind. In the other complex they took the stairs. A robust fellow, Mitchell went two at a time, Tromp matching him bound for bound. They marched down the hallway to a door that opened after a single knock.

"Gentlemen, this is Romy Tromp." Mitchell said. "Romy, meet my producer, Stan Wofford, and cameraman, Bruce Myer."

Without ceremony, Wofford said, "Let's see this footage, kid."

The sun went down quickly, as Kathy had explained to Glenn it did near the equator. She readied her things: the plastic bag with her clothes, the bundle of money, the handcuffs, and her room key. An assortment of vessels returned to the dock, unloaded their fishing gear, and the crews ambled off to the bar where they drank and watched TV. Soon after dark, the boatyard emptied.

The bar stayed open later than she anticipated. A lone customer drank himself stupid, until he practically fell off his stool. The bartender tired of his antics and waved him out. Kathy watched the action with the binoculars, counting the cars in the parking lot until only one remained. This she figured belonged to the cook whose face she hadn't seen all day. Whoever it was worked on the other side of the window through which the platters passed to the bartender.

At last the cook came out. He carried a beer bottle in one hand and a cigarette in the other. Taking a seat on the customer side of the bar, he sipped and smoked, watching the television perched above the liquor bottles.

Kathy strained to see what was on TV. She recognized the Global News Network logo filling the screen. She knew they ran news stories twenty-four hours a day but the picture was too small to make out other than the general shape of faces.

She sat back on the settee to wait a while longer, hoping the cook would soon depart. Famished, she stared longingly at the can of beans on the shelf in the galley. Losing weight was one thing, starving was something else. Yet, she didn't want to take anything from the boat or leave any clues to her presence. She went back to the porthole to see if the cook had gone.

He had switched off the television and was in the process of closing his business. After putting all the stools atop the bar, he lowered the awnings that protruded out from the roof like huge flaps. Then he went inside through a door, presumably to secure them in place. Minutes later, he came out, locked the door, and headed for the parking lot. He paused at the corner of the building and stuck his hand into a potted palm for a moment before taking the wheel of the last car in the lot.

Anxious to break out and end her ordeal, Kathy took a final look around to make sure she'd closed the portholes, obscured her prints in the dust, and not forgotten anything she'd brought. Then she peeked out the schooner's door, listening for any voices or signs of human activity. Nothing.

She left the boat behind, padding along the dock, her ankle giving her less trouble than it did earlier. With only a scant number of security lights in the boatyard, she felt invisible among the dark shapes of the boats. Plus, she wore her swim-suit, which would seem normal to anyone who saw her.

"Just got back," she would say, and leave it at that.

Not even the stray dog, who slept under the nearest boat on blocks, bothered Kathy when she got to the corner of the building with the bar. He raised his head for a sniff, then went back to sleep. Resting her ankle, she leaned on the potted palm. Reaching into the plant to see what the cook had put there, her hand brushed a slim metal object which, as she suspected, was the key.

In all her life, she'd never stolen anything until now. As for the drugs Kathy took from the pharmacy, they were considered trash. In her mind, she was recycling not stealing when she used them for her purposes. However, since arriving in Aruba she'd taken five thousand dollars, handcuffs, and now calories. Using the key to the side door, she entered the kitchen in search of a snack. Whatever she ate wouldn't be much, just enough to keep her going until she pretended to come ashore.

Kathy went to the first refrigerator in sight. Plastic containers of potato and macaroni salad sat on the center shelf. She grabbed one, carried it to the counter, and peeled back the lid. With a giant spoon from a stainless steel rack, she dug in like a five-year-old with a bowl of ice cream. Plain old potato salad never tasted so good. She traded for the macaroni salad, so as not to eat a quantity of either that the cook might notice missing.

In hindsight, she should have gone to the bathroom for a quick cleanup, but Kathy was overcome with curiosity. Feeling much better, she crossed into the bar to check out the TV. She couldn't resist the idea that her disappearance had made the news. Local stations in the States often reported on missing persons and on occasion those stories went national, especially if they had an unusual or sensational element. Had her case made it to GNN? After a scan of the bar, she determined the shutters were sealed tight enough that no one outside would see the glow from the television. She took the remote from beside the cash register and tapped *On.*

As it had been all day, the set was tuned to GNN. A rerun of the Judge Nadine program filled the screen. Kathy noted the *Taped Earlier* banner in the upper right corner. Judge Nadine, her eyes blazing, taunted a defense lawyer who represented a recently convicted double murderer.

"Your client used a shotgun to kill two people," the judge fumed.

"My client is a disturbed individual who needs ..."

"He needs something all right. The electric chair!"

"The death penalty is not a deterrent ..."

"Says who? Says defense lawyers like you who are looking for more clients to ..."

Kathy skipped to other channels in search of more news. Colombian and Venezuelan reports given in Spanish were interspersed with infomercials and sporting events. Going back to GNN, Judge Nadine had finished with her lawyer guest.

"When we come back," the judge teased, "more trouble in paradise. Clive Mitchell is live from Aruba with exclusive footage."

Suddenly Kathy was enveloped in a fantasy. She sprawled on a deserted beach, the water lapping her feet, the sun about to set, a lone palm tree in the distance. She was barely conscious. No, she was unconscious, her face covered by strands of hair caked with sand. A man comes along. He scoops her limp body in his arms and pushes the hair away from her face. He sees she's breathing. Gently he strokes her cheek. She opens her eyes to find the man holding her is Clive Mitchell.

"You're safe now," he says just before he presses his lips to hers.

Blinking at the TV, Kathy saw the real Clive Mitchell reporting from where she and Glenn had gone in the water. His safari shirt showed not a single wrinkle, amazing given the heat and humidity.

"Here at this rocky point," Mitchell said, "two people went snorkeling, Kathy Barrow and Glenn Hogan. Friends. Travel companions. More than that we do not know because Kathy Barrow is missing and Glenn Hogan has been arrested."

"Arrested!" Kathy shouted then slammed an open palm over her mouth. The scene changed to show a handcuffed Glenn led down a short flight of stairs by a loading dock and put into a van.

"The Aruban police wasted no time tossing this joker in the slammer," Judge Nadine interjected. "What are the charges?"

"Unlike the United States, Aruban law allows for temporary incarceration without charge," explained Mitchell. "A person can be held for up to sixty days, after which a judge may rule that he can be held for another thirty days if the prosecution shows new developments."

"So this man has sixty days to think about his story," commented the judge. "What does his lawyer have to say?"

"Mr. Hogan has yet to retain counsel."

"He better get someone quick."

"I'm sure he will, your honor," Mitchell agreed, "and when he does, we'll be the first to speak with him."

"Tell us more about these people," Judge Nadine continued. "Who are they, where are they from?"

"Kathy Barrow and Glenn Hogan live separately in Media,

Pennsylvania, a western suburb of Philadelphia. Sources tell us they have been dating for a while, but we're waiting for further confirmation on their backgrounds. Here in Aruba, the search continues."

Ever bossy, Judge Nadine barked, "Get on it!" She cut away from Mitchell to another story about a missing teen in Vermont.

Catching herself before she again shouted with joy, Kathy pounded the counter with her fists. Glenn had been arrested. He was in jail. It happened all by itself. Maybe the cops tricked him into a confession. Or, he might have been groggy from the drugs and said something by accident. Either way, he was locked up, which is where he belonged for attempting murder.

To celebrate, Kathy helped herself to a shot of rum. As the liquor warmed her gut, she reconsidered her plan. She relished the idea of Glenn rotting in a cell. It put her back in control, which is what she'd sought in the first place, a few minutes of absolute power over an abusive man who needed a taste of his own medicine. Chuckling at the pun, she poured a second shot. While the accommodations aboard the schooner weren't the most comfortable, she wouldn't mind another day of rest. Her ankle had improved and another twenty-four hours would help even more.

By the time Romy Tromp got home, his brain ached worse than when he drank half a bottle of Old Parr once on a dare. The GNN producer, Stan Wofford, ran him ragged. First it was the questions. General info about Aruba: size, population, language, government, religion. Things then got more specific. Name of the prosecutor. Names of the cops and witnesses. Where did Hogan's rental car come from? Which hotel had he stayed in? Do you know the room number? What about the beach? Deep water, strong currents? Have you been swimming there? Do you know anyone who fishes there? Has anyone else gone missing or drowned there?

Tromp expected Mitchell to ask for this information, but the reporter sat listening on the couch, occasionally jotting a line in a small notebook. Cameraman Bruce worked a Macintosh laptop connected to a satellite antenna no bigger than a box of cereal. From a lounge chair on the balcony, it pointed at a spot in the sky.

"New York has the footage," Bruce interrupted.

"Be sure they spell Romy's name right," Mitchell said.

From behind a thumbs-up, Bruce released a slack smile. He reminded Tromp of a high-school classmate who was a notorious prankster.

"How many hours of daylight left?" Wofford asked getting up from his chair.

"Two, more or less," Tromp replied.

"Let's go."

They went. To the Caribbean Club for a look around. To the rental car agency at the airport. To the courthouse. To the police station in San Nicolaas. They ended where Tromp had photographed Glenn Hogan with the fisherman.

"Not much of a beach," Mitchell said as he walked amid the rocks and scrubby grass. "Why do they call this Baby Beach?"

"It's not Baby Beach," Tromp corrected him. "Baby Beach is over there."

"What's this called?"

"That's the old Esso Club. My father told me it was quite a place back in the fifties. He said Frank Sinatra once sang there."

"That's interesting," Mitchell said, "but I need an identifier for the beach, something easy for people to remember."

At that moment, Bruce, with his big, shoulder-mounted video camera, stumbled but managed to stay on his feet. "Damn rocks," he groaned.

"Rocky point!" Mitchell crowed.

"Works for me," Wofford seconded.

Not half an hour later, Tromp watched as Clive Mitchell went live on *The Judge Nadine Show,* the first one to take the story to the world.

If his day had finished there, Tromp would've been telling his excited mother all about it over a late dinner, but Judge Nadine was only the beginning. There were three more programs in line after her, taking up the hours to midnight, at which time the network ran the cycle a second time until their morning show started the day all over again.

"The twenty-four-hour news cycle," Wofford commented at ten-thirty when Tromp was starting to flag. The producer held smartphones in each hand and managed to punch out instant messages and answer emails on both simultaneously. Once in a while he took a call, too.

Just after midnight, while Bruce packed up his camera and satellite gear, Wofford laid out the next day.

"Clive, you have a stand-up at six-twenty. Then we're clear until forty past noon. In between, we'll get the prosecutor and the cops and find that fisherman. Bruce already has the B-roll of the hotel and various stuff around the island, except the prison. We'll have to fit that in somehow. Then, we pin down his lawyer."

"Do we have the lawyer's name?" Mitchell asked, notebook

at the ready.

"No, the prosecutor will give us that," Wofford answered.

"Why not give Romy a digicam and have him get exteriors of the prison?" suggested Bruce.

"Can you handle that?" Wofford asked Tromp.

Before Tromp could answer, Mitchell said, "Romy should be with us. Who knows the island better than him?"

It took Tromp two full seconds to realize that all of them were staring at him, an eighteen-year-old kid, bleary-eyed and burned out from a post-adrenaline high at being in the presence of the newsman he aspired to be.

Wofford took Mitchell aside for a private conference. They came back not a minute later.

"Listen, Romy," Mitchell said, "we want you on our team. That means you're working for us, for GNN."

"Yeah, I always wanted …"

Wofford cut him off. "Everybody says that until the other networks find their number. Then they get crazy and start trying to feed all the lions. You know what happens then?"

The Discovery Channel recently ran a show about lions. Tromp watched it three times, including the part about how lions fought over territory and females.

Mitchell made it clear. "In this business, *exclusive means everything*. If you're going to the dance with me, Romy, you can't dance with anyone else." He held out his hand. "Deal?"

"Deal," Tromp said and shook.

"You're on retainer as of now," Wofford informed him. "Day, night, until this thing ends or we cut you loose. The rate is four hundred per day plus expenses and no receipt equals no reimbursement. Get some sleep and meet us here at the rocky point at six."

"I'll be early."

"Don't forget, Romy," Wofford said, "if NBC waves some facetime on the *TODAY* show in front of your nose, you tell them thanks but no thanks. The same applies for all the networks in the alphabet soup. Got it?"

"Got it."

Tromp drove home counting the number of photos he'd have to sell to make four hundred dollars. He was lucky to make that much in ten days, let alone twenty-four hours. He forgot to ask how much they were giving him for the arrest footage. And no one said anything about being on the air, which to him was worth more than the money. Unable to recall a time when he hadn't watched the news, Tromp believed he could bring something fresh to it. He resolved to pitch his ideas tomorrow after Mitchell did the first report.

After setting two alarms, Tromp fell onto his bed and slept in his clothes.

9

Driving to the station the next morning, Chief Calenda recalled a conversation with his girlfriend, Agnes. They had been talking about her job when he asked how they keep track of planes when they're moving hundreds of miles per hour. Radar was the simple answer, but there was more to it than that: procedures, communications, and specific routes.

The chief knew that solving a crime, like air traffic control, involved many factors and that physical evidence alone could not paint the whole picture. He quarantined what they had so far to himself and Bakker. Not even his secretary, Julisa, knew more than the broad strokes. The videotape from the room was a critical element, one he feared would be broadcast to the world as soon as he put it in the prosecutor's hands. No doubt one of the staff lawyers would leak it to the press, if not *Diario*, then *Bon Dia* or one of the many news outlets that gorged themselves on people's misery like sharks joining a whale kill.

Driving on Bernardstraat past the police station, the chief saw the feeding frenzy had already begun. Five cameras on tripods pointed at the building like soldiers in a firing squad. Correspondents with microphones talked at lenses, while producers jockeyed cellphones and tablet computers.

What do they have to talk about? Calenda wondered. Nothing other than a woman was missing and a man had been detained. The rest was pure conjecture. Unlike pilots, most reporters needed less specific information to make their way. Preface an entire paragraph with *alleged* or *rumored,* and they were free to ramble on with the kind of speculation that would get the chief fired for misconduct. He dreaded having to deal with them, but he would because Eddie, in his blunt, Dutch manner of speaking, might tell them to piss off. The prime minister warned Calenda against such a faux pas.

"The carnival wagons have come early," Aruba's elected leader had said referring to the news teams. "Let's be sure they see our best. We don't need a repeat of the last time."

Diplomatic skills won the man the election. A successful conclusion of this case would prove the island's reputation as that rare, safe, vacation spot where the electricity and water were reliable. Calenda had traveled to many other islands and parts of South and Central America. Not many rivaled Aruba when it came to infrastructure. Well, he wasn't in charge of the Department of Public Works. He was a police commander, and if he wanted to do his part for the island, he best stick to his purview.

He went around the block, parked in a lot abutting the Fire Station, and walked to the rear door of his building unmolested. The reporters were too busy to bother with him, having gleaned all they needed from their few hours on the island. Maybe they had already solved the case, too, and were ready to give him the details.

Sarcasm in check, he went to his office, where Julisa had left him a steaming cup of hot chocolate, the one vice he allowed himself to indulge. The first sip hadn't passed his lips when Bakker came in.

"Prosecutor will be here soon. I've made a copy of the video for him."

"Lose it," the chief said, adding, "they'll leak it."

"Something this serious?" Bakker jeered. "I don't think so."

"It won't be their fault. A computer tech, a secretary, a friend of a friend who works for one of those circus clowns out front ..."

"But what if he asks for a copy?"

"Computer problems. Unrecognized format. You're doing your best."

A by-the-book detective, Bakker viewed misleading a prosecutor as a dubious proposition. He said, "The defense attorney may leak it anyway."

"Why?"

"To tarnish this woman's character."

"It's one thing if the defense portrays her as a floozy, it's something else if our side allows that to happen."

This made sense to the detective. He said, "If the defense does let it go public, it may signal Hogan is trying to show himself as the victim."

"A victim of what? A woman who lured him to Aruba to disappear? She's the one missing, not him."

"I was thinking more along the lines of him being a victim

of wrongful prosecution. He claims confiscating the video was an invasion of his privacy. It makes us seem aggressive."

Calenda contemplated this angle for a moment. "We *are* aggressive, Eddie, and we're about to get downright nasty after he picks a lawyer and we drag him in here."

Julisa tapped the door, stuck her head in, and told them the prosecutor had arrived.

The three men sat in front of the monitor on Bakker's desk. The video from Glenn Hogan's camera played in the center, an image large enough to leave no doubt as to the identity of the people or location.

"From the perspective, I would say the camera was on the shelf in the armoire that holds the television," Bakker said, "and that's right where we found it when I searched the room."

Clad in nothing but boxer shorts, Glenn Hogan went to his suitcase beside the bed. He opened the lid, held the clothing back with one hand, and extracted a set of as-yet-to-be-located, fur-lined handcuffs. He swung them in front of the camera, smirking like a teenager.

"Notice the color," Bakker said.

"Who could miss it?" the prosecutor snorted at the hot pink fur in Hogan's hands. "They're like something from an Amsterdam bordello, not that I would know from personal experience."

Hogan tucked the handcuffs under a pillow on the bed. At this point Kathy Barrow entered the room, naked but for a towel wrapped around her body. The two started kissing.

"I don't think she knows the camera is on," Evert said.

The chief nodded in agreement. Barrow appeared comfortable as the towel fell away. Unless she was a part-time porn actress, she was oblivious to the fact that her companion had let the camera roll on their antics. They moved to the bed, where Hogan kicked off his shorts and rubbed himself against Barrow's thigh. He had her on her back, which she didn't seem to mind.

"No sign of distress," noted the prosecutor.

"None in the entire video," confirmed Bakker.

The prosecutor shifted in his seat, embarrassed at the prospect of watching such a scene to its inevitable conclusion.

Hogan next reached under the pillow and brought out the cuffs. "What do you say to these?" he cooed.

Barrow didn't answer. Did she show a flash of anger? Calenda couldn't be sure. He'd watched that second of tape over and over the day before without arriving at a firm opinion. Whatever she'd been thinking, Kathy Barrow didn't allow Hogan to cuff her. She grasped Hogan's wrists and flipped him on his back.

"Strong woman," Evert remarked. "Athlete?"

"We don't know." Calenda said.

Next Barrow took the cuffs in hand, twirling them overhead while she ground her hips into Hogan's. He placed his hands on her hips, shifting her into the right position. Over and over, he thrust upward.

"Ride 'em cowgirl!"

Shaking his head, Prosecutor Evert said, "And I thought this only happened in dirty movies."

Barrow rubbed the fur-lined cuffs over Hogan's chest. At one point it looked as if she might use them to choke him. This was another thing the chief had watched several times. It was difficult to discern her intentions because the angle on the pair was skewed to the foot of the bed, giving a better view of the couple's joining parts than anything else. Hogan must have set the camera this way on purpose because he said something to Barrow and she got off him, repositioned on the bed, then slid on top again. This time, everything was in full view.

So it went for another ten minutes until the groaning stopped and they took turns going to the bathroom. While Barrow was out of the frame, Hogan took the handcuffs from the floor where she'd dropped them. He returned to his suitcase, replacing them in the same location from which they'd come. His last act on video was to mug for the camera, beating his chest like a gorilla, then showing a devilish smile before reaching up and switching off the device.

The screen glowing cobalt blue again, the prosecutor said, "Tell me your theory."

"I searched the entire room, including inside the toilet tank," the detective said. "The handcuffs weren't there."

"We're not convinced they were used in the commission of a crime," Calenda added. "Although, as soon as we asked Mr. Hogan where they were, he requested a lawyer."

Bakker continued the thread, "When we opened the safe in his room, Mr. Hogan had a startled reaction. Something must have been missing."

"We all just watched him put the cuffs in his suitcase. You think he relocated them?" the prosecutor wanted to know.

"Impossible to determine," admitted Eddie. "The point is, he deflected the issue of anything missing from the safe. If something's gone, it leaves loose ends. Was the safe robbed? Did Mr. Hogan misplace something? Is someone else involved, someone with knowledge of the safe's combination? Someone who assisted in the disposal of evidence used in the commission of a crime? Again, impossible to determine."

The prosecutor took off his glasses and said, "Before I tell the prime minister we have this man under arrest for more than kinky habits, give me something concrete."

The chief waved for Bakker to explain the rest of what they did and did not find. The detective accomplished the task with true Dutch efficiency. If Glenn Hogan's account of events was to be believed, then Kathy Barrow rode with him to the other side of the island wearing just her bathing suit, which is unlikely because the security cameras in the lobby at the Caribbean Club show her leaving in a nice sundress with a big flower printed on it. Along the way, she also lost her footwear. No witnesses saw the two of them enter the water. One person, fisherman Dennis Rosina, who admits to consuming about a case of Balashi that afternoon while fishing from shore, found Mr. Hogan disoriented on the beach with slight injuries.

"Combined, these facts point to a woman gone missing under curious circumstances that may involve her companion," concluded Bakker, adding, "and the handcuffs are nowhere to be found."

Prosecutor Evert smoothed back his hair and folded his glasses into his jacket pocket. "This could all be an accident, in which case we're the villains for locking up a hapless fool."

"The body hasn't been found," Chief Calenda put in.

"Finding the body is your job," the prosecutor said. He took several sheets of paper from his briefcase and gave them to the policemen. "I believe these documents, courtesy of the FBI and the Pennsylvania State Police, will give you more to consider."

"Credit report," Bakker said as he scanned the pages. "Casino debt: twenty-five thousand dollars. Numerous credit cards totaling fifteen thousand. A mortgage with a hundred thirty-eight thousand outstanding. Car leased."

Another sheet of paper was passed around, as Bakker whistled, "One-point-five-million travel insurance policy."

"The insurance won't pay without a body," Calenda said looking up from the document.

Retrieving his glasses, Prosecutor Evert said, "Use these for the fine print." Seeing the impatience on the chief's face, he replaced the spectacles over his eyes and gave a short dissertation on the nature of the unusual policy taken out by Glenn Hogan. It covered a wide range of possibilities, including many that are normally excluded such as suicide, death from civil unrest, and most important, disappearance from a ferry, cargo vessel, cruise ship or other waterborne activity. Even if a body is not recovered, after ninety days it paid the full amount.

"What kind of company issues a policy like that?" Detective Bakker asked.

"Be sure your lady-friends don't find out," Evert returned with uncharacteristic levity. Turning serious, he added one final dimension. "There are actually two policies, one held by Mr. Hogan and one by Ms. Barrow. Each named the other as beneficiary."

Bakker said what his boss, the chief, was thinking. "What do we know about her?"

"Precious little. She has some college loans, which are not delinquent. She lives in a rented apartment, also paid to date. She's a pharmacy technician, which means she's passed a background check for drug abuse, stealing, and psychological impairment. The FBI is locating next of kin and will be conducting an interview of her co-workers today."

"This thing could have gone either way and somebody would walk away a millionaire," Chief Calenda muttered as he rose out of his chair.

"Assuming either party was inclined to harm the other," Bakker countered.

"Assume nothing," Calenda finished.

Soon after a breakfast of burnt coffee and buttered toast, a nerdy gentleman with a clipped name and heavy glasses visited Glenn. Prosecutor Evert, he called himself in an officious tone that smacked of the last kid picked for intramurals. Evert gave Glenn a list of lawyers, from which he was supposed to pick one to represent him. He ramped up his hurt-boyfriend routine, acting like he didn't need a lawyer and saying he would answer any question, even take a lie detector test. The nerd was unimpressed, stating that he should select counsel, use the prison telephone to call the lawyer, and arrange for a meeting as soon as possible. In the afternoon, he would be taken to police headquarters in San Nicolaas for more questioning.

"I'll be there while Chief Calenda and Detective Bakker conduct the interview," Evert said right before he left.

"I bet you get your jollies watching old episodes of *Law and Order*," Glenn said to the door after it closed behind the prosecutor.

Half the names on the list were unpronounceable. Two consonants like D and J were next to each other. How was he going to talk to someone whose name made no sense? Then there were some women's names. The last thing he needed was a woman telling him what to say and do. On second thought, maybe a woman would make him look better in light of his past behavior. It would show how much he'd put his mistakes behind him. No, it wasn't worth that. Go with a man who understands what it's like to put up with a nag like Kathy. She was the one who wanted to go snorkeling. She was the one who sent him to the gift shop for the gear. Cost him two hundred bucks. Ridiculous. He did it to keep her happy. And her big idea got her lost at sea. Wasn't his fault. He tried to save her. She nearly pulled him down. Smacked him in the face when he attempted to drag her to safety. He nearly died himself. Just ask that fat fisherman, he saw me lying there half-dead. Why aren't there signs posted on the beach about the dangerous currents?

Glenn went over it a hundred times before the nerd got there and fifty more after he left. Weighing the pros and cons of not hiring a lawyer at all occupied him for at least an hour. On one hand, he knew if he kept his mouth shut or just stuck to what he'd already said, there was no way they could pin anything on him. On the other hand, a sharp lawyer could get him out of this box and back into Suite 1406 at the Caribbean Club until he could go home. If he was going to be stuck on an island, he'd rather have a view of the girls at the pool.

He ran his finger over the list a couple more times when he was interrupted by a rap on the door.

"Visitor!"

Glenn sat up as the door swung open, prepared to tell whoever it was to leave him alone. In walked a man wearing a beige suit jacket over a white shirt with an open collar. He carried a briefcase, the kind with no sharp corners, which he placed on the bed. Before the door closed, he stuck out his hand and introduced himself.

"Good morning, Mr. Hogan. My name is Arnold Koolman, Attorney Arnold Koolman."

With feigned indifference, Hogan shook the proffered hand. For all he knew, he could be a plant sent by the cops. He looked slick enough, with the polished skin and manicured fingers of a frequent visitor to the spa. Glenn liked the idea of a spa so long as it came with a certain amount of *hands-on* treatment at the end of the massage. He went to places in Philly where they never let him down.

Anyway, Glenn wasn't going to trust a jailhouse lawyer who showed up uninvited with hands softer than a girl's. He'd rather play eeny-meeny-miny-moe on the list from the nerd than take a chance on some shyster preying on his ignorance of the local heavy-hitters. He was just about to tell him to get the hell out when he heard words that instilled more faith in Glenn than if Moses had appeared cradling the Ten Commandments in one arm and the baby Jesus in the other.

"Jeff Nedd asked me to see how you're doing."

"Arnold Koolman," Romy repeated into his phone. "At the police station in San Nicolaas at three this afternoon." He disconnected and faced Clive Mitchell.

"Let's hear it."

"My aunt's friend says Arnold Koolman showed up at the prison."

"Who's Arnold Koolman?" snapped Wofford, who was showing signs of wilting in the heat.

They were parked outside the courthouse, which had been relocated to a bland building near the airport while the original structure downtown was undergoing renovation. Their fleet expanded from a single Honda CR-V to two. Bruce busied himself with a game on his computer inside one vehicle, while Mitchell, Wofford, and Tromp stood outside the other. The morning started great, the live shot at the newly named *Rocky Point* coming off without a hitch or duplication by the other networks' personnel who now crawled the island like infiltrating commandoes. Then they set up outside the courthouse in anticipation of the formal arraignment that was supposed to happen that afternoon. Mitchell refused to run the air conditioner for fear of aggravating his sinuses, and Wofford couldn't bear the incessant nursery-school music of Bruce's video game. The producer paced the parking lot which was akin to being roasted on a spit now that the sun was well above the horizon.

Then Tromp got the call from his aunt's boyfriend, who delivered supplies to the prison. Wofford saw the young man with the phone to his ear and jogged over to find out what was happening.

"Koolman is a criminal lawyer," Tromp replied to Wofford. "I took his picture in January. He defended a couple of smugglers caught by customs agents at the port. Fake whisky sent from China."

"Win or lose?"

"Lost, but a reduced sentence in a slam dunk case. He convinced the judges his clients were duped by others up the food chain."

"Was it true?" Mitchell queried.

"I don't know, but Koolman is at the prison talking with Hogan right now. They're going to interview him at San Nicolaas headquarters at three."

Wofford crushed his phones. "You're sure?"

"The driver of the police transfer van told my aunt's boyfriend they're moving him there."

"Bruce!" hollered Wofford as he rushed to the other vehicle. "Change of location!"

Jeff Nedd didn't chase ambulances. He took the toughest cases, went up against the most brilliant prosecutors, and racked up a line of wins that made him famous. Glenn should have thought to memorize his number, but that might've made him look bad. No matter. Nedd must have seen it on the news and decided to throw his hat in the ring. Good thing for Glenn he paid the extra premium, bumping the insurance policy to one point five from a million even. Nedd would want a pound of flesh, but he was worth it. He was too smooth for the movie screen. He froze enemy lawyers in their tracks while melting hearts in the jury box. He was sliced bread made whole.

Emboldened by this development, Glenn asked when Nedd was scheduled to appear.

"Mr. Nedd is not licensed to practice law here in Aruba. I'll take care of the official matters, in consultation with him, of course, until he arrives, which will be soon."

"Of course," Glenn repeated. He felt a rare twinge of sympathy for Kathy. She never had a chance, not really, not up against his luck. She was doomed the moment she gave him the eyes at Iron Hill Brewery, where he sat at the bar, shoving a cheeseburger into his mouth, when she took the seat next to him.

"Anyone sitting here?"

"All yours," he said, checking out her rack and not caring

that she caught him at it.

"Are the burgers good here?" she'd asked.

He wanted to smack her for that stupid question. Wasn't there one on the plate in front of him? Did he look like the kind of moron who didn't know a burger from a pile of horse manure? She looked dumb enough to make that mistake not on purpose, but she was also too cute to ignore. So he told her they were good, she ordered one, and wolfed it down. He was impressed. Next thing he had her number; she had his. They were in the sack three weeks later. If it had taken another week, he would have kicked her to the curb. He never waited a month to get laid.

Glenn wished he could have a burger like that right now instead of having to retell his story one more time. It's good practice he reminded himself right before he repeated his version of events to Koolman. He inserted none of the emotions he worked up for the cops.

"Nothing worse than bad luck," Koolman said when Glenn wrapped it up. "I'm sorry you lost your companion. I'm sure she was a sweet lady."

"I'm sorry, too," Glenn went on. "Sorry to be locked up here. How much are they asking for bail?"

"We don't have bail here," replied Koolman.

"No bail? This isn't some banana republic. You got an airport big enough for 747s and water that's safe to drink. What do you mean you don't have bail?"

"The legal system here is different from what you may be used to in the States, Mr. Hogan."

"Sure it's different, but everybody has bail."

Smiling, Koolman said, "With some maneuvering, I should

be able to get you out tomorrow, perhaps the next day. We'll agree to house arrest at a hotel. It will reduce the cost of your incarceration to the government."

Glenn was liking this local fellow more by the minute, which was only natural given he was associated with Jeff Nedd. "I was staying at the Caribbean Club, in a suite," he mentioned.

"I'll see what I can do. Today, when you enter and exit the police station, you'll hear lots of shouting. Reporters from every network have descended upon the island, and we have more than a few homegrown ones as well. Say nothing to them. Walk with your head up. Do your best not to appear angry even though you are suffering an extreme inconvenience given your loss."

For one point five million, it was a stroll down easy street, Glenn told himself after Koolman departed. Then he cursed himself for not asking how much the lawyer charged.

10

―――

The risk of cleaning up both herself and her living quarters was that if she were found, Kathy wouldn't look as if she'd been lost for more than two days. At the same time, her personal funk was getting offensive, worse than anything she experienced at the gym. In high school, track and field appealed to her, but she wasn't lean enough to compete in any of the running events. One of the coaches, who also helped with the swim team, suggested she might do well in the water given her body type. She earned a place on the team, befriending a new set of girls who all cut their hair short for the season. Her father hated it.

"Now I have a lesbian for a daughter," he complained. "Don't expect me to take a picture of you and your dyke girlfriend on prom night."

"All the girls on the team cut their hair," her mother said in defense.

"As if I need proof from you this country's going down the shitter."

Every time Kathy took her place at the edge of the pool, she imagined herself a warrior, and not the Amazon her father thought she was turning out to be. In her Ancient Cultures class she learned Athena had been the Greek Goddess of War and Wisdom. She focused her anger at a point at the far end of her lane, aiming at the petty ignorance of her father. Stoked on bitterness, she often launched farther than her competitors, earning her a team record. She also took a handsome boy to the prom. Her father wasn't there for pictures; he was busy helping his buddy change a transmission. Kathy screwed her date in his car parked right in the driveway, hoping her father would catch them, proving she wasn't a lesbian. No such luck.

In college she gave up sports for academics. It wasn't as if she had a scholarship riding on it. She wished she would have stayed more active. Stints at the gym or an aerobics class would have fought back the freshman fifteen. Her paycheck from working behind the register at the local pharmacy didn't go far and before long she'd run out of money. Her mother was making barely enough to keep the house, the car, and food on the table. Her recently unemployed/retired father refused to take even a part-time job to help. He'd also changed his mind about Kathy's sexual proclivities.

"You want me to take some job bagging groceries so she can finish college?" he spat one evening after dinner, before he left for the Cozy Corner, his regular watering hole. "What's she going to do if she graduates?"

"A career," her mother pleaded. "She's got excellent grades."

"She gets out of school, some loser knocks her up, and then

what happens to my hard work, my money? Down the shitter. She'll be using that degree to wipe a baby's ass. She's better off quitting now and getting on with it."

A promotion at work came with a nice pay raise that allowed Kathy to move out that summer. She took a garage apartment in nearby Swarthmore, and transferred from Temple to Delaware County Community College. With the credits she already earned it took her a year to complete an associate degree.

After leaving her parents' home, she begged her mother to divorce her bastard father and come live with her. Her mother wouldn't do it, which perplexed Kathy more than the chemical compounds in the drugs she dispensed. At least they could be figured out according to the rules of the physical universe. Her mother's decision to hang on to a man as pathetic and miserable as her father was incomprehensible. He treated her worse than an old doormat, and whenever Kathy pointed it out, her mother went quiet. Kathy alternately fantasized about shoving her father down the stairs and slapping her mother back to reality. Then she would feel guilty, angry for thinking the way her father acted. Move on, she told herself, ashamed of her lack of control.

And Kathy did move on, getting another promotion and a transfer to a bigger pharmacy. She found a one-bedroom apartment and was saving for a condo. In need of licensed pharmacists, the company put her in line for their corporate development program, which meant eventually she'd have the chance to get her graduate degree. This time, she wouldn't have to loan or beg, the company would pay for everything, including the books, as long as she maintained a B average. Easy.

Her father's death provided some relief. She anticipated good times with her mother, making up for the lost years menaced by her father's presence. Then her mother collapsed with the first stroke which, as the doctor predicted, was followed by the second. Absurd as she knew it to be, Kathy blamed her father. No, he wasn't responsible for the strokes. He wasn't a specter ruling his widow's life from the grave. Nonetheless, he deprived mother and daughter of too much to escape unnamed as a source of misery.

Looking back, Kathy saw this as the last turn of the screw, the trigger. She would never forget the day her mother entered Clearwater Lodge. After a tearful parting, leaving her mother in a comfortable but institutional room, she stopped at the supermarket for groceries. She tossed the *Delaware County Times* into the basket. Later, reading it while hovering over a bowl of cereal, she saw the case of a man sentenced to six months in jail for spousal abuse. *Six months.* In light of the damage done, half a year was no big deal. It was an extended vacation, an opportunity to workout and catch up on some reading. Yet, it was more than her father got. He went to the grave without so much as an apology.

She threw the newspaper in the trash. Being a swim team champ didn't make her a superhero, nor did two years of college education, but they did prepare her for exacting a little revenge on knuckleheads who threaded the needle of the legal system or dodged justice entirely.

At first, she felt like one of those cardboard cutouts set up by the pharmaceutical reps. The aloof doctor in his white coat holding a box of pills with the answer to whatever ailed you. Is that who she wanted to be, the smiling avenger? Not exactly, but she wasn't going to be a miserable bitch waiting for old age to catch up with these malefactors. She was going to tamp them down, one at a time, in a way that gave her a great deal of personal satisfaction.

Wading through her textbooks, warning pamphlets, and literature left behind by drug reps, Kathy conjured up a one-two punch of a cocktail. It tranquilized and induced amnesia, thereby giving her control over the person and rendering him unable to remember what happened. If she wanted to, she could dress them up like baby dolls, snap some pictures and post them on the Internet for all their macho buddies to see. They'd never know how it happened, but there they would be with lipstick, a lacy bustier, and a parasol, an attractive getup for a cellmate. Although a great idea, she came up with something better, something scary.

Next, she outlined a method to select her marks. Similar to how pharmaceutical companies conducted a drug study, the person had to meet specific criteria. For her purpose, that meant an abusive male with better-than-average looks, subject to legal action, and as arrogant as possible. The first two categories came easily from the newspaper and court reports. Pictures weren't always published, which required Kathy to pay some visits to the nearby towns where these men lived, spying on them. Most were trolls hunting for a bridge under which to live. But there were some stunners, too, men she would never have suspected of taking a hand to a woman. She confirmed their arrogance by inserting herself into their social life, bumping into them at a bar or even in the aisle at the grocery store as she did with her first target.

"Can you reach that tomato sauce?" she asked Phil Ryan.

She'd been watching him power through the store like an Indy car. He darted around mothers with children, old ladies, and pensioners mumbling at the meat counter. Since he was in a hurry, it pleased her all the more to stop him in his tracks with her cart blocking the entire lane between the shelves. Her scoop-neck blouse and push-up bra, that could have doubled as a medieval torture device, put her chest on full display.

With a roll of his eyes, Phil signaled his extreme displeasure at having to do something to earn the right to ogle her tits. "That stuff sucks," he said. "Try the one two shelves down." He moved to go past her cart, but she bent over, bumping it with her ass. It wedged him into the pickles.

"You mean this one?" Kathy asked, holding up the wrong jar on purpose.

Stuck, Phil huffed her way, unable to focus on her ass, her face, or the jar of tomato sauce. His eyes settled on her backside for a second before he pointed to the correct row.

"The next one up," he said, wiggling against the front of her cart, still trying to get by.

She didn't mean to whack the cart's handle a second time. It happened by accident when she bent over again. Phil had had enough and shoved it out of the way. He came up beside her in one lunge, and grabbed a jar of sauce.

"This is the stuff," he snarled.

A little afraid, Kathy stuck to her goofy personae. "Are you Italian?" she asked, her voice higher pitched than usual.

"In certain places," replied Phil with a lecherous grin.

"I had a boyfriend whose mother made the best lasagna."

"Maybe you should pay him a visit for some of mom's home cooking," Phil said, moving down the aisle at last.

"Bet you know a good Italian restaurant," Kathy called after him.

"Popi's in South Philly."

It took her two more weeks to get his attention at Stacey's Grille, where he watched baseball and drank lager two nights a week. She wore the exact same outfit, a detail he failed to recall even if he seemed to have the shapes beneath memorized.

"You're that chick looking for something Italian," he said after several obvious eye-locking exchanges.

With pick-up lines like that, no wonder Phil sat alone during most of the games. Kathy admitted she was the one, telling him she hadn't been to Popi's yet.

"Yeah, why not?"

"I'm not going alone," she said.

Here the arrogance kicked in, confirming Phil as an appropriate target. "That boyfriend of yours too cheap?" he mocked.

"That boyfriend of mine shipped off to Afghanistan."

"Really? Why?"

Arrogant and dumb, Kathy had thought. Perfect. "We broke up anyway."

"Too much temptation around for you? Couldn't handle him being away?"

Hearing his response, Kathy tacked asshole on to arrogant and dumb. If she hadn't been luring him into her ambush, Kathy would have dumped her drink over his head. Rather, she acted coy with a dip of her eyes and a lick of her lips for a touch of glistening sultriness to lock him in.

The next Friday they were at Popi's together. He paid the check and tried to feel her up in the car later that night. She held him off a month before contriving an overnight stay in nearby Cape May, New Jersey, insisting she pay her half. On the beach, she dosed his bottle of Yuengling Lager. Ten minutes later, Kathy was waving for him to join her in the water. She flashed him her boobs, which got him up and running, pumping the drugs into his system. Swimming just hard enough to make him work for it, she allowed him to get his hands on her. Soon confusion overcame his mind as his arms refused to cooperate. He tried to crane his neck to keep his face above the sea as he dipped down on wobbly legs.

Using the life-saving stroke, Kathy towed him back to shore. When he didn't revive, she worried she'd gone too far. At last he blinked and started babbling. Poor Phil. He couldn't figure out what happened.

If he had screamed it would have been the perfect scene from a slasher flick. Only Phil wasn't about to get the knife. He was about to drown, which was just as terrifying. He couldn't make his arms and legs go. He forgot he was in water barely eight feet deep. He lost track of the way to the beach. The last part of his brain to work was the fear reflex, and Kathy glimpsed it in full splendor. It was fight or flight and he could do neither.

Although he behaved better after the incident, Kathy was finished with Phil Ryan. She told him her boyfriend had sent a letter from Afghanistan. She was going to try to make it work with him.

"Forget him," Phil said making an effort to hold on to her. "You need someone like me looking out for you."

They didn't stay the night, which cost her half the rate at the bed and breakfast. A better hundred dollars she hadn't spent in years.

Kathy reveled in the memory of duping Phil Ryan. Success with him gave her the confidence to pursue others. It also instilled a sense of invincibility, which led her to miss the warning signs with Glenn Hogan.

Now, flexing her ankle on the schooner's settee, she swore on her mother's life she would never do it again. She'd had her fun. She accomplished her mission by teaching a few people a lesson. In no small way, she recognized the psychological transformation she'd made from the time she started tempting fate to the present moment. She understood it wasn't her job to punish one person for the sins of another. Her father's tyranny was her problem. She should have done something about it when he was alive.

Of course it was too late to deal with him, but it wasn't too late to extricate herself from the current situation. She took up the binoculars and peeked out through the portholes like a stowaway, occupying her time with the operation of the marina and resisting the urge to eat the can of beans staring out from the rack in the galley.

Sometime after noon, a huge boat on a trailer passed through the gate. Then a strange contraption like a cross between a spider and grizzly bear rolled over top of the boat. It traveled on four giant tires at the bottom of legs tall enough to raise its body above the boat. Heavy slings hung down and they were positioned under the hull of the waiting vessel. As the slings were tightened, the machine lifted the boat off its trailer. With much yelling and waving the truck yanked the trailer out, leaving the boat hanging in mid-air.

There it hovered because the engine quit as soon as the operator tried to move the contraption. He cranked the ignition over and over to no avail. The others scrambled to make a quick repair with no success. It dawned on them that the boat was dangling precariously over the concrete ramp. More shouting and gesturing sent everyone scrambling for blocks, which were tucked under the hull for support.

With everything secure, the crew retired to the bar for beer.

"Nothing better to do," Kathy said, wishing she could walk over and join them for a cold one.

"Here's how it goes," Romy Tromp began. "I take the digi-cam in an underwater housing and go straight in the ocean. Water comes up over the lens, giving the audience a point-of-view look at where this happened. I swim out, twenty meters, maybe fifty, then look back to show the rear of the Esso Club in the distance. It's getting farther away. I swim some more. Look back. Farther away. Maybe put a fisherman there for scale or put Dennis in, you know, the witness. Somebody else could play the boyfriend. I spin the camera to show him. Then, bob up and down, move inshore a bit, water laps over the lens. Cut!"

"You want to do a re-enactment?" Wofford asked.

Catching his breath, Tromp replied. "Exactly."

They were seated around a table at the Hollywood Smoke-house, an incongruously named eatery at the east end of San Nicolaas, a place that served beef brisket and pulled pork in a style beloved by the expatriate refinery workers from Texas. Earlier, while the other networks crammed in front of the police station's main entrance, Bruce was positioned in the alley out back near the Fire Department. The van carrying Glenn Hogan cruised in behind the station, and when the door slid open, Bruce recorded twenty seconds of Hogan walking to the rear entrance escorted by Attorney Arnold Koolman.

Clive Mitchell introduced the footage during a live, top-of-the-hour stinger, at three. It was likely to be the last exclusive GNN got. Because they monitor each other's broadcasts, the competing networks swarmed the back of the building for Hogan's departure.

"Where's Kathy?" a reporter shouted.

"Was she pregnant?" another hollered.

"What were her last words?"

"Did you love her?"

The van sped away, leaving more reporters than policemen congregating on the sidewalk.

Through the deft use of his smartphones, Wofford had broken through Koolman's resistance and arranged for an interview at five-thirty, giving them plenty of time to enjoy a late lunch at the Hollywood.

"Point-of-view. Realistic. Back and forth between a stand-up with Clive and my footage." Romy wasn't used to using his idol's first name. It came out after a moment's hesitation, which he disguised with a nod inviting the man to join in. Mitchell held court, but didn't engage the discussion.

"Too distracting," Wofford said. "For straight news we use a tripod." Dismissive, the producer was on his feet. "Let's get to Koolman's office and set up for the interview."

Because he'd been talking, Tromp's meal sat untouched. He shoved a forkful into his mouth then got up. Mitchell pulled him down with a tug on his belt.

"Good work today, young man," Mitchell said. "Finish your lunch, go home, get some rest."

"But …"

"An interview with a lawyer is easy. Stan has it under control. We need you to keep your ear to the wall for the tough stuff."

Despite the delicious aroma, Tromp had lost his appetite. He was pissed. He put Bruce in the perfect spot for the van's arrival. He got them Arnold Koolman's secretary's private cell-phone number. He gave, GAVE, them the footage of Hogan's arrest, something none of the other networks had or could get. And they sent him home like a kid without his homework, mitigated only by Mitchell's kind pat on the head. For this he took a nice paycheck, but he'd run afoul of *Diario*'s editor and had yet to appear on camera.

"Call us if anything develops. If not, we'll meet you at the Renaissance for breakfast," Mitchell said.

The crew pulled out, Bruce in one vehicle, Wofford and Mitchell in the other. Tromp shoved his food around, giving them time to get down the road.

"Tough day," a voice said from over his shoulder.

At first Tromp thought it was Mike Bislick, Hollywood's owner, talking to him. When he turned to reply, he saw someone else, an Americano by the look of him wearing old-style, tortoise-shell glasses. His skin shone pink from unprotected exposure to Aruba's equatorial sunshine, and he donned a New York Yankees baseball cap that seemed out of synch with his spectacles.

He sauntered in from the doorway. "Buy you a beer?"

"I don't drink beer," Tromp replied.

"Shot of whisky?"

Wincing at the thought of Old Parr, Tromp shook his head.

"Well, I'll get you a Coke because I never drink alone." The man paid the bartender with a ten-dollar bill, waved away the change, and sat down uninvited at Tromp's table. Relaxed, he took a long pull from his beer and studied the room.

Tromp got the impression his new tablemate was trying to make him uncomfortable, and it was working. Who walks in a place, pretty much demands to buy a drink for a stranger, then sits down and waits for the conversation to begin? A full minute later, Tromp found out.

"My name is Zach McCabe. Call me Zach."

Tromp raised his Coke to meet McCabe's tilted bottle of Balashi.

"With whom do I have the honor of sitting?" McCabe continued.

"Romy Tromp."

"Pleased to meet you Romy. Now that we've both had a sip of jungle juice, let's get down to business. I figure you're the reason GNN has beaten us to the punch every round since this sordid affair began. Am I right? Don't answer. You don't have to. Just nod your head. That way you won't have to deny agreeing or disagreeing with me. You can claim you were stretching your neck."

Before Tromp had a chance to bail out of his seat, McCabe shifted his chair, blocking his easiest path to the door.

"My network is in the pole position for this race, and I think you're the key to winning. I don't know what GNN is paying you or maybe they're not paying you anything because they have pictures of you with a goat. Hey, take it easy, that's a joke. You just take this pen here and write the figure on that soiled napkin and whatever it is, I'll double it."

A gleaming silver pen appeared in McCabe's free hand while the other lifted the bottle to his lips.

If Tromp remained honest, he could double his salary in the two seconds it took him to write a number. If he wanted to stretch the truth, he might get away with tripling it. And if he wanted to find out if McCabe was a bluffer or desperate or just plain crazy, he would write a one with three zeros behind it. At that price, he'd have a top-notch video rig in a week. It wouldn't matter what Stan Wofford thought of his ideas. He could piece the video together himself then send it to the world via YouTube.

"Come on, son," McCabe pressed. "Take the pen. Scratch a number there nice and neat for me."

Tromp grasped the pen. The weight of it impressed him, as did the brand, Mont Blanc judging by the six-pointed white star on the cap. There was a Mont Blanc store at Palm Beach Plaza on the tourist end of the island. Tromp photographed the grand opening.

"My beer's almost gone," said McCabe after a series of gulps.

Flattening the napkin on the table, Tromp wrote a number. Even on the flimsy texture, the Mont Blanc missed not a single curve.

McCabe set his drink atop the napkin, obscuring Tromp's writing. "Can't be bought," he said. "Is that what you mean?"

"Money isn't what I want," Tromp said.

McCabe lifted his bottle, leaving a damp ring around the zero Tromp had written on the napkin. After draining the last of the contents, he said, "Keep the pen, and when you change your mind, let me know. A clever person like you will know where to find me."

When McCabe's shadow left the threshold of Hollywood's door Tromp got up from the table. The weight of his camera bag cut into his shoulder. Mitchell was right, he was tired, but he wasn't going home to bed. He was going to buy a week's worth of safari shirts, and work his sources, using McCabe's pen to write notes.

11

The perverts made him watch the video, the whole thing, right to the end where he did the gorilla routine. Koolman protested. Detective Bakker sat stone-faced. Prosecutor Evert all but dozed off. Chief Calenda said it was relevant to the questioning.

Glenn answered one by one. They set obstacles in front of him, challenging his answers, many times asking for clarification. It was like playing miniature golf. He putted around the obvious hazards until the ball fell in the cup. He was under par when the handcuffs came up.

Bakker, the lanky dude who tossed his room like a cat burglar on meth, asked flatly, "So, where are the handcuffs?"

"You saw me put them in my suitcase," Glenn answered.

"They weren't there when I searched your room."

Koolman pinch-hit for him with, "My client does not have control of his hotel room. Other people come and go when he is absent."

"A maid stole them?" posited Bakker while Calenda drilled holes with his eyes.

"It's not my job to catch thieves," Koolman replied. "That is your responsibility."

Glenn wanted to stand and clap for that one. He stayed in his seat, locking eyes first with Calenda then with Bakker who had a follow-up.

"Would Mr. Hogan like to file a complaint? I'd be happy to get the form for him."

"My client may wish to do that at a later time."

Damn right, Glenn wanted to shout. *One pair of handcuffs and five thousand bucks!*

"The clues are going stale," Bakker chirped.

Because you morons ... Glenn cut the thought short, thanking God these guys weren't as sharp as the characters he watched on TV. He couldn't help but wonder if that stuff was real or made up to give the coiffed stars a chance to figure it all out by five before the hour, right after the last commercial break.

They moved on from the handcuffs, biting into the meat of the insurance policy. Koolman told him that he didn't have to answer, but Glenn decided to take the lead because he knew more than the chief and his number one brave.

"I always buy travel insurance," Glenn said. "You never know what can happen."

"Something did happen," countered Bakker.

"Yeah, I got locked up for an accident."

"You named Kathy Barrow as beneficiary and she named you."

"Correct."

Koolman fidgeted in his seat, giving his client a convenient moment to demonstrate his unshakable poise.

"You need the bathroom, counselor?" Glenn asked, pointing at the door behind the two cops. "You sure? Okay. The insurance. You're right, I named Kathy and she named me. I told her to write in her mother's name. Anyway, she laughed and put me down. We filled out the paperwork at the pharmacy where she worked. The other lady there, I don't know her name, she let us fax it to the company. Give her a call."

Prosecutor Evert piped up for the first time. "We will," he said, scribbling a note on his pad.

Glenn hoped they would talk to Kathy's co-worker. She had called him a *keeper*. He resisted the urge to crack a smile, a good thing, because next Bakker clobbered him with a question that came out of nowhere.

"Do you remember the dress Kathy was wearing?" Bakker asked.

"Yeah," Glenn said, thinking this was another dead end they were leading him to in an effort to force an error. How could he forget the dress? She put one on, then another, then shorts, then a third dress with a big flower on it that he thought was sexy because you could almost see through it.

"When was the last time you saw it?"

Another lay-up. "When we were driving to Baby Beach."

"Did she wear the dress into the water?"

Glenn resented Bakker for not looking at him as he ticked off these questions. A real detective would be nose to nose. Just the same, he knew every question had a point, and the nature of this one escaped him.

"Did she wear the dress into the water?" repeated Bakker.

"Have you ever seen a woman swimming in a dress?" Glenn answered, buying time to think.

"Did Kathy Barrow wear her dress into the water?"

"No," Glenn replied.

"Did she take it off in the car?"

It's a trick, Glenn told himself, *just like the handcuffs. Stick to the truth and you're out of here in no time.*

"It was a flimsy thing," he said, throwing in a detail to demonstrate how he'd paid attention to his date. "She stood between the car and the door and pulled it over her head. I don't know, I guess she draped it on the seat."

"Thanks for clearing that up," Bakker said with a nod to his boss.

There was another fifteen minutes of back and forth that went nowhere. Glenn displayed a fair amount of indignation at being held in jail when all that happened was a horrible accident. Koolman requested his immediate release but was rebuffed by Evert. The cops walked him back to the van.

Outside, the flashes fired like machine guns, odd considering he was standing in broad daylight. He cocked his head for the reporters, adopting the same expression he used when landing a pair of kings atop two aces during the final shoe at the blackjack table. Of course, he was a winner. He always won. Soon he'd be sitting on the couch or the chair or the whatever they put under his ass for an interview with the big-name talent that didn't schlep around to sweaty islands. They stayed in the air-conditioned studio, talking via satellite to those losers who were trying to climb the ladder into that same studio with shouted questions. Punters every one of them, except for Clive Mitchell. If Mitchell wanted to do a sit down from his cell or his suite at the Caribbean Club, Glenn was ready.

At the prison, Koolman asked for an explanation of the handcuffs. "You didn't mention anything was missing from your room when we spoke earlier in the day," he said.

"I don't want to accuse some poor maid of taking something that maybe she just borrowed for a tryst with her boyfriend."

"They were stolen?" Koolman deadpanned.

"Must have been," replied Glenn.

"That's unusual. Hotel employees go through a background check and those working at the Caribbean Club must sign confidentiality agreements."

"One of them has sticky fingers. I'm missing the handcuffs and my winnings from the casino. Five grand."

Shocked, Koolman blinked several times before saying, "And you didn't report the loss to the hotel or the police?"

"I didn't know until that skinny cop made me open the safe."

This detail Koolman processed with a scratch of his chin then both hands rubbing his temples. Finally, he said, "Is there any other part of your visit to Aruba that has been unexpected?"

"I'd say it was going great until Kathy dragged me down there to go snorkeling."

"Nothing else you think or even suspect was odd. Perhaps a person bumped into you, made a strange remark, or asked a peculiar question."

Glenn showed his empty palms the way the blackjack dealers do before leaving the table. *See? Nothing to hide.* He said, "No one but those cops who have been hassling me. They don't seem to know the difference between having fun and being out of control."

"Detective Bakker asked about Kathy's dress. Any idea why he would do that?"

Lifting one shoulder for a lazy shrug, Glenn said, "I have some kinky habits, but wearing women's clothes isn't one of them."

Koolman remarked, "It seems Chief Calenda and Detective Bakker are wasting their talents on a tragic accident."

"Maybe they'll find Kathy, and I can get out of here."

"They'll find her, Mr. Hogan. Sadly, a person who drowns in that area always washes up nearby."

Inside, Glenn was beaming. A body, three days moldering in the ocean, then tumbled ashore by a wave, it would make collecting on the insurance policy much easier, and dial up the sympathy factor for him. He might get a book deal, or he could advise a production company making the movie of the week. If anybody could set the wheels in motion on that angle it was Jeff Nedd, which is why he asked Koolman about Philadelphia's most famous lawyer.

"What about Nedd? When am I going to meet him?"

"Tomorrow."

All day they worked on the travel lift, as Kathy learned the machine was called. Through the open vent, she overheard a bunch of fisherman talking about it. By dusk they thought they had it fixed. At the turn of the key there was a belch of black smoke then nothing. The repairmen retired to the bar for beer to drown their frustration.

"Parts are on the way," someone said.

The crew stayed late, pointing to the travel lift every time a new group of people showed up via boat or car and wanted to know why the thing blocked the launching slip, another of Kathy's new vocabulary words.

She was settling in on the schooner. Forced to live aboard it, she grasped the functionality of every item. The portholes were for light and ventilation. The settee doubled as a storage compartment. Wherever possible, a vacant space became a shelf or drawer. Tables converted to cutting boards and disappeared into slots. The tiny bunkrooms provided a coziness the expanse of a bedroom lacked.

If she spent a week cleaning and polishing the wood, the schooner would be a pleasant abode to spend a few days. Aside of the trip on *Consuela*, Kathy had never been sailing, certainly not on a boat of any kind out of sight of land. The idea frightened her. At the same time, she wondered if she might enjoy a cruise. Something different than a plane ride between airports before camping out in a hotel room, most of which were similar enough to be clones.

At last, the cook closed his kitchen and shooed away the repair crew. He chatted with the bartender while the TV played. They pointed at it a couple times and Kathy strained behind the binoculars to see what was showing. It was GNN, but more details were out of range. For all she knew, her story had been bumped by a nuclear disaster, an earthquake, or a plane crash.

Kathy's aching stomach nearly drove her to smash open the can of beans with a hammer. Every minute the cook loitered with his pal, she felt like gnawing on the edge of the porthole. Her ankle was doing much better. It was more stiff than painful now and showed only minor swelling. As for her body odor, the flies stayed away.

Unlike the previous night, Kathy wasted no time waiting to see if the yard was vacant. Once the cook left, she moved to the potted palm for the key, then to the kitchen, and sat herself down before a plate of cold chicken breast from the fridge. The taste brought tears to her eyes. In no time, she devoured several large bites and a scoop of macaroni salad. Only after did she realize how much she had consumed. Covering her misdemeanor by rearranging what remained, she went to the TV in the bar.

Her stink followed her, wafting along in a pungent cloud. The news could wait, she decided, and went to the kitchen for a bar of soap before stalking outside to where there was a hose coiled against the back wall. She'd seen people using it to rise out their coolers.

After a glance around, she turned the hose on herself, daring to step out of her bathing suit. Lathering up gave her an almost sexual sensation, a tingle she savored as much as the food she'd just consumed. The simple things, she told herself, that's all you need. For good measure, she rinsed her suit as well.

Minutes later, she sat naked in front of the television with her swimsuit drying over the kitchen sink. The intro to *The Judge Nadine Show* tumbled across the screen at the top of the hour.

"Tonight, live from Aruba, we go to Clive Mitchell." A box popped up showing Mitchell standing among palm trees. "Clive," Judge Nadine said, "Tell us the latest from paradise, or should I say paradise lost?"

"Well, your honor, the sad fact remains that Kathy Barrow has not been found."

"Are they still looking?" the judge interjected, her shrill voice shaking the bottles of booze near the TV.

"They are but the search has been scaled back."

"Do I have to send someone down there?"

"A helicopter and several boats are patrolling the waters off the rocky point where Kathy Barrow was last seen with her companion, Glenn Hogan."

"Tell us, how is Mr. Hogan doing?"

"Yeah," Kathy said to the screen. "How's that bastard doing in prison?"

Mitchell's face was replaced with footage of Glenn being walked into a police station. The voice-over continued. "Glenn Hogan was questioned today by police and the senior prosecutor. Of course, the Aruban authorities are withholding all comments because this is a continuing investigation. However, just hours ago in an exclusive interview, I spoke with Mr. Hogan's attorney, Arnold Koolman."

The view changed again to a medium shot of a beautifully decorated office.

"My client maintains his innocence with regard to any wrong doing," Koolman said. "A tragic accident has occurred. He prays for Ms. Barrow's safe return."

"I'll bet," Kathy said.

"Mr. Hogan has answered all the questions asked of him. He has cooperated in every way possible. Tomorrow, I will file a petition for his release, with the condition he remain on the island to lend his continued assistance to the police. I am confident the authorities will grant this request when they see there is no evidence of foul play."

"Stop the tape! Stop the tape!" hollered the judge. "Clive,

does this lawyer take us for fools. If they let him go, he'll be on the first boat to China."

"A condition of his release will be the surrender of his passport," Mitchell informed the judge.

"Whatever."

The interview with Koolman rolled again, "At his own expense, Mr. Hogan will remain on the island until such time as Ms. Barrow is found or the police recognize he is in no way responsible for her unfortunate disappearance, which, as I said, is the truth of the matter."

Judge Nadine's face filled the screen, her trademark scowl in high definition blistering with anger. "The truth of the matter? This lawyer wouldn't last a minute in my courtroom. His client swims to shore and leaves his girlfriend behind. There's something wrong with that. The man's a coward at the very least."

It took Mitchell a second to absorb the host's diatribe before he dared to counter her argument. "Mr. Hogan, through his attorney, maintains the currents were strong off the rocky point. We're going to interview a local fisherman to get an accurate assessment of this contention, but in any case, he insists he did everything he could to rescue Ms. Barrow, but that it was her idea to go there in the first place."

"Now he blames the victim," the judge moaned then slapped her desk. "I've heard enough, Clive. We're digging into this up here and tomorrow night we're going to show just who this guy is, and I hope the Aruban authorities are watching."

Kathy swallowed a shot of rum then switched off the TV. She took her damp suit off the rack in the kitchen and retreated to her cabin aboard the schooner. How many days could she survive in the water? Two? Three? More than that was stretching it. As much as she was reveling in Glenn's torture, she understood the reality of the situation. If she went too far, she would have some explaining to do. And the Arubans would be angry about spending the resources searching, only to find out it had been a prank. There might be real distress cases out there.

One more night, after that, she was re-entering the world, sore and a few pounds lighter, but alive. The first thing she would ask for is a visit with her mother. That would look good on *The Judge Nadine Show*. A daughter who cheated death, who, when all hope was lost, never forgot the importance of family. Unlike Glenn's story, it was true. Kathy thought of her mother again and again. Her first stop after getting off the plane in the United States would be Clearwater Lodge.

"Did he do it?" asked Agnes.

Chief Calenda marveled at his girlfriend's ability to get straight to the point. He was less certain about the answer.

"I don't know," he said. So far, he and Bakker proved nothing but Glenn Hogan's lack of forthrightness regarding the disappearance of his handcuffs and Kathy Barrow's dress. There might be an explanation. Given his retention of Koolman as counsel, Calenda expected Hogan to produce a story soon. Koolman didn't mind defending guilty clients, but he rarely tolerated one who held back and thereby set him up for embarrassment in court. In this instance, Calenda suspected Koolman might make an exception. Hogan was an American, and a great deal of international exposure could be leveraged into higher fees. Crooks watched the news more than regular folks, and when they got pinched, they believed a lawyer seen on TV was better than any other no matter what the cost.

Agnes sipped her hot chocolate. "I have a confession," she said next.

Calenda engaged the joke by saying, "The jail is full."

"I've been watching the news."

It was her way of teasing him into telling her more, which Calenda recognized and countered with his own polite rebuff. "Don't believe everything you see," he said. Then, to demonstrate his trust, asked, "Would you go swimming in a dress?"

"I'd go swimming naked if the moon was full and you asked me," she replied.

"Where would you put your dress if you drove to the beach and then went snorkeling?"

"In the car. The trunk so no one would see it."

"You wouldn't put it under a rock near the shore or something like that?"

Agnes set down her empty mug but remained seated at the table, indicating her desire for more information. When Calenda stayed tight-lipped, she posed a theory of her own.

"You didn't find the dress," she whispered. "If you don't have the dress, then Kathy Barrow may not have gone in the water. Clive Mitchell reported no witnesses saw the couple together, and that a fisherman found the man alone. Could she be somewhere else?"

"Perhaps."

"Awful," concluded Agnes.

"We have to look."

12

——

"You're putting a lot of trust in this kid," Wofford said as he drove past the Essoville gas station.

"Ye of little faith," Mitchell returned.

"The kid's got stars in his eyes, Clive. He wants to be you."

"Better he wants to be me than to be Matt Lauer."

They rolled up the hill, paralleling the refinery wall, to Esso Heights. Bruce followed close behind. After turning three rights they entered what remained of the Lago Colony: overgrown asphalt streets, a former high school converted to a rehab center, and an assortment of homes that were alternately lived in and abandoned.

"Must have been a nice place in its day," Mitchell reflected. "Colony living in the Caribbean. From what I've read, Esso provided expats with all the comforts of home, right down to the village church."

It was there that Wofford stopped, in the lot on the east

side of the church where the Lago residents held their weekly services. Romy Tromp was waiting, leaning on his car. Mitchell moved with remarkable liveliness, jogging across the short distance.

"*Bon dia,*" the reporter said, shaking Tromp's hand.

Wofford cringed at the sound of his network's most highly rated on-the-scene reporter adopting the local patois. Watching him admire the kid's shirt, which apart from its color was identical to Clive's own, gave the producer more reason to worry. Did Mitchell say, "Nice duds?" He did. Tromp was the stray puppy the reporter's own father hadn't allowed him to adopt. Then Tromp hauled out a narrow steno pad just like Clive's and the two compared notes. Wofford moved closer, fearing he may have to conduct an intervention before this got out of control.

His mother was proud of him and that's why Romy Tromp called Clive Mitchell late in the evening to tell him about the land search for Kathy Barrow. Tromp told his mother about the offer from the man named McCabe, the smug American who bought him a Coke at the Hollywood. His mother whistled through her teeth upon hearing how much money her son let go. She put her hand over her boy's and told him he was wise to turn it down.

"Who knows?" she said. "Maybe this man wants to give you a piece of silver for your gold. You see him again, give him back the pen."

Feeling brave, Tromp kept McCabe's pen, knowing it to be worth hundreds of dollars. He thought about returning it, but decided to keep it for another purpose, which, at the moment, was more important than drawing a diagram of the Lago Colony environs. He used it to point to the east northeast.

"They're going to search the old phosphate mines up there," Tromp said, noticing Wofford's attention on the pen instead of the direction it was pointed.

"Phosphate mines?" Clive asked, squinting in the morning sun. "They're not sealed off from the public?"

"Not all the entrances. I used to play in them, which made my mother crazy when she found out."

"Dangerous?"

"She told me a boy got lost down there and was never found, but I think she just made that up to scare me."

Wofford stepped closer, saying, "When is this search supposed to start?"

"Eight-thirty."

"We need something for top of the hour," Wofford said, looking at his watch.

"The fire department rescue team will be up there soon. The police are going to use new recruits to examine the abandoned houses here in the Colony, which is a more likely place to hide a body."

"Hold on," Wofford said. "Why would Hogan hide the body on land when he can let it drift away in the ocean?"

No one had an answer, but Bruce broke the silence. He hefted his camera onto his shoulder and said, "Who cares? Let's get some video."

Beyond the Lago Colony streets, the adjacent openings to the phosphate mines, and a strip of houses fronting what had once been a small airport, Glenn Hogan woke up after a terrible night's sleep. He'd been awake several times and not to relieve his bladder, which could hold half a case of beer before he had to break the seal. He fretted over those last questions from the detective, the ones about Kathy's dress.

He'd parked the car behind the old building with the dive shop, not directly behind it, about a hundred feet away where the two tracks through the scrub grass ended. Kathy pointed over to the spit of land.

"I think I remember that," she said.

Glenn knew he was in the right spot to do what he'd planned to do ever since his bookie clamped down hard on him at the end of football season. He stopped the rental in sight of where *Consuela* had taken them snorkeling, purely a coincidence as far as he was concerned. It didn't matter which stretch of water he dunked Kathy in, so long as it was somewhat secluded and too deep to stand.

But why couldn't he remember what happened?

He started over again with parking the car. Kathy fetched a couple beers from the cooler in the trunk. When they were empty, she started in about snorkeling. He got out, tossed his shirt onto the driver's seat, went to the back seat for the snorkel gear. Kathy did her thing on the other side. He paid no attention. He was busy ripping open the packaging around the snorkels. The plastic was impregnable. Why didn't they make airplanes and army tanks out of the stuff? He got the first one open after a struggle then turned to the second, cursing under his breath at how much they cost. Then he thought about the one point five million, and looked up at Kathy with a smile.

There it was! A clear image of her in the one-piece swimsuit. She knew better than to risk a bikini. Where had she put the dress? He didn't know.

"All set!" she beamed, brushing back her hair, the fabric of her suit stretching tight over her nipples.

Next, Glenn locked the car. He pressed the key fob, saw the lights blink, heard the horn chirp. Useless as ever, Kathy didn't help him with the snorkel gear as he reached under the bumper to hide the key. She soaked up the sun, fiddled with her hair, and posed as if modeling for the *Victoria's Secret* catalog. A mask fell out of his hand, landing in the gravel by the front tire. He dropped the smile for a sneer, letting his anger smolder at her lack of consideration. Just like all the women in his life, Glenn thought, waiting for a man to do something for her.

It came back to him as real as the key fob in his hand. His contempt for her stewed hot and bubbly at that moment, especially when she told him to hurry up.

"The sun goes down quickly near the equator," she had to remind him as she started for the water without offering to carry her own snorkel.

Did she leave the dress in the car? She must have. Kathy was ahead of him, her chubby butt winking in the suit, the dress nowhere in sight.

Like the end of a movie, Glenn's memory soon faded to black. He relived the brutal emotion of those last thirty seconds. A feeling of repugnance came over him. Every annoying comment Kathy ever made piled on top of her irritating habits until he could hardly wait to pull her into the abyss. She was just like his ex: always right about things, usually paying attention to something else instead of him, and never giving as much as she took. Case in point: the trip to Aruba. It had been his idea, but she didn't volunteer to pay for her ticket. He had to shame her into it by acting like he cared about equal rights for women. Then, in the Caribbean Club Casino, as soon as he started winning, she had her hand out for money to lose in the slot machines. Did he offer it to her? Yeah, he did. But she could have turned it down. Did she? Hell no! Equal rights? Yeah, right. He was supposed to cough up, and if he didn't, he looked like a cheap bastard in front of the rubes, like that old bitty who said what a cute girlfriend he had. Dining out? A pain in the ass every time. Hold the mayo. No onions. More ice. Diet Coke not Diet Pepsi. But a dip into her purse? Not once. That kind of thing wears on a guy, Glenn and his pals often said.

Putting up with all of it had been worth it, but he would never do it again. From now on it was going to be one night stands, maybe a week playing honeymoon, and on to the next one. He couldn't take it, and because he couldn't take it, because he let these things build up like a flood behind a dam, it was much easier to push her under the water, which is what Glenn was one hundred percent certain he'd done to Kathy. He released his pent-up rage, every bit of it from his first botched date in high school to his final lost bet on the Eagles.

As for why he couldn't remember committing the act, Glenn had a reason for that, too. It was like the time he got into a car crash on his seventeenth birthday. He saw the light turn yellow, stomped on the gas, and boom! The cops told him he was T-boned by a panel truck in the middle of the intersection. Despite totaling his car, he never lost consciousness. Yet, he couldn't recall the fire department cutting him out of the wreck even though they were talking to him the whole time. His first memory after that yellow light was the doctor assessing him in the emergency room. For all he knew, Glenn could have been abducted by aliens. He learned later from the investigating officer what happened. Such was the situation with Kathy here in Aruba. It was a traumatic event, an unholy struggle, which explained the fatigue afterward and the blank between his ears.

Suddenly, Glenn felt liberated now that his system was purged of worry. Lying down on his bunk, he took a deep breath. He wasn't concerned about Kathy's dress, the lost handcuffs, or being tripped up by the police. He had this thing beat. With Jeff Nedd at his side, how could he lose?

Around the middle of the day, the repair crew was successful and the travel lift started. Kathy watched the gangly machine roll over the slip and then lower the boat into the water. Cheers rose up from the men, who availed themselves of yet more beer supplied by the case courtesy of the boat's owner. The party wore on into the afternoon, until many of them were sprawled on the dock not fifty feet from where Kathy sat in the schooner.

Despite the primitive bath the night before, she was far from clean. Every time she moved about the cabin, bits of grit and filth clung to her skin. In the stifling air, her hair turned to an old mop left to dry dirty. She was starving, not literally, but she hadn't had a balanced meal in three days.

If the lockup in Aruba was anything like the States, Glenn was enjoying clean sheets, three meals a day, access to exercise equipment, and plenty of hours to watch television. Kathy didn't have so much as a radio. Clean sheets and room to stretch her legs? No quite. Making it worse were those men on the dock, coming and going with coolers of beer, having a back-slapping good time turning wrenches and killing fish depending upon whether they were working on the travel lift or manning one of the boats accessing the marina. They emptied their bladders off the end of the dock while their friends joked about the size of their dicks. Kathy squatted over a coffee can because she didn't know how to make the schooner's toilet flush. Although the breeze brought some air inside, it stirred up the reek of her urine.

Who was she punishing with her vigil, Glenn or herself?

I'm writing the script of this movie, Kathy told herself, *not Glenn.* He thought he was. He thought he had it all planned: her drowning, him being the forlorn boyfriend, her found dead, him collecting the insurance money after her body was shipped home for her mother to cry over at the funeral. *No way, asshole.* Tonight the tables turn. I'm coming out of the ocean, walking right up to Clive Mitchell, and telling him what happened. He said, she said? Maybe, but I'm going first and you'll have to talk your way out of it. When Judge Nadine gets you on the stand, you'll wish you had drowned and died a hero.

Kathy unfurled her sundress, holding it up to gaze at the big flower. She'd have to get rid of it or else the cops would figure out she'd been back to the car. Glenn's casino winnings? She wasn't going to ditch that. She would put that under a rock and come back for it once she was in the clear. It wasn't as if she had a chance at collecting any insurance money. Glenn was alive and well, snug in his prison bunk with a full belly.

"Enjoy it while it lasts," she said to her own empty cabin.

"Are there buzzards on the island?" cameraman Bruce asked Tromp.

"No."

"Then a body down one of these holes would never be found." Bruce edged precariously close to the rim of what appeared to be a wide sinkhole. He once covered such a depression in Pennsylvania that sucked down half a block of houses when the coal mine beneath it collapsed. This pit wasn't as big, but it was surrounded by prickly bushes that cast camouflaging shadows. Getting the right exposure was a losing battle. Capturing detail in the dark areas was all but impossible without blowing out the brighter ones.

Tromp led them to several places he knew from his days as a marauding pre-teen. Not only sinkholes, but empty houses, abandoned phosphate mine shafts, even concrete gun emplacements atop Colorado Point left over from World War II.

From the last stop, Clive Mitchell commented, "One hell of a view."

Bruce recorded several stand-ups with the search party in the background. He panned to the left of Clive, and zoomed in on the police and fire personnel as they fanned out like soldiers on a battlefield. Tromp watched the playback monitor, thrilled that Bruce pushed Wofford to shoot from Colorado Point instead of closer to the actual search area.

"From up here," Tromp had told Bruce, "you can see the rocky point and the area where they're searching."

Bruce glanced in both directions, using his hands to frame the shot, then gave Tromp a slow nod, his professional acknowledgement of the younger man's understanding of the job.

The other networks rushed in an hour late, after Mitchell's face had already explained to the world this new phase in the

Kathy Barrow Case as it was now called.

"Aruban authorities are providing no reason for this change in tactics," Mitchell said. "Perhaps there's been a break in the case, something they have discovered that leads them to believe Kathy Barrow may be somewhere on the island instead of in the water. For now, we can only wait ... anxiously ... to see what happens."

No sooner had Mitchell finished than Stan Wofford told them the next stop was the courthouse, where Koolman was going to argue for Glenn Hogan's release from jail. Tromp lent a hand to Bruce, noting the type, brands, and model numbers of all the equipment. It was high-end stuff worth tens of thousands of dollars. He wondered if Sandeep might find a few of the essentials on the used market somewhere.

Then, just as they were ready to pull out, Wofford threw a fit. He tilted his head toward the sky, screamed, and shook his smartphone-clutching fists. Mitchell and Bruce seemed nonplussed. They must have seen these tirades before, but when Wofford glared at Romy Tromp, the aspiring reporter went cold in the blazing sun.

"Remember what I told you about trying to feed the lions?" Wofford said as he stomped up to him.

"*Sí,*" responded Tromp, falling back on his native Papiamento.

"So what's McCabe paying you?" asked Wofford. "I saw the pen, and don't deny he gave it to you because it's McCabe's trademark."

"He's not paying me anything."

"Nothing?" Wofford snorted. "Oh, I get it. He made you a promise, a stand-up with his on-the-scene clown. Your face is broadcast for all your friends to see. Is that what you did it for?"

"Did what?"

Mitchell interjected, "Take it easy, Stan. I have no doubt Romy's on our team."

"Really?" Wofford said turning his head for a fraction of a second before zeroing in on Tromp again. "You're a decoy."

This comment caused Bruce to raise his eyebrows, and he'd once seen a paranoid producer accuse a source of secretly recording conversations to give to another network. Looking at Romy Tromp, wearing a one-size-too-big Clive Mitchell shirt, Bruce doubted the kid was up to anything other than a side-by-side with Clive. The pen put the monkey in the wrench, but McCabe handed them out like slices of cake at a wedding reception.

"You dragged us away from the airport, down here to this sweating rock to watch the authorities poking in the weeds."

"We were here first," Tromp countered.

His face exploding, Wofford said, "We're going to be last for an interview with Jeff Nedd."

"Let's go," Bruce said grabbing Tromp's arm, pulling him out of the line of fire and into his vehicle.

In the passenger seat as they followed close behind, Tromp learned from Bruce the details of Jeff Nedd. A *Philadelphia Lawyer*, the cameraman called him, which apparently meant something important in legal circles all over the United States. Except Nedd took it to the next level, making himself a *TV Whore*, a term which needed no explanation. No celebrity murderer, nor multiple child molester, nor crooked politician escaped Nedd's able counsel. Although he needed three attempts to pass the bar, he augmented his staff with brilliant strategists, public relations experts, and jury sifters, all of whom enabled him to weasel victories in several famous cases. Afterward, he appeared on any television program that would have him, which was all of them because the ratings pegged the needle thanks to half the audience who hated Nedd and the other half that loved how he goaded prosecutors.

"He'd defend the devil on trial in Saint Peter's court, which isn't so bad except that when Lucifer got convicted, Nedd's appeal would say it had been God's fault for making the universe so easy to exploit."

Tromp, still smarting from Wofford's accusation, ignored the analogy and defended himself. "I kept McCabe's pen after I turned down his offer."

"How much are we talking about?"

"Whatever number I wrote on a napkin, he said he would double it."

"And you stuck it up his ass by keeping his pen?"

Minutes passed before Bruce said, "I'll tell you what's happening in the other car. Wofford's telling Clive he wants to leave you at the next bus stop, which would have happened already if I hadn't pulled you in with me. The thing is, Wofford has so many suits kicking him in the head he feels like a soccer ball. But don't worry, Clive thinks you're the real deal and that's what matters."

A smile formed on Tromp's face. Clive thought he was the real deal.

"Doesn't mean you're out of the shit," Bruce continued. "You're on probation."

Lowering the window, Tromp took McCabe's pen out of his

pocket, and would have tossed it out if Bruce hadn't stopped him.

"Why throw away a perfectly good pen?" the cameraman argued, raising the window using the control on his side. "This is a game, Romy. Here's the part you missed. McCabe marked you with the pen. He was confident enough you'd keep it because it's five hundred dollars worth of high-class design and ten cents of ink. Soon as Wofford saw it, he pegged you for having talked to McCabe, which is what McCabe wanted. If he can't have you, then he sets it up so nobody wants you because they think he does have you. Are you following me?"

Tromp said, "That's like a guy who's not catching fish pissing in the cooler so no one can drink the beer."

Roaring with laughter, Bruce almost sideswiped a dump truck parked along the road. "Tell that one to Clive," he said. "Just make sure it's the right time. Anyway, you're doing a good job following the story, Romy. Don't worry about Jeff Nedd. He never does exclusives because he wants his face on every channel. He'll give McCabe first dibs then make the rounds like the fame slut he is."

"What about Wofford leaving me at the bus stop?"

"Wofford has a short memory. Come up with something good and he'll forget about today. Until then, let's hope Clive calms him down."

Shaking hands with Jeff Nedd was like grabbing a bull's tail. Glenn couldn't let go for the fear, awe, and excitement the man inspired. He pumped the lawyer's hand over and over, entranced by the brilliant green eyes and luminous capped teeth he'd only seen on TV. And the hair, precisely combed and held in place by magic because there wasn't a glimmer of oil. As for his suit, it was a lightweight number with a crease sharp enough to cause a paper cut. He skipped the tie, giving the appearance of a man ready for serious work.

"First thing I want to say," Nedd began, "is that you're walking out of here tonight."

"Tonight?"

"Tomorrow afternoon at the latest. Mr. Koolman, my local associate, is up there working wonders in front of the judge. It's not like you should be in here anyway, right?"

"Right," Glenn parroted.

"I took the liberty of doing some homework on your companion, this Kathy Barrow."

"You did? I mean, good, I'm glad you did."

A fatherly arm around Glenn's shoulder, something he never could have gotten away with in a Philadelphia lockup, Nedd said, "Son, what were you thinking?"

"Thinking?"

"Getting yourself tangled up with a woman like her."

"She was …"

"She was dangerous, Glenn."

"Dangerous?"

"I know, love is blind and all that, but she works at a pharmacy with drugs, controlled substances, things people aren't supposed to have without close supervision, medical supervision."

"Yeah, but …"

"Yeah, but you put her down as a beneficiary on an insurance policy, one with very liberal terms I might add, worth more than a million dollars, payable upon your death or demise."

"I did," admitted Glenn.

"Signed the form in front of a reliable witness, namely the pharmacist with whom Kathy Barrow worked side by side, a woman named Margie Taylor, who told my snoops you were a *keeper*."

"Well, what I meant to do was ..."

"You meant to show what kind of man you really are," Nedd interrupted. "Sure, you have a restraining order regarding some mistakes you made with your ex-wife. Since then, you're a choirboy. You did the community service, paid the fine, got a commendation at work. Hosting a diversity training seminar shows how enlightened you've become."

"How did you find out about ..."

Nedd shook his head, patted Glenn's shoulder, and said conspiratorially, "Be glad I'm not your proctologist, okay?"

"Okay."

"Let's talk mano a mano," Nedd went on. "We can't attack Kathy no matter how many pills she filched ..."

"She stole drugs from work?" Glenn cut in.

"That's just it, Glenn. We don't know. Nobody does. Everyone assumes she was pure as the driven snow and you're a big old rusty plow that pushed her out of the way to get the dough. But it's just as likely she was trying to get at you, isn't it?"

"Maybe."

"Of course it is! We can't say it because all the weepy blankets in the media will think we're beating up on the memory of an honest woman, one they never met but you certainly did."

"That's true."

"It is true and truth is our weapon, Glenn, our sword, our hammer. The truth about Kathy is going to come out by way of those same media animals that are trying to tear you limb for limb, including Judge Nadine herself."

In addition to the food she ate and rum she drank, Kathy owed the cook a water glass. She fired it at the TV, missed, and it shattered against the wall, shards ricocheting into her hair. They hung there until she watched the entire *Judge Nadine Show*, right to the top of the hour when the headline update began.

"Glenn Hogan released!" Judge Nadine shouted to begin the show. After the music finished and the logo did its dance, she stared out through the flat screen into Kathy's eyes.

"Justice is in peril, ladies and gentlemen. Glenn Hogan has been released from jail in Aruba. Let's go to Clive Mitchell for the latest."

In front of the courthouse stood Mitchell looking somewhat tired under the lights. Kathy knew Judge Nadine was live at eight and that Mitchell also supplied reportage to the early morning shows, making for a long day. Regardless, his baritone was steady.

"Judge, we know that Aruban authorities have released Mr. Hogan to the custody of his lawyer, Jeff Nedd."

"That bozo?" shouted the judge from the inset box in the lower right corner of the screen.

Continuing without missing a beat, Mitchell said, "Remember, Hogan also has a local attorney, Mr. Koolman, who argued before a judge earlier today that his client has done nothing wrong, has cooperated fully with police, and has agreed to give up his passport as a condition of his release."

"He gives up his passport. That's it? No monitoring bracelet? No house arrest?"

"There are strict conditions as to Mr. Hogan's movement," answered Mitchell. "He is confined to his former suite at the Caribbean Club that shared with Kathy Barrow, where he will remain at his own expense. In addition, he must check in with police every six hours, and cannot leave the property without a police escort."

At this point, Kathy almost threw the glass, but managed to hold off.

"Have you spoken to the cops?" asked the judge.

"San Nicolaas Police Chief Jules Calenda is in charge of the investigation, assisted by Detective Eduard Bakker. Our producer has made repeated attempts to arrange an interview but they have refused comment due to the continuing investigation."

"That's standard," huffed the judge. "What about the prosecutor's office?"

"There we've made more progress."

The screen changed to show Milo Evert at his desk, the vibrant blue Aruban flag in a corner behind him. He wasn't going to be on the cover of *Gentlemen's Quarterly* anytime soon, but Kathy thought he spoke like a competent man.

"Of course, I am disappointed by the judge's decision," Evert said in heavily accented English. "Let's be clear. Mr. Hogan is not exactly a free man. We have his passport, and he is confined to a specific geographic area. American authorities have provided us with background information that we are processing as part of this case. Mr. Hogan is a person of interest and will remain so until such time as we resolve the matter of Ms. Barrow's disappearance."

Mitchell came back on. "Here's where things are getting

interesting judge. Let's go to our affiliate in Philadelphia."

A snapshot of Glenn Hogan filled the screen, one of him standing outside Lincoln Financial Field, where the Eagles play. The voice-over coming from the speakers was one Kathy recognized, a reporter who covered the Philly crime beat named Josh Russo.

"Who is Glenn Hogan?" Russo's disembodied voice asked.

"I'll tell you," Kathy replied.

"Hogan is employed by the State of Pennsylvania, Bureau of Licenses and Inspections. His colleagues tell us he does his job well. His superiors recently gave him a commendation. His friends speak of an avid Eagles fan who is the life of the party."

"He's a real hoot," put in Kathy longing for another shot of rum instead of the water in her glass.

"But is there more to Glenn Hogan?" inquired the still faceless narrator. "Court records indicate he pled to a reduced sentence for spousal abuse. His ex-wife refused to speak with us."

Finally, Russo appeared on screen. He stood too close to a white door that opened no more than a crack into which he tried to shove a microphone.

"Tell us about Glenn," Russo said.

The door slammed and the screen went back to the snapshot of grinning Glenn in his Eagles jersey.

"As part of his plea deal, Hogan performed forty hours of community service, cleaning up trash along streets and assisting Media Borough personnel with the planting of trees. He also paid a fine. Since then, Glenn Hogan has been a model citizen, earning the respect of his superiors for organizing a diversity training seminar that included a segment on women's rights in the workplace."

For the second time in ten minutes, Kathy held back, saving the glass for something worse, which she swore there couldn't be. Then Judge Nadine appeared to tease the rest of Glenn's background after the commercial. While the ads ran, Kathy took a sturdy plastic bag from the kitchen into which she stuffed a handful of crackers for later.

"We're back," Judge Nadine called from the TV. "Let's see the rest of Glenn Hogan's story."

The grinning photo dissolved to a red-faced bartender Kathy recognized as the brewmaster at Iron Hill, the micro-brewery were she roped Glenn.

"He's one of my regulars, sits over there. I've known him for at least five years. Loves cheeseburgers and always pays his tab. Tips like a champ. Throws some extra on top at Christmas time or if the Eagles win."

"Did you see him come here with Kathy?" the off-screen reporter asked.

"They met here. Hit it off right away. Lots of smiles, drinks, kind of like love at first sight. I saw it in their eyes."

The urge to vomit overcame Kathy, but she couldn't afford to lose the few calories she had managed to ingest.

"Too bad what happened down there in Aruba," the bartender said. "I thought they might come back married."

Running to the sink with her hand over her mouth, Kathy choked back the puke at the last second, rushing to the TV so as not to miss a second.

"Is this the real Glenn Hogan?" Judge Nadine was saying. "Football fan and loverboy who whisked a girl away for a Caribbean vacation. Or is somebody else lurking behind that smile? We'll be right back."

The commercials ran an excruciating four minutes. When the program returned Judge Nadine sat with a psychologist, a brassy-haired woman with eyes too close together and a patterned shirt that gave Kathy a headache. Or, maybe it was the stress combined with the lack of food. Either way, she was feeling drained while the expert guest talked about doppelgangers and the Jekyll and Hyde Syndrome. Then more commercials to be followed by Clive Mitchell.

Judge Nadine introduced the segment by asking Mitchell, "Did you catch all that about Glenn Hogan?"

"I did, your honor, thank you."

"What can you add?" prompted the judge.

"Due to contractual agreements, Attorney Nedd wouldn't speak to us today in a formal interview."

"Which means a less scrupulous network is paying him for first dibs," fired the judge.

"I don't know about that," Mitchell said, "but I managed to question him outside a local eatery."

Handheld footage filled the screen. Mitchell followed Jeff Nedd along the tall glass windows of a fancy restaurant while startled diners on the other side of the partition gawked in the background.

"Has Glenn Hogan told you what happened?" Mitchell asked.

Without stopping, Nedd glanced sideways to reply. "Mr. Hogan has told me everything, Clive. The man is distraught. I'm hiring a nurse to care for him. The last thing I want is a suicide to follow an accident."

"I should be so lucky," Kathy groaned.

"What happened that fateful afternoon?" pressed Mitchell.

"We'll get to that soon. First, I have to consider my client's well-being, which may have been in danger since the moment he met Kathy Barrow."

"Please clarify that statement."

Stopping abruptly, Nedd looked at his shoes than directly at Mitchell. "You should know, Clive. There's always more to the story, and I'm wondering why your network has not investigated Kathy Barrow."

There went the glass. Kathy put all her might into the throw, which would have qualified her as a Major League pitcher.

"Are you saying she is in some way responsible for her own demise?" Mitchell asked, not hiding the skepticism in his voice.

"I'm saying the media always jumps to conclusions," replied Nedd. "Good police work takes time, and I intend to help the Aruban authorities do an investigation so thorough that Sherlock Holmes would be impressed. Now, if you'll excuse me, I need to check in with my client."

"As you can see," Mitchell said, rejoining the live feed to the studio. "Mr. Nedd has raised an interesting angle on the case."

"He's full of you-know-what," boomed the judge. "It's smoke and mirrors."

"Tomorrow, I'll have more with Jeff Nedd."

"Soon you'll have more with Kathy Barrow," Kathy growled.

13

When he should have been sleeping, Romy Tromp was busy rehearsing his stand-up presence. He faced the mirror, held an imaginary microphone up to his chin, and spoke with the voice of authority.

"Romy Tromp, reporting live from Aruba. Back to you, Clive."

Hard as he tried, he couldn't relax his vocal cords enough to get the resonant bass tones any self-respecting in-the-field reporter had. He fought back tears at the reflection of his reedy voice. What if he was stuck a permanent tenor and never grew into a thundering baritone like his father? Turning sideways in the mirror, he considered that maybe his weight was the problem.

"If you want to have pipes like a Mack Truck, you have to be built like a Mack Truck," he said, vowing to eat more starting with a big breakfast and to begin lifting weights.

Tromp was also bitter at having been branded by Zach McCabe. He wished he'd thrown the pen in the Hollywood's trashcan right in front of him. That would have made the point and denied Stan Wofford a reason to doubt his intentions. No, he'd kept what was a trinket for McCabe and marked himself a traitor.

But he wasn't a traitor. He was loyal to Clive Mitchell. Stan Wofford? Who was he? GNN might replace him tomorrow or send him on another assignment in New Zealand. People out there didn't know Wofford's name. They knew Clive Mitchell, whose familiar face talked to them in their living rooms every day, connecting them to the world.

"You're doing a good job following the story," Bruce had said, which is why Tromp fended off jibes from his editor at *Diario* who was both threatening never to buy his photos again and begging him to give him something. Tromp also ignored calls from his friends to join them in their nightly antics and turned down a freelance corporate job that would've earned him a nice chunk for his video rig. Instead, he called every source he knew: bartenders and janitors, patrol cops, electricians and car rental clerks.

It was a taxi driver who came through with a claim that sent Romy Tromp sprinting to his car.

"I saw that woman, Romy, the Americana, the one gone missing in the water."

It never ceased to amaze Agnes how fast her boyfriend dressed. From the time he answered his phone until the moment Chief Calenda finished tying his shoes, ninety seconds might have elapsed. Having his uniform on a rack beside the bed helped, as did the familiarity of wearing nothing else for most of his life. She guessed he could don his clothes in complete darkness and stand ready for inspection without a single button out of line. The only thing he didn't do was slow down to polish his shoes before bolting out the door at half past eleven.

Calenda covered the distance from his home in Savaneta to the Marina Pirata restaurant in nearby Pos Chiquito in a matter of minutes. He was the first policeman on the scene, arriving ahead of the two patrolmen he called en route to secure the area, and before Eddie Bakker, who had to drive all the way from Noord, near the far end of the island. Romy Tromp was there when the chief pulled in, but the photographer didn't stick around. His rusty Nissan sped away just as Calenda got out of his cruiser. A confirmation that whatever information the chief was about to get would be on tomorrow's front page.

Squaring his cap, the chief faced a chubby, middle-aged man seated on the bench outside Marina Pirata and said, "Tell me what happened Floyd."

"I just gave Kathy Barrow a ride from the airport."

Floyd Dunham received a call from the General Aviation Terminal located on the west side of the Queen Beatrix Airport. Corporate and private aircraft collected and discharged their passengers there at all hours, so Floyd didn't find it unusual to get a call just before eleven. He took his last fare from downtown to the Hyatt and was on his way home when the call came.

"Directly or via dispatch?" asked Calenda.

"Direct. My cellphone," answered Floyd. "My cards are posted in the General Aviation building."

"Then what?"

"I pulled up and a woman was waiting there. She asked me in English to take her to Marina Pirata."

"Was anyone else there?"

"I don't know. Isn't there always someone working with the planes?"

"Go on."

"Near the Balashi Brewery, I remembered that Marina Pirata closes at eleven. I told her this, and she said it didn't matter. Her boyfriend was waiting for her. I thought that was strange and asked if she was sure he would be there. She got a little testy telling me to keep an eye on the road."

"How did you know it was her?"

Pointing to his taxi, Floyd said, "I have *Diario* from two days ago on my passenger seat. Her photo is on the front page. And one of the man she was with, too."

"You're sure it was her?"

"She was wearing a big hat and sunglasses, like one of those Venezuelan stars from the telenovelas."

"How could you see her face then?"

"I didn't see it until we got here. She paid me cash money, a hundred-dollar bill, and I thought maybe she was a movie star from the States because she flew in private, the money, the attitude, and covering her face."

Calenda nodded that it made sense.

"I was making change when she got out and the breeze caught hold of her hat," continued Floyd. "She grabbed it just in time, but knocked off her glasses. When she looked up, I saw her face clear as day under the lights here."

"What did you say to her?"

Shaking his head, Floyd replied, "I didn't recognize her at first, so I just said, *'Masha danki,'* and handed her the change." The taxi driver chuckled, then added, "I asked her if she was sure her boyfriend was around because it gets quiet this time of night."

"Did you see him?"

"No. She told me they had a fight but patched it up."

That happened all the time, Calenda agreed with a nod as he listened to Floyd's account.

"I told her to call me quick if he didn't show. I would come back and take her to a hotel. So, I drive down the road to the Chinese joint by Mangel Halto, thinking I'll have a beer before I go home. Those places are always open late."

"They are," the chief said. Only minutes ago, he'd driven past the place Floyd mentioned. It was called Nam Yong.

"Nobody was inside, so I take the newspaper to look at while I'm sipping beer."

Impatient, Calenda cut to the end. "That's when you realized the woman you picked up at the private terminal was Kathy Barrow."

"*¡Exactamente!*" cheered Floyd. "I dropped a full bottle of Balashi when I saw her staring up at me from *Diario's* front page."

"What was she wearing?"

"A dark dress, kind of long, like something my daughter would wear."

Busted by a cab driver!

Kathy almost jumped into a stand of cacti after seeing the taxi come back around the corner. It was the same Chevy

Tahoe, which she thought was more unusual than even the Mercedes that had picked her up at the beach. This driver had shown genuine concern for her safety, and he must have stared at her in the rearview mirror more than he watched the road ahead. She didn't want to chastise him, but she was worried about getting into an accident this close to ending her ordeal.

Then the stupid hat almost blew away. She flailed like an idiot, knocking off her glasses and dropping the bag. She pressed the hat to her head, and reached into the Tahoe for her change. Letting him keep a hundred would've been a ridiculous tip and drawn more attention or else she would have just walked away. She hesitated when she saw the newspaper on the seat and her face looking back. Then the cabbie wanted to chat, asking about her fictitious boyfriend. She took the change and spun away.

At first, Kathy thought the driver hadn't recognized her. Their eyes had met just as the money changed hands. It was only for a second, and she doubted there was enough light for her features to be discerned. When the taxi passed out of sight, she scouted Marina Pirata to make sure no one was there. The restaurant was down a set of stairs and seemed to be built right at water level, perfect for what she had planned. Satisfied that she was alone, she pulled off her new dress in preparation to cut it to shreds and stuff it in Marina Pirata's dumpster along with the rest of the contents in her Bamboo Bazaar bag. The cuffs she would take with her into the water and throw them as far away from where she intended to come ashore as was practical.

To this point her plan came off without a hitch. She'd found a bunch of magazines in the schooner. *Island Temptations* contained an article about the new General Aviation Terminal opening at the airport to serve private planes. It mentioned courtesy phones available for passengers to arrange ground transportation. A map showed the terminal's close proximity to the Varadero Marina, where some passengers were expected to meet waiting boats. The same magazine contained an ad for the Marina Pirata Restaurant, located on beautiful Spanish Lagoon. Tables sat on a platform over the water. A framed nautical chart in the forward cabin showed Spanish Lagoon to be near the center of the west side of the island.

With this information, Kathy took a pair of scissors from the galley and placed them in the plastic bag from the Bamboo Bazaar along with her flowered sundress, the handcuffs, Glenn's casino money, and her flip-flops. She wore her new sandals and dress, the long black one she bought on the day she cheated death. From the marina, it took her about ten minutes to walk to the General Aviation Terminal where a lone security guard dozed on a comfortable chair. Taped beside the courtesy phone was a card for a taxi service. She dialed the number and asked to be picked up.

On the ride to Marina Pirata, the driver asked too many questions, but Kathy thought she had mollified him. Now, she was out of the black dress, standing there in her swimsuit, ready to cut the dress to shreds and throw it in the dumpster, when a set of lights came up the road, forcing her to crouch behind the trash bin. It was the Tahoe, its driver peering out the front window, obviously looking for her. He stopped, got out, walked to the entrance of the restaurant, even went down a few steps, then returned to his car. She waited in fear as he backed up and his high beams panned the metal box shielding her.

As the headlights turned down the road, she made a break in the opposite direction. She didn't get far before the Tahoe made another slow circuit in front of Marina Pirata. The only direction Kathy thought to go was back to Varadero Marina, which couldn't be more than three or four miles away. She couldn't be found anywhere near here, not after the taxi driver had seen her. Worst of all, she would have to hide out for a while longer, until his story blew over. The best she could hope for was that no one believed him. Otherwise, she'd be in jail for fraud or whatever they called it in Aruba.

Thankfully, her ankle held up, at least for the first part of the journey. She skirted the darkest streets until she was back on the main road. There she had no choice but to move as fast as she could, picking out spots to duck into every so often when a car came by. She did pause going over a little bridge, thinking she should toss everything in the water, but decided it was too late. The best thing she could do was get back to safety on the schooner and come up with another plan.

Along the road she went, tucking herself into bushes and twice dropping flat in a ditch when cars came along. Her ankle weakened, making the last half hour a torture test that had her wishing she'd lifted some Oxycodone along with the other pills.

Several times, she sat on the ground, rubbing her ankle and wanting to giving up. What did she hope to achieve? Teach Glenn a lesson? Fat chance of that happening. The bastard was just plain lucky. He won at the casino, no small feat in itself, and got Jeff Nedd for a lawyer along with a local person who sprung him from jail in no time at all. So what if he beat her at this game? He would forever be a schmuck, loved only by his pals because he rooted for the same team and bought rounds at the bar.

With the iron gate at Varadero in view she was ready to surrender. The next morning she would slip into the water then call out to the first person she saw. It would be over. She had nothing to explain but how she survived the past several days. One look at her was all it took to know she'd been eating little and had not engaged in regular personal hygiene.

Jeff Nedd's insinuation that she stole drugs from the pharmacy was unprovable. Kathy took her stock from expired lots destined for disposal boxes. Her technique of palming tablets was indiscernible to the overhead cameras because she was supposed to be touching the drugs anyway. She was the one entrusted with the task. She was also required to wear a white lab coat with long sleeves which further disguised her maneuver. She once saw the security footage when the police came for evidence to apprehend a chronic shoplifter. The display in the back room showed every camera, including those focused on her and Margie. All she needed to do was keep her hands moving in an ordinary way and everything appeared normal, the appropriate disposal of expired lots into the red plastic bins.

Limping into the boatyard, Kathy stopped at the kitchen door. It must have taken two hours for her to walk from Marina Pirata. She longed to go inside, make herself a huge sandwich, and guzzle orange juice, but if she was going to look like a starved castaway, her diet had to remain limited, if only for a few more hours.

She got to the schooner feeling dizzy and parched. Drinking half a bottle of water helped, giving her a moment of clarity during which she considered an aspect of the situation so obvious that she'd missed it entirely. Glenn had tried to kill her, and he was still alive. She wasn't worried about him making another attempt with her. She feared he would prey on another woman, someone without the benefit of having first given him a wicked dose of tranquilizers.

She stretched out on the bunk and asked herself, *Can you live with that?*

Romy Tromp did not have time to back up his video of Floyd Dunham. He drove straight to the Renaissance Hotel where he sat in his car to watch it before rapping on Clive Mitchell's door.

"How can you be sure it was Kathy Barrow you saw tonight?" Tromp asked from behind the camera but audible.

Floyd held up *Diario*, tapped it with his hand, "I had this newspaper in my taxi. Her picture has been staring at me for two days."

His editor would forgive him for everything thanks to *Diario* seen worldwide by millions of GNN viewers.

"After you realized it was Kathy Barrow, you came back to look for her," Tromp prompted.

"For fifteen minutes, I searched the area then I called the police," Floyd said, waving his hands to show where he had driven. "How far could she go?"

In sync with Floyd's gestures, Tromp had zoomed out showing a deserted lane illuminated by insufficient streetlights. Although it was a consumer-grade camera, the video captured the emptiness of the dim thoroughfare.

Satisfied, Tromp grabbed his phone.

"Mitchell," came the voice on the second ring, scratchy from being asleep.

"Sorry to wake you, but I'm downstairs with some material you have to see," Tromp said.

"Bring it up."

Mitchell roused Stan Wofford and Bruce, both of whom sat, grumpy, on the couch in the living room of the suite. Tromp hadn't been expecting them. He wanted to review the piece first with Clive and get a reaction before bringing in the others, especially Wofford.

"You get a job as the town crier?" the producer scolded Tromp.

"Plug his camera into the big monitor, Bruce," Mitchell requested.

The cameraman connected the cables before retaking his seat on the couch.

While the video played, Tromp watched Wofford and Mitchell. The producer perked up like a Doberman on point, while GNN's star reporter showed little reaction.

"Are we finished?" Floyd Dunham said to Tromp at the end of the recording. "I think that's Chief Calenda turning the corner."

The screen went dark. No one moved. Clive Mitchell said, "Upload it to New York. Tell them I want to use it in the morning."

Was that his ticket to the big time getting punched? Romy Tromp thought so.

Chief Calenda and Detective Bakker worked through the night, from the time they arrived at Marina Pirata until dawn when they retreated to the chief's house for breakfast. Agnes overheard them talking about Floyd Dunham's account, the reason Calenda rushed out of a comfortable bed in the first place. She answered questions about general aviation traffic, making calls to her counterparts who confirmed that there had been two arriving and one departing flight between ten last night and six this morning. Immigration officials on that side of the field had not seen a woman matching Kathy Barrow's description, but there were several women passengers who walked through their station.

"You think Floyd was confused?" Bakker asked.

"No, he believes he saw her, but that doesn't mean he did. It just means he's not making up a story."

"His description of the dress doesn't match," Bakker reminded him.

Calenda pushed his plate aside and asked Agnes, "How many sundresses with big flowers are there out there?"

"I have one," Agnes answered.

"How about calf-length dark dresses?"

"Take me to dinner and I can show you one of those, too."

"Because we didn't find her doesn't mean she wasn't there," suggested Bakker.

The chief waited to elucidate on his theory until he and Bakker were driving to the prosecutor's office an hour later. It wasn't that he didn't trust Agnes, it was that he counted on her to be an unbiased sounding board for his ideas. The less background she had on how they developed, the more accurate her feedback.

"Is it possible these two are working together?" Calenda said.

Bakker went further with, "One point five million and no one dies."

"How does she stay underground long enough and then escape without being discovered?"

"Lots of boats along the shore here. Take one to Venezuela for a while ..."

"Two people keeping a secret is difficult. Three? Impossible."

"Then we're back to a taxi driver mistaking one woman for another," Bakker said.

"It's the most probable answer. An honest mistake," confirmed Calenda. "Let's see what our American friends have to say about her before making any more inferences."

They visited Prosecutor Evert's office where they gave a detailed report of the night's activities. Dour as he normally was, Evert seemed upbeat to have stacks of paper from the Federal Bureau of Investigation. Kathy Barrow, unlike Glenn Hogan, was a model citizen. She held a degree from an accredited school, passed a background check for her job, and paid her bills on time. She was neither in serious debt nor subject to any legal action. Her immediate supervisor and co-worker described her as, "great to work with." She visited her mother in a nursing home every weekend. No pets. No other boyfriends anyone knew about. Landlord stated no wild parties, no signs of illicit drugs, no heavy drinking, no damage to her vehicle parked in the driveway.

Evert offered his own assessment. "Unless she fell in with Hogan and allowed him to convince her to scam the insurance company, I would say it's unlikely she's the person Mr. Dunham delivered to Marina Pirata."

"Anything new about Hogan?" inquired the chief without commenting on Evert's position.

"The FBI is investigating his cellphone activity. They tell me it will take a day or two to sort this information and provide a summary."

"Nothing else?"

"Only what I see on television."

"Are you watching GNN?"

Jeff Nedd called from his suite down the hall to Glenn's, which was 1406, the same one he had shared with Kathy.

"I was sleeping," Glenn said.

"Wake up!" Nedd hollered. "Put on GNN."

After sleeping on that board in prison, Glenn was only too happy to remain in the middle of a king-sized bed, wound into the covers, and dreaming of European chicks. Jeff Nedd had other plans. Unable to find the television remote, Glenn got out of bed and pushed the button on the set itself. Clive Mitchell's voice came through the speaker.

"Last night there was a possible sighting of missing Pennsylvania woman, Kathy Barrow," Mitchell said.

On came grainy video of a local fellow explaining how he'd driven his taxi from the airport to a restaurant. He held up a newspaper with Kathy's picture on it.

"It was her," he said.

The phone rang again, sending Glenn tripping over the covers he'd left on the floor.

"A cab driver saw her!" Nedd blurted. "I'll be right over."

A knock on the door came so fast Glenn didn't have time to pull on his pants. He let in his lawyer then dressed while

Nedd thundered on about Kathy being a black widow.

"You're in danger," Nedd warned. "We'll have to get you security, two big guards at the door. Maybe another one to sleep on the couch."

"It wasn't her," Glenn said. "She was lost in the ocean."

"I know you're still in love with her, but you have to see what's going on here. Kathy's stalking you, Glenn," the lawyer said, lowering his voice to a whisper. "She could be in the next room. You go to sleep tonight, she slips in and suffocates you with your own pillow. It's happened. I had a case years ago where the ex-wife killed her old man with an aluminum baseball bat. She only got a year of probation thanks to my closing argument."

"Kathy could never do that," insisted Glenn.

His voice rising, Nedd took his client by the shoulders. "Wake up and smell the coffee! If you want to get off this island alive, you have to look out for yourself. Are you listening to me?"

The lawyer's voice was loud and clear, but Glenn knew there was no way the taxi driver gave Kathy a ride. She was gone, shark bait, crab food. He had read that within days a body dumped in the water would *bloat and float*. The decomposition process created gases inside the corpse, causing it to rise to the surface. Assuming none of the sea creatures availed themselves of an easy meal, she should be washing up on the beach right about now. And if the crabs or sharks or barracuda took her apart, well, she would never be found. In any case, she wasn't in the back of some taxi. She couldn't be. Glenn himself barely made it out of the water, and he was closer to shore. But he wasn't going to say all this to Jeff Nedd.

"I can take care of myself," Glenn said.

"What would guys like you do without guys like me look-ing out for you?" Nedd asked.

We'd have a lot more money, Glenn almost replied before he picked up the phone and ordered breakfast.

The long walk to the schooner depleted the last of Kathy's energy. She slept until noon, evidenced by the workers in the boatyard taking lunch. Her ankle throbbed and her crooked gait had made her back ache. Hiding from passing vehicles re-sulted in scratches that covered her arms and legs. She could hardly hold up the binoculars to look out the window.

Slumped on the settee, she eyed the cans of soup on the galley shelf. She no longer cared if the boat's owner caught her eating his food. Her health was in danger. Taking a can in hand, she smiled at the pull tab on top.

"Thank God for modern design," she sighed.

Opening the lid, the smell of Campbell's chicken noodle wafted to her nose. She sipped the cold broth then added a little water. In no hurry, Kathy drank her way to the bottom, savoring every drop. Still, she felt weary and heavy-limbed to the point where she dropped the empty can into the sink, limped to the forward cabin, and collapsed on the bunk.

Half asleep, she had a memory of her father. He'd come home late from his favorite tavern. Glassy-eyed and cantan-kerous, he snatched the remote away from Kathy and flopped onto the couch hard enough to make her side jump.

"Stupid girlie shows," he complained. "Why don't you watch something intelligent for a change?"

He rode up and down the channels until he came to a pro-gram about World War II. *Battle for the Atlantic* it was called.

Black and white film of ships plowing through storms alternated between current interviews with now-elderly men who had served aboard the vessels. Then there was a rare color shot of a tanker on fire, huge yellow flames cast freaky reflections on the water. Kathy got up to leave the room.

"Real men fought that war," her father said to her back.

She recalled wanting to ask him why he never joined the military, why he hadn't stepped up to the plate to be a *real man*. She even turned to pose the question, which she intended to do as a polite inquiry to drive the point home. She knew for all his bluster he didn't have a good reason for not being one of those who risked life and limb for the country. He was a wife-beater and a miserable prick.

"You got something to say about it?" he challenged her, not removing his eyes from the television.

"Goodnight, Dad," she said and climbed the stairs to her room.

She hadn't sparred with him that night because a witty exchange wouldn't have earned his respect. He would have twisted it around to make her look stupid or ungrateful and claimed another victory in the battle for their household, which ran stifling hot or bitterly cold depending on his mood.

Now, as she lolled on the musty bed, Kathy realized she was, in the most bizarre way imaginable, at the same point she had been on the night when she turned her back on her father. This time she wasn't going to walk away. She no longer sought revenge, nor did she want to teach anyone a lesson or get a thrill. Justice motivated her, a belief that she had to take responsibility for the situation and do what only she was in a position to do.

She possessed the will, but accomplishing her mission required more than blind ambition. There was physical strength, which at present was too low to be reliable. She had to recover, and when her body regained its potency, her mind would function better. Above all else, she needed a workable plan, one that gave her control over Glenn while seeming as if what she wanted to happen had been his idea exclusively.

Growing drowsy, she flashed back to *Battle for the Atlantic*. A merchant mariner, grown old but wearing a peaked cap with service ribbons pinned to it, spoke in her dreams. He said he'd been adrift at sea for six days, clinging to a chunk of crate wood, before a passing ship rescued him.

Could she last six days without food or water? In her semi-delirious state, she thought she could. Another part of her brain, the section that had put her on the dean's list at Temple University, told her she might not have to.

His mother had the good grace to tell him what a brilliant job he'd done taping Floyd Dunham's interview, but Romy Tromp knew she was disappointed that his voice and face were not part of the GNN report early that morning. An adept editor in New York had sliced it up, inserted a handful of quick dissolves, and rendered a shortened account that fit neatly into thirty seconds. Aside of his day rate, they granted him a byline: *Video Courtesy Romy Tromp* in tiny white letters in the lower left corner.

Tromp's ticket to the big time was still in his pocket. For this he blamed Stan Wofford, who had paced the suite with his cellphones alight, annoying Bruce to the point where the cameraman decided he might as well clean lenses instead of listening to the incessant chatter, bings, and bongs coming from the producer. Tromp played it cool, mimicking Clive Mitchell's poise, which never seemed rattled. Suddenly, Wofford dismissed him, with a comment about everyone needing some rest.

"Check in with us after lunch," Mitchell said to Tromp at the door, one eyebrow raised and the other dipped in conspiratorial confidence.

On that pair of bushy hooks, Tromp hung his hopes that he would soon be featured in one of the reports from Aruba. Watching Mitchell's morning stand-up and witnessing his own evaporation from the segment, he wondered, had Mitchell known New York would delete his side? Perhaps, and that's why he did the bit with his eyebrows. He was saying, *don't give up.*

Tromp held on. He went to his room, put his batteries on chargers, and stretched out on the covers. He asked himself what he would do if he was Chief Calenda. After all, getting ahead of the story, figuring out where it was going, would put him in the driver's seat with GNN. Tromp knew Calenda, but he couldn't step up to him for questions either on or off the record. The chief made it clear he was saying nothing about the case until it was over. The same went for Detective Bakker.

They don't believe Kathy Barrow is alive, Tromp thought, or one of his tipsters would have made his phone ring.

But what if she is? Backtracking, he came up with a more important question. Why hide out in the first place? Collecting insurance money was one option, but disappearing required a new identity, not an easy task in the modern world. Plus, it was the most obvious solution. Fake a death. Get the money. Move to Colombia and live happily ever after in a pleasant Bogotá barrio. Did Kathy Barrow even speak Spanish? Doubtful. And what if Hogan decided not to share the cash? She'd be guilty of fraud along with him and in for a rough ride with the legal system.

No, Tromp concluded. If Barrow is still alive, she's not pulling a scam. Assuming she's up to something else, either with or without Glenn Hogan, then where could she be? Tromp knew Aruba from the dunes in the shadow of the California Lighthouse to the rugged trails leading to the surf at Colorado Point. Caves, abandoned houses, buses left to rot at the end of dirt roads, he could put himself in any of those places in a matter of minutes. None of them fit with a place for an Americana to hide because they lacked any facilities from a toilet to air conditioning. From what he knew about Kathy Barrow she was not a trained survivalist. He couldn't see her camping in the cunuku under the stars.

He came back to the beginning. Why?

There were crazy people, those who did diabolical things their friends and neighbors never imagined they'd do. Was Kathy Barrow one of them? Was she one of the rare breed bent on manipulating others for her own twisted purpose? Or, was his imagination grasping for something to keep him in the limelight instead of pursuing the facts wherever they led.

Maybe Floyd made a mistake. Maybe Kathy Barrow was lost at sea. Maybe Glenn Hogan did nothing worse than lose sight of her. It didn't make for a good story, but it was as likely true as any other explanation. And if that's what happened, he'd be back to snapping pictures for *Diario:* car crashes, tourist spats, and the occasional grand opening. He might as well return the video camera to Sandeep for a full refund.

Dozing off, Tromp refused to give up. His skill and good luck brought him this far. It would carry him to the end, which had to be something more dramatic than a coward abandoning his girlfriend.

14

———

Glenn ate every edible speck on his plate: a cheeseburger piled high with lettuce, tomato, and onions, a double order of French fries, two whole pickles, and a huge scoop of white rice.

"Who serves rice *and* fries?" Jeff Nedd asked.

"Who cares?" Glenn shot back. It was one damn good burger: real meaty flavor, juicy, cooked to perfection, and a million times better than some soy-meal patty soaked with leftover pan grease. If they were going to keep him cooped up in his suite, he was going to eat one of those for lunch and dinner every day, just to give the reporters something to wag their tongues about. In that vein, Nedd was pushing for a press conference and not about dietary habits.

"We have to get ahead of the story," Nedd began. "I've got friends working for every network. They're calling me day and night for a statement."

"I don't have anything to say," Glenn told his lawyer, who

still hadn't said how much he charged.

"You don't say a word," Nedd reminded his client. "I do all the talking."

For one point five million, Glenn resolved to keep his mouth shut forever. Getting caught was almost always preceded by saying something stupid, and so he resisted his lawyer's idea.

"There's nothing to talk about," insisted Glenn.

"The video is what we must talk about," continued Nedd. "If not, they're going to make you look like a pervert, a weirdo. Is that what you want?"

"If you watch it, you'll see Kathy had no problem with a camera in the room. She's having as much fun as me, maybe more since I did all the work."

On this point, Nedd stood his ground. "Which is why we need to get it out there before it comes from the cops."

"The cops aren't going to release it."

Here Nedd took a deep breath, casting an eye over the room to a non-existent yet sympathetic audience who understood the difficulties of his job.

"How many cases have you tried?" the lawyer asked Glenn.

"Only the one with my ex."

"And that didn't go to trial. You pled. Had I been your lawyer, there would have been no fine, no community service, no public apology."

The apology in open court had been the part Glenn hated most. His dull-pencil attorney at the time told him to give it his all, "be contrite, speak like a man so the whole world knows you understand what you did was wrong." But all he did was punch his wife. Yeah, he gave her a shiner, a ripe black ring around her left eye. She practically stepped into it when she bounced off the wall after he shoved her. And why did all this happen? Not because of what he did. No, he wasn't the one who handed over a dozen custom suits to Goodwill. Stealing is what she did, and he was the one in court apologizing for solving the problem with a quick jab instead of wasting time in small claims court.

"I've tried and won more cases than there are coconuts hanging over that beach right now," Nedd was saying, his arm waving at the expanse of Palm Beach. "Did you ever consider that Kathy wanted you to video her in order to use it as evidence against you later?"

Glenn had not thought of that possibility, and he wasn't about to ponder it now. He wasn't going to admit to Nedd that Kathy was one of those basically sweet girls who lacked attention from real men like him because she wasn't quite thin enough or hot enough. Thus, she was stuck with the second string, the less confident losers who didn't mind sitting through chick flicks or doing the dishes in order to get in the sack. Nor would Glenn say that he brought her along for that exact reason. He perceived her neediness from the moment she spoke to him at Iron Hill. If he hadn't been planning a whopper of a payday, he would have sent her down the bar without so much as a glance.

"Step up to the mirror, Glenn," the lawyer said, backing away from the table where they shared lunch. "You have the look of lost love in your eyes. You miss her. You dream about her. Doesn't mean she wasn't your worst nightmare in the making."

Glenn shook his head.

"Here's what's going to happen," Nedd went on. "The

prosecutor or the police are going to leak parts of the tape. They'll have a good reason to keep their own asses out of hot water, something about getting help from the public. This is a bullshit excuse for their lack of courage to accept the reality of the situation, which is the following: Kathy Barrow was making half your salary. In the past, she's only taken a cheap seat to the Bahamas and has never been to a place as swanky as Palm Beach, Aruba. She was a potential gold digger. She may be a black widow setting you up so she can collect the insurance money you were so gracious to provide thanks to forethought and honest consideration of the hazards of modern travel."

"I hear you," Glenn said, just to give Nedd a moment to catch his breath.

"But are you listening?" questioned Nedd. "Let me fill in the rest of the details for you. Kathy knew about the video. The camera was sitting there beside the television in plain view. Is that correct?"

"I told you it was," answered Glenn.

"Of course. You both enjoyed an adult experience and confirmed a few things she will use later."

Frustrated and losing patience, Glenn said, "Use later for what?"

"Think about the facts you've given me, Glenn. One, the police asked you about her dress, which implies it's missing. Two, a pair of handcuffs are also unaccounted for, and they can be seen in the video. Three, you tell me you won thousands of dollars in the casino, and the money is gone. Put that all together and tell me what you come up with?"

His head spinning from eating too much, Glenn burped

his answer. "She threw away her dress, dumped the cuffs, and helped herself to the money. Then she disappears? For a meager five grand?"

"No, to stick it to you in the court of public opinion. Here's a headline: *Bad Boy Does It Again*. She shows up, and mark my words, she's going to show up any day now, and you'll be begging me to fend off the civil suit."

"Civil suit?"

"Emotional torment, pain, suffering, the whole spiel."

"She can sue for that?" Glenn wondered aloud.

"Don't you read the papers?"

He read the sports pages. The rest was political bullshit and feel-good garbage.

"Once it goes that far, you might as well be back in front of the judge apologizing even though you did nothing other than take a girl on vacation. Then we're sitting in her lawyer's office, and you'll be wishing the settlement was as cheap as alimony. The best you can hope for is a number you can pay with a second mortgage and the help of some generous friends, whom I can introduce you to if it comes to that."

Although he'd never admit it to Jeff Nedd, Glenn still could not remember what happened to Kathy once they were in the water. He figured his rage had caused him to blank it out. It didn't matter because he was left thinking Nedd could be right. Kathy could have escaped him. She might be in the suite next door laughing her chubby ass off.

"Glenn? Glenn? Glenn!"

Somehow Nedd was in his face, peering into his eyeballs.

"I'm calling a doctor."

Snapping out of his trance, Glenn said, "You really believe

she set me up?"

"Do you want to take a chance she didn't?"

Kathy awoke late in the afternoon. She hesitated not one second before eating another can of soup, taking her time to get to the bottom. It was during this skimpy meal that she acknowledged the necessity of action.

The most difficult part was time. On the day she and Glenn had first seen the schooner on the way to *Consuela*, the crewman had said the owner would return on Monday, two and a half days from now. He hadn't said morning, noon, or night, which constrained her to execute her plan by dawn.

She asked herself if it was believable that she had been drifting around the ocean for days and had suddenly made it to shore. Yes, it was possible, but no, it was not believable. She would need another reason to be out of sight and yet discoverable by another person. However, it couldn't look as if she'd been deliberately avoiding the authorities.

While she contemplated a number of scenarios, she rummaged the boat for fabric to support her ankle. Her swim coach had once demonstrated the proper way to wrap all the body's joints, from wrists and elbows to knees and ankles. In a drawer under the bunk, she found a bunch of rags. Using one, she reinforced her weakened appendage, holding the cloth in place with a piece of duct tape. Already she felt stronger, moving about the cabin with new confidence.

Next, she counted out the pills she had, the ones she used for her knockout cocktail. There were enough left for one big dose, which wouldn't kill a man, but would render him unconscious if taken together. By her calculations, she could incapacitate

Glenn for up to two hours. The trick was getting him to take the pills. She couldn't shove them down his throat like a dog. And once he was out, what was she going to do with him?

She did have the handcuffs. Beneath the faux fur, was a set of hardened steel loops, designed and built to restrain a grown man. So, if she could get him to swallow the medicine, wait for it to take effect, and cuff him, it would then be possible to force him to confess when he awoke. He had a video camera, although he left it in the room instead of taking it along on the *Consuela.*

Taping his admission with his own camera gave her a reason to cheer, but she didn't because the hair-brained scheme of getting a confession was unworkable. All he needed to do was start screaming and hotel security would come to his rescue. For the laughs, she thought about making a blackmail tape. Slip him the mickey, shave his chest, legs, and genitals, and then dress him up in her panties. Tape that and put it on the Internet.

With the coming sunset, Kathy made another sober assessment of where she was and what she wanted. Glenn had tried to kill her. There was no doubt about it. He'd pressed her down and put all his weight on her shoulders. When she tried to get away, he yanked her foot, and not like he was playing, either. He pulled and twisted, intending to do damage. Did a thug like that deserve to be the victim of a practical joke, or was he deserving of something worse. And if something worse was the right choice, was she the one to do it?

If she needed more convincing, it came at eleven when she caught up on the news of the day on the vacant bar's flat screen. It was Kathy Barrow for the full hour on *The Judge Nadine Show.* The opening teaser featured Jeff Nedd.

"My client has been unfairly incarcerated, detained unnecessarily, and defamed by a news media that chases fresh blood like a pack of wolves."

"Ladies and gentlemen," Judge Nadine said, "You just heard Attorney Jeff Nedd describing the situation as he sees it for Glenn Hogan, the man who allegedly went snorkeling with his companion in Aruba. He made it to shore. She is missing. Tonight, you decide as we review the case from the beginning."

Theme music, rolling clips of Judge Nadine shouting down guests and hugging victims, and finally a dolly shot rolling in through the studio filled the screen.

"Let's go to Clive Mitchell in Aruba," the judge said. "Clive, what kind of garbage was Nedd peddling today?"

Mitchell raised his microphone. "Your honor, call it what you will, but Attorney Nedd laid out a scenario this afternoon that has everyone, including the Aruban authorities, scratching their heads. Before we get to that however, let's hear what Prosecutor Evert had to say."

The man with the heavy glasses stood behind a podium. Beside him was an easel holding several large photos.

"Today we are asking for your assistance in helping to find Kathy Barrow who was last seen on Tuesday. To my right are stills taken from a security camera and also from a video made in Mr. Hogan's hotel room. These pictures have been enlarged to show detail and the clarity has been enhanced. You'll note in the first one, a dress."

The camera panned and zoomed in on a shot of Kathy in mid-stride crossing the Caribbean Club lobby wearing her flowered dress on the day she disappeared. The same dress now hung on a peg in the forward cabin.

"We believe Ms. Barrow may still be wearing this dress," the prosecutor said off screen.

"For four days?" someone called out.

"In the ocean?" another voice asked.

Ignoring the questions, Evert tapped his pointer on the next image. "Here you see a bright pink color. Upon closer examination, you will be able to discern what appears to be fur-lined handcuffs."

Kathy gasped as a reporter armed with a camera rushed the easel to shoot a photo before being hauled away by a policeman. It wasn't the reporter that shocked her; it was sight of the handcuffs. Taken from a video made in the room according to the prosecutor, which meant ... which meant Glenn had recorded them having sex.

"You rotten bastard!" she yelled.

"These items have not been located," Evert continued. "Mr. Hogan has informed us they are no longer in his possession but has given no further explanation. Members of the public, those of you who enjoy safe activities in our tranquil Aruban waters, may come upon one or both of these objects. If you do, we ask you to please notify police immediately. That is all."

Twenty shouted questions hit the prosecutor at once.

"No comment. Thank you."

He left under a second volley of fire, which dissolved into a one-shot of Clive Mitchell.

"The island is abuzz with speculation as to how the dress and a pair of fur-lined handcuffs figure into the disappearance of Kathy Barrow."

Shaking her head, twisting her mouth, and clearing her throat with a less than subtle cough, Judge Nadine went on to say, "And this animal is in the same hotel suite he checked into before this happened? He's there instead of a jail cell? Handcuffs and her dress are missing. A man with a restraining order from an ex-wife. Do we need to connect the dots?"

"Connect the dots is what Jeff Nedd did in his immediate response to this informational release by Aruban Authorities. Here's what he had to say."

Wearing a jacket so carefully cut it left almost no room for the folded sheet of paper he took from the inside pocket, Jeff Nedd dramatically scanned its words then used it as a prop.

"My client has been dumbstruck by some of the developments that have occurred in recent days." Nedd spoke as if giving a speech in the well of Senate. "Nothing has been more egregious than the release of images, without his permission, from his private video recordings. I'm going to warn all of you to be careful in the use of this material. Defamation and libel are serious issues, which my client intends to pursue. That aside, I ask for you to not pre-judge my client through the lens that the prosecution is using to fry him like an ant."

"He's going to fry," Kathy said, "if I have to light the fire myself." Before the trip, they had been intimate against her better judgment. She'd done it the last time to make sure he wouldn't back out of going to Aruba. It happened at his place. Did he have a tape of that, too?

"My client may enjoy certain lifestyle choices that you may not entertain yourself. So be it. What the prosecutor has not told you is that Kathy Barrow was a willing participant in those activities. In fact, she initiated them, and in doing so, has left my client in a compromised position with regard to his employment, friends, and future acquaintances."

"I initiated?" Kathy fumed. "I wasn't the one with the video camera running, and they sure as hell weren't my handcuffs!"

"There are other things the prosecutor left out," Nedd was saying. "Things about Kathy Barrow's job, her access to powerful narcotics, and her potential to …"

Judge Nadine interrupted, "Stop the tape! What is Jeff Nedd implying?"

"I followed up on his assertion," Mitchell said.

"Fast forward to Clive's question," the judge instructed.

A moment later a medium two-shot of Mitchell and Nedd came on. "You mentioned Ms. Barrow had access to prescription medications. Are you saying she may have misused her position at a pharmacy to obtain drugs?"

Nedd tapped the folded sheet of paper he had taken from his jacket at the beginning of the press conference. "You are saying that, Clive. Not me."

"I'm asking …"

"You're insinuating that I implied something, when nothing could be further from the truth, which is what we all need to find out here and not just in regard to Mr. Hogan."

"You did comment about powerful narcotics," Clive reminded the lawyer.

"As you know a pharmacy technician has access to controlled substances. I did *not* imply anything about Ms. Barrow or her job performance. I stated a fact about the conditions of a particular job. Although, let me clarify that the police should be conducting an investigation into all the circumstances surrounding this situation. If they need help, I can give them references."

Nedd walked away and Judge Nadine rejoined Mitchell.

"The nerve of this guy. Incredible."

"We go now to our Philadelphia affiliate to learn more about Kathy Barrow," Mitchell said, handing off to Josh Russo, the reporter who had profiled Glenn. On came a photo of Kathy that had been taken for her Employee-of-the-Month award.

"Kathy Barrow. Single. Living alone, here, in a one-bedroom apartment. She drives this two-year-old Chevrolet Impala. A normal life by any standard. Working at this pharmacy in Devon, Pennsylvania."

Russo stood with Margie Taylor in the parking lot. "You were Kathy's boss."

"I was her co-worker," Margie said, her voice apprehensive. "We were … are … friends."

"Tell us what it's like to work with Kathy?"

"She's cheerful, fun, you know, always willing to jump in and help."

"Did she ever show up late? Or leave early?"

"Once in a while to see her mom."

A cutaway to Clearwater Lodge popped onto the screen with the reporter's voice speaking over it. "Kathy's mother lives here, in a shared room. Staff would not let us speak with Mrs. Barrow, but they confirmed she is aware of the situation involving her daughter."

Kathy's fury dissolved into sadness as she thought of her mother, alone at Clearwater Lodge, mourning the loss of her only child.

Returning to Margie at the pharmacy, Russo asked, "If there's one thing you could tell Kathy, what would it be?"

"We miss you Kathy," Margie croaked. "Come back soon."

Crying through the commercials, Kathy steeled herself for the next segment.

"Clive," the judge said, "give us some good news."

"Late last night, a cab driver reported seeing Ms. Barrow," Mitchell told her.

"I saw your report."

"It turned out to be a mistake."

"I said I wanted good news!" bellowed the judge.

Cocking his head, Mitchell replied, "Supposing Ms. Barrow's dress is missing, she may still be wearing it."

"Let's hope so."

"The police continue to search the waters along the coast of Aruba. In my research for this story, I found cases of people lost at sea for more than a week who lived to tell about it. So, it is possible that Kathy Barrow may be found alive."

"Thank you, Clive, that's what I wanted to hear," the judge said, softening her tone.

Don't worry. I'm going to live to tell about it, Kathy vowed.

It was Romy Tromp's footage of Prosecutor Evert that ran on GNN. Wofford sent him there to record the official event while Bruce and Clive covered Jeff Nedd's statement. It was boring stuff, except for the handcuffs and the dress. There was no mistaking the flower on the front, even in the grainy image from the lobby surveillance video.

Could Kathy Barrow be alive? If he found her, there was nothing Wofford could do to keep him off the air. GNN, and for that matter all the networks, would want him. Zach McCabe would have to ante up more than a silver pen and short-term cash.

As their workday ended with the live spots for *The Judge Nadine Show,* Wofford told Tromp that tomorrow they would be doing a series of stand-ups at the various locations where Barrow and Hogan had been on the island. To get between them as fast as possible, Wofford wanted Tromp to do the driving.

"No problem," Tromp said thinking it would give him the opportunity to trace the couple's steps for his own investigation.

"You think we can get that done by noon?" Wofford asked.

"Absolutely," Tromp assured him, anxious to be free the rest of the day.

On grounds of professional integrity, Chief Calenda had refused to release evidence he thought would be better kept out of public view. Prosecutor Evert insisted the opposite was true. Bakker saw both sides of the issue and refused to break the tie. In the end, the prosecutor ranked higher and used his position to make the decision, with the blessing of the prime minister, who wanted something done immediately if not sooner.

As expected, Floyd Dunham called headquarters to insist the dress from the video enlargement was not the one he'd seen on the woman taken to Marina Pirata, but that it was the same woman. He demanded to speak with the chief, who took the call, assured Dunham he would personally revisit his claim, and then sent four patrolmen to roam through Pos Chiquito, Spanish Lagoon, and western Balashi to prove his sincerity. Also anticipated were the flood of crank tips about lost sex toys, oddball claims of female ghosts, and one report of aliens landing to steal a herd of goats. If he didn't know better, the chief would have thought his island home had been converted to an asylum, if not for the insane, then for the chronically bored looking to try their hand at comedy.

Calenda paged through reports of areas searched on land and at sea, noting only the recovery of flotsam and jetsam that spoke ill of those who needed a lesson in public stewardship of the natural environment. He asked his secretary, Julisa, to call *Diario* and remind them to run the public service advertisement about using trashcans, an order that indicated his own level of boredom.

Then he picked up Bakker's case summary and read every word. His last thought before closing the file was that it might have been an accident after all. Even though it fit with the other pieces of the puzzle, an accident didn't explain the missing dress and handcuffs. Taking his hat from the rack by the door, the chief ruminated on possibilities that accommodated the facts.

On his way home, he feared he'd lost his good sense to the power of suggestion. Hogan's American lawyer, Jeff Nedd, made the comment about Kathy Barrow's access to drugs. Was he a sharp advocate deflecting blame, or was he providing, either deliberately or not, a way into the case that had been overlooked?

Calenda had been one of the first on the scene to speak with Hogan. His initial impression was that of an exhausted swimmer. The fisherman's statement of finding a man weak and disoriented supported the assessment. How far would a person have to swim to wear themselves out? Currents or calm, it would have to be a fair distance and Hogan was not a flabby fifty-year-old. He was thirty-seven, in the prime of his life, and a regular at a fitness club.

Already on dangerous ground, the chief took another step. He created a scenario in line with Nedd's assertion that Barrow used one of those drugs she has access to as a tranquilizer.

Somehow, she doped Hogan right before they went into the water. While snorkeling, the chemicals took effect, incapacitating Hogan to some degree. He feared for his life and got ashore while she moved out of sight. Maybe he passed out for a while. She would know from her college studies and work background exactly what to expect. She retrieves her dress and the cuffs and goes into hiding.

"Why?" he said aloud.

What he knew about Kathy Barrow came from the reports provided by his American counterparts. According to them, she was an exemplary citizen, a loving daughter who visited her mother every week, a conscientious co-worker who was on her way up the company ladder.

So what was she doing with Glenn Hogan, wife-beater, gambler, and amateur pornographer?

The chief would have chalked it up to a good girl looking for a thrill on the wild side, but when he reclined on his bed late that evening, side by side with Agnes who had just watched her round of news programs, Calenda asked for a second opinion.

"Did you ever date someone who turned out to be like Glenn Hogan?" he asked.

"Sounds like you want to sleep on the couch."

15

———

Although he slept soundly in bed next to Agnes, Chief Calenda was on duty early, called to the airport by FBI Special Agent Bernie Griffith. Cynical, Calenda guessed that an agent arriving without warning in Aruba on a Saturday had less to do with expediting a case than it did with enjoying a few extra days under the sun.

In size and attitude, Griffith reminded Calenda of Romy Tromp. Both were young, thin, and unabashedly striving for greatness. Whereas Tromp had his cameras, Griffith toted a badge and a gun when within the bounds of his own jurisdiction. Coming out the door at Queen Beatrix Airport, he wore a fashionable linen blazer but heavy shoes more suited to a colder climate.

"A real pleasure to meet you," Griffith said, shaking hands with a powerful grip.

"This is Detective Bakker," the chief introduced Eddie.

"From Holland, right?" Griffith posed, demonstrating some of his own detection skills.

"Right," Bakker replied.

Driving to Prosecutor Evert's office, Griffith gave them a preview of his findings.

"We ran Hogan's cell calls back two years. You're going to love what we found."

Calenda marveled at how casually Americans used the word *Love*. A tasty meal or evidence of criminality, either one, you'll *love* it. However, he couldn't be critical of Griffith when it was clear he took his job seriously.

"You know he's an elevator inspector for the State of Pennsylvania. Anybody with an elevator, new construction, retrofit, whatever, they have to get an inspection to certify compliance with the Uniform Construction Code. That's Glenn Hogan's job. He's supposed to go out to the site and make sure things are done right."

"Does he do his job?" Bakker asked.

"He does it well, with lots of follow-up, I can tell you that."

"Follow-up?"

"You want details or should I wait until we're all in the same room?"

"Save it," the chief said.

Once inside the prosecutor's office, Agent Griffith took the floor for a one-man stage show. The playbill was a bundle of papers in triplicate, mostly telephone records, but also a map of building sites where Glenn Hogan had performed inspections and a handful of photographs for good measure.

"Here's the upshot," Griffith told his new Aruban acquaintances. "Hogan has a state-issued phone for official work, and he uses it judiciously. Nothing but business on that number, which is more than I can say for other people in various departments. Anyway, I compared his work calls to those made from his personal cell. Some of the numbers matched. I asked myself why is he calling job sites with his personal phone. To save the taxpayers money?"

No one believed that.

"Right, so it's easy enough to find out who these numbers belong to. The phone company coughs up that kind of stuff in thirty seconds. The numbers all lead to one place."

"There is a reason this helps us with Kathy Barrow's disappearance?" Prosecutor Evert put in.

"I think so, sir, if you'll give me time to explain."

The prosecutor waved for Griffith to continue.

"Hogan's credit report shows a twenty-five thousand dollar marker outstanding at an Atlantic City casino. That's a lot of money to me. What it tells me is Glenn Hogan is a regular gambler. Intuition also tells me these phone numbers have nothing to do with elevator inspections. I mean, he's calling after the elevator is complete. What? He's following up with a courtesy call? Doubt it."

"His bookie?" Bakker asked.

"Amazing system this bookie has going. I staked him out yesterday. He sits in the office trailer on the job, acting like he's doing real work. Even wears a hard hat. People come and go and no one says anything. He answers the phone for business and to take bets."

"How did you confirm he takes wagers?" inquired Bakker.

"I asked," Griffith responded with a Santa's-elf grin. "Up pulls the roach coach, you know the lunch truck, I get in line with the rest of the guys on the job. No blue blazer yesterday, jeans and sneakers so no one pays any attention. I get a sandwich and ask the vendor selling the chow if he knows someone local who takes action on football. 'You new on this job?' he asks me. 'Couple of days ago,' I answer, because that's when the call came in from Aruba. He hands me a card for Fairline Lift Works, tells me to call the second number, ask for Billy."

"I'm guessing no Billy is employed by Fairline," the chief said.

"Not one Bill, Billy, Will or William. But when you call the number and ask for Billy, which I did, you get a job offer. He tells me to stop by the site for a personal interview. I figure it's his way of staying undercover. A dude walks in he doesn't know, he vets him then and there. If I show up, he's going to say I'm not strong enough for the job, and he don't know nuthin' about no gambling."

Prosecutor Evert summed up. "You're assuming Hogan is in debt to this bookie for a substantial amount of money. In order to pay off the debt, he lured Ms. Barrow into the water, killed her, and will thus collect on the insurance policy to pay off his illegal gambling debts."

"More or less," agreed Griffith. "Depending on how you want to play it, I'm going to get Glenn Hogan here in Aruba, or back in the States when you're done with him."

Kathy didn't gorge herself after the latest GNN report, but she ate more than she had all week. She knew she couldn't execute her plan on an empty stomach.

Her first order of business was to organize her wardrobe. Before returning to the schooner, she rinsed her flowered dress as best she could then went to a closet in the back of the kitchen searching for a hanger. She found one among a rack of chef's whites, some still bearing tags from the laundry service. Paging through them, she realized a solution to one of her biggest problems was at hand. Kathy took a jacket and a pair of pants.

Aboard the schooner, she hung her dress to dry, and tried on the whites. Her chest filled out the jacket, but the pants were quite long. Using the galley's scissors, she cut them off, tucked in the ragged edges and secured them with duct tape. A length of cord served as a belt. Thankfully, the jacket hung down far enough to cover the hobo ensemble.

Kathy assumed her every move would be recorded by security cameras, especially in hotel lobbies. She intended to use this to her advantage by beginning the day in her new black dress and ending it in the chef's whites. Thanks to the prosecutor, everyone was fixated on the flowered dress. They weren't looking for an itinerant cook or tourist in a dark flowing number. Afraid of being addressed in Papiamento while wearing the chef's whites, she prepared a simple answer. She was an American chef visiting the island for a demonstration. Where? A private home. In your uniform? It's all I ever wear.

Good enough, Kathy told herself and moved on.

She next assembled her knockout cocktail. Instead of the combination of medicines she had used on Glenn at the beach, she retrieved the remaining Ambien she'd taken from the nightstand in the Caribbean Club, as well as two of his Valium tablets. To make sure the pills would dissolve fast, she ground them into fine powder within a sheet of plastic wrap taken from the kitchen. Like a drug dealer preparing an individual dose, she wound the wrap into a tiny satchel, securing the end with a tight knot. Just like those street-level dealers, she could toss it away if she had to, thereby ridding herself of incriminating evidence.

The tricky part was getting Glenn to take the medicine. She would have to be in place at the Caribbean Club from around five until well after dark, which could be difficult with or without a disguise.

Finally, Kathy gathered the empty soup cans, water bottles, and other items that indicated how long she'd been on the schooner, placing them in the galley sink. If she wasn't careful, she'd be caught in a lie against irrefutable evidence, which would ruin any satisfaction she got from dealing with Glenn. Confident in her preparations, the only thing left to do was get some sleep, and to that end she climbed into the forward bunk.

Kathy awoke to loud voices drifting in through the open portholes. They spoke English, too.

"I wouldn't mind owning a boat like that."

"Pfft ... garbage."

"Couple coats of varnish. Some new sails. I'd be riding the wind."

"You'd be broke is what you'd be."

Then Kathy caught the familiar timbre of a voice she'd heard the last four nights in a row.

It was Clive Mitchell who said, "Gentlemen, let's get this shot so we can enjoy a nice lunch."

Unable to control her curiosity, Kathy pressed her body into the shadows and peeked through a porthole. She could see Mitchell, wearing his trademark, two-pocket safari shirt. With him were three other people, including a skinny teenager wearing aviator sunglasses, a man shouldering a bulky camera, and the fourth person, a stern fellow with white zinc painted on his nose.

It became apparent they were doing a report with the *Consuela* in the background. Clive Mitchell strode along the dock, speaking to the camera that followed his every move.

"It was to this pier at the Varadero Marina that Kathy Barrow and Glenn Hogan came to board a sailing boat named *Consuela.*"

"We did," Kathy whispered.

"Under the watchful eye of Captain Hubert, the couple enjoyed a fun day of sailing, snorkeling, and sunshine."

Had she been with any other man, Kathy admitted, it would have been the perfect day. *Consuela*'s captain and crew treated them like movie stars. Drinks and fresh fruit were served on platters. No one bothered them as they snorkeled. Plenty of areas on the boat to enjoy the sun.

Thinking of the best parts of the trip, Kathy confirmed her earlier decision to move on with her life. No more plotting revenge and grousing about injustice. She accomplished what she wanted to in those areas, and whether or not it worked out as she hoped in this final episode, she was going to focus on the future. A graduate degree and a decent boyfriend were two things on the horizon. After all, it was better to pursue goals that made her life better instead of making someone else's life worse.

Isn't that why you wanted to be a pharmacist in the first place? she asked herself. She liked science in general and chemistry specifically. Yes, she had originally enrolled at Temple to become a pharmacist because medicines helped people. Their powers ranged from soothing a simple headache and drying up a runny nose to eliminating harmful bacteria and reducing cholesterol. She'd abused her privileges for a selfish purpose, which was all the more reason to end this chapter with Glenn the way she planned, with her penance served aboard this schooner in the interim.

Buoyed by her prospects, Kathy listened to Mitchell wrap up his report. Then the skinny kid took a call on his cellphone and said something that sank her spirits into the bilge.

"The FBI is on the island."

"Why would the FBI fly someone down here to talk to you?" Nedd asked Glenn.

Off the top of his head, Glenn thought of three reasons. No, four. The FBI might want to discuss his extra-curricular gambling. Then there were the elevator certificates he provided his slumlord pal in exchange for buying time with the bookie. They may also want to discuss his minor extortion of expensive dinners at a certain rooftop restaurant where the elevators were a necessity. And of course, there was this business with Kathy: the insurance policy, her disappearance, and whether he drowned her. On the last point he was most confident because he still couldn't remember how it happened. If he was lucky they would hook him up to a lie detector. He'd pass with flying colors and laugh all the way to the bank.

Jeff Nedd was not smiling, let alone laughing. He was doing that eyeball-to-eyeball stare of his, the one that made Glenn feel like he was up against his ex-wife who could stare dry a full bucket of paint. He had to slap her just to make her blink. He felt the urge to smack Nedd, but held off to give him the standard answer.

"I don't know," Glenn said.

"Anything going on at work?" the lawyer queried.

Another question his ex would have posed, except for the tone. She cranked up the operatic soprano when she wanted to badger him. It was like sitting in the dentist's chair.

Sounding more aggressive than he wanted, Glenn retorted, "Are you saying I'm on the take? Shaking down building operators for elevator certificates?"

Nedd lowered his voice, "Not you, Glenn. You wouldn't do something like that without telling me up front because you know a lawyer can only do his job if he has all the facts."

Is this shmuck insulting me or being straight? Glenn wasn't sure but he listened anyway.

"Maybe you know of some other people at work doing those things. Is that a possibility, Glenn? Is that why the FBI is here?"

"My co-workers wouldn't think of risking their pensions for a few hundred bucks to sign a certificate."

"Is that what the building operators offer, a few hundred?"

Dodging the trap, Glenn replied, "I wouldn't know."

"All right. It's nothing at work." Nedd spread his arms wide. "What could it be?"

"It's about Kathy. The insurance. I don't know."

"Let's go over it again," pressed Nedd.

"I'm not going over it again," protested Glenn. "They want to ask me questions, I'll answer every one like I did for the Aruban cops."

Surprisingly accommodating, his lawyer said, "Okay. I'll tell them we'll meet this afternoon at three."

"Do I have to talk to them today? It's Saturday, isn't it? Don't I get a day off like everyone else?"

Back to the ex-wife routine, Nedd whined, "I thought you wanted to answer their questions. Get all this behind you."

Glenn flashed back to the day he heard about his favorite suits going to Goodwill. The bitch telling him his stuff was gone with a sneer that begged for a punch. And he would have driven Jeff Nedd's expensive dentistry down his throat if he wasn't a lawyer and the only thing standing between the door and the FBI. Was now the time to tell him about the gambling, or should he wait? Glenn couldn't decide.

"What do you think I should do?" Glenn asked.

In full control now as the provider of advice, Nedd relaxed. He wasn't the ex-wife anymore; he was the brilliant lawyer from Philadelphia.

"I think you should tell me everything," Nedd began before taking a long pause. "Start with the day you were born and don't stop until this moment. Otherwise, I'm going to cut my losses and get the next flight off this rock."

To stay on budget, GNN reduced their fleet to a single vehicle. Wofford rode in the front passenger seat while Bruce drove. Clive joined Romy Tromp in the back. They were on the main highway, bound for the Holiday Inn where Tromp's source said Special Agent Bernie Griffith had checked in. As usual, Wofford was juggling his cellphones, when he suddenly shouted at Bruce.

"Pull over!"

Knowing it was best to obey without question, the camera-man braked hard and swerved off the road. Before anyone could ask why, Wofford was outside yanking open the rear door where Tromp was sitting. He grabbed the upstart reporter, tearing his shirt as he dragged him out.

"You're working for McCabe. All morning we're bouncing around this island of yours, doing nothing that we haven't already done, and you're laughing the whole time because it's exactly what McCabe is paying you to do."

"I told you ..." Tromp tried to explain before Wofford cut him off.

"Yeah, that you wouldn't take his money. Blah, blah, blah. But this is the second time McCabe scooped us here, and both times we're running in the opposite direction when he's got an exclusive."

"What's McCabe got?" Mitchell asked wearily.

"One of Kathy Barrow's ex-boyfriends," the producer spat, "who conveniently arrived on the island a few hours ago. In other words just in time to tape a segment for *Night Watch*, McCabe's Saturday night favorite that will top the ratings because we'll be lucky to have a 'no comment' from some FBI drone."

No one attempted a word for fear of Wofford's wrath, not even Mitchell, who scratched his famous chin. Tromp was finished talking anyway. It wasn't his fault he had no contacts in the States. Wofford should have been on top of those leads. Furthermore, Tromp wasn't about to explain or make excuses or beg. He reached over the back seat for his camera bag, hung it on his bony shoulder, and turned to Clive Mitchell.

"A pleasure working with you, sir," he said and then looked

at Bruce. "Thanks for the camera tips."

Walking down the road, Tromp turned onto a narrow path hotel workers used to get from their neighborhood to the high-rises. Taking out his phone, he scrolled back through the received calls, saw Floyd Dunham's number, and pushed send.

"It's Romy Tromp calling," he said when the taxi driver answered. "I need a ride."

16

Kathy enjoyed the distraction of watching the GNN crew. In person, Clive Mitchell cut a figure more handsome and confident than on the TV screen. His ability to speak to the camera as if it were another person was impressive. It not only lent credibility to his report but also sincerity, something she always wondered about. Did these newsmen care about the things they reported, or were they mercenaries? Mitchell came across as the former. His teenage sidekick seemed to believe in the cause as well. The kid stared at Mitchell, sometimes striking the senior man's pose.

As the news crew departed, Kathy resisted the urge to call out to them. *Hey, Clive! Over here!* If things went her way in a day or so, she'd be on with Judge Nadine herself. She felt the same tingle that surged through her body right before a swim meet, a combination of anticipation and nervousness that she always managed to channel into improved performance.

To pass the hours until the yard emptied, Kathy flipped through the magazines stuffed under the settee. There were issues of *Sail, Motor Yacht,* and *Boat International.* She learned the difference between Bermuda and gaff rigs, trawlers and yawls. The photos displayed elegant yachts equipped with the latest electronic gadgets as well as a special section about tugboats converted to pleasure craft. All the brass and woodwork required plenty of hands on deck to keep things in top condition.

Admiring the potential of the schooner, Kathy considered whether the cost to restore it would be worth the final result. At the end of each issue there were advertisements offering vessels for sale and charter. The prices astounded her. If she owned this derelict, she'd be swabbing the deck, polishing the brass, and stitching new sails. Instead she left things as they were to the best of her memory.

Was this going to be my fifth night aboard the schooner? Kathy asked herself. Yes, it was. The first four she ate next to nothing, and now running her hands over her thighs, she knew a few ounces had come off. It wasn't the healthiest way to lose weight but it was effective. Tonight she would limit her intake to just enough slow-burning protein to get her through tomorrow's mission.

When darkness fell, she made her way to the kitchen. To her dismay the selection in the refrigerator was sparse. The chef had used up his perishables to make room for fresh supplies when the new week began. Perusing the cans and jars on his shelves, Kathy selected the smallest tin of beans available, but it was still the colossal, institutional size. She microwaved a bowlful to make a bland meal.

The TV also disappointed her. GNN's regular programming had been replaced by a special about the Taliban. She went up and down the channels, through several from South America, until English came from the speaker. It was *Night Watch*, a Saturday newsmagazine type of show.

The presenter spoke about a new computer that did everything Kathy's current machine did but faster, and it would fit into the palm of her hand. If they got any smaller, how would she type on them? Next came a report about home repair scams. She was hardly paying attention and more interested in the odd brands of liquor on the shelf behind the bar when she heard the word *Aruba*.

"Today, there's been a development in the case of Kathy Barrow, the American who's missing in Aruba."

Kathy turned up the volume two notches.

"A former boyfriend arrived on the island and spoke exclusively with our correspondent, Gerald Wakefield."

Reeling back from the TV, Kathy saw Phil Ryan walking side by side with Wakefield. They were at the site where she and Glenn had gone in the water.

"She's alive," Ryan said. "I feel it. I feel her presence."

When it came to feeling things, Ryan preferred her boobs. A wave of nausea rolled through her stomach as the dolt she rescued in the ocean off Cape May spoke of her like a long-lost lover.

"We connected, Kathy and I. We had something special."

"How long were you together?" Wakefield inquired.

"It was short. Too short. We weren't ready for each other then, but now? Now, I feel this is a reminder about finding the best in people. Kathy found it in me, and when she comes home, I know I'll find it in her again."

The camera pulled back showing the sun low to the west. The voices remained close, which left Kathy gagging.

Wakefield said, "You have to know Kathy's been missing for almost a week and the chances …"

"I taught her some water-survival skills," Ryan interjected, "during a visit to Cape May. We stayed a week."

"One day!" Kathy yelled at the screen.

"Every day we swam, and that's the Atlantic up there, not a mill pond like here."

"There have been reports of strong currents off this rocky point," Wakefield said.

The camera went in close on Ryan.

"Kathy could handle it. I know she could. While we were in Cape May, this boy went out too far. There was no lifeguard, so Kathy rushed out to save him."

"What?" Kathy said in disbelief.

"I was at a snack stand, one of those carts that sells hot dogs and stuff. I saw her run into the water. At first I thought she was crazy or something. So right away, I sprint across the beach and see the kid in the distance, her headed for him, put two and two together and go in myself."

"Wow, what a story," Wakefield acknowledged.

"Yeah, of course, I'm a faster swimmer," Ryan explained, "and got to the kid first, but Kathy was nearby. I brought him in over my shoulder like a fireman would."

"Are you kidding me?" Kathy raged. "You lying sack of shit!"

Ryan wasn't finished. He added, "Kathy was tired. Who knows? She might've got into trouble herself, but she was brave going out into open water like that. After I gave the kid mouth to mouth and knew he was going to be okay, I went back to her. She was in shallow water by then, but I carried her to the beach, you know, just to make sure."

"Incredible," gushed Wakefield.

"Just a day at the beach," Ryan remarked. "I'm writing a book about stuff like this."

"Really?"

"Don't egg him on!" Kathy shouted.

"This thing with Kathy is just one chapter, a sort of day in the life of my adventures."

The view widened a bit, showing Wakefield with Ryan, both of them at the water's edge.

"I'd like to read that some day. So, based on your experience in these types of situations you think Kathy is out there somewhere."

"No doubt about it."

"Well, Mr. Ryan, what are your plans now that you're here in Aruba?"

"I'm going to search for Kathy. Help the police, the Coast Guard, put my skills to work, and bring her home."

Softly, Wakefield said, "Are you prepared for the worst?"

"No matter what," Ryan replied, tapping his chest with two fingers, "a piece of her is in here forever."

"In Aruba, the search goes on," Wakefield said, looking straight at the camera.

"Not for long," Kathy added.

From behind the wall at the former Esso Club, Romy Tromp watched McCabe play mother hen to the recently arrived Americano, Phil Ryan. Thanks to a ride from Floyd Dunham,

Tromp was able to retrieve his car from the Renaissance and drive immediately to the *Rocky Point*. He had a hunch they would shoot the interview from the place where Barrow went missing and his instincts were spot on. McCabe first directed the cameraman and correspondent, then walked Ryan through the paces of the segment. It took the Americano five takes to get it right.

In addition to the equipment and techniques used, Tromp saw McCabe give Ryan a shiny flask when the taping finished. They both drank liberally while the cameraman packed up.

"I don't care if you go over to GNN," McCabe said to Ryan, "but if you want to plug that book you're writing, I suggest you lose their number."

Later, viewing the finished segment on *Night Watch*, Tromp heard Ryan mention his book and put it together with what McCabe had said over the swig of whisky. He also figured Wofford never had a chance at landing Ryan. Why would he want him anyway? He was an obvious exaggerator, if not an outright liar. Rescuing a kid in the ocean then going back for Kathy? Did anyone believe that? Tromp didn't, nor did he think Ryan bright enough to fill out the immigration form on the plane that brought him to Aruba without help from a flight attendant. How was he going to write a book? Perhaps McCabe's staff included a ghostwriter. Otherwise, this fool had served his purpose.

Tromp spent a solemn evening in his room. He was less angry with Wofford than he was frustrated with how much was out of his control. Every time he got a good tip, somebody upstaged him. When he scored an interview no one else had, like the one with Floyd, it turned out to be irrelevant. Worse than that, he'd lost interest in what happened to Kathy Barrow.

Are you a reporter or a dog chasing cars?

If you're a reporter, what should you be doing right now?

Following the police?

Eddie Bakker lived in Noord, where many of his fellow Hollanders took up residence when they moved to the island. Among their hangouts was a restaurant called Bingo, where lanky Dutch girls served enormous mugs of beer. But, when it came to divulging information, Bakker was the only person less likely to squawk than his boss, Chief Calenda. It was a dead end.

On the other hand, an FBI agent alone on a beautiful night might want to brag about his latest case to a young man interested in law enforcement.

Tell his whole life story is not what Glenn did. He knew damn well what the FBI wanted to talk about. For all he knew they caught Billy with a crib sheet and he gave up his entire book. Be that as it may, Glenn was not confessing to anything least of all to a lawyer until he knew what the charges were.

Throughout his betting history, he'd been careful. The numbers he called to speak with Billy were all justifiable on official business. He was an enthusiastic regulator, determined to protect the public. You can never let up on these people, he would say. They know I can shut down the job. Maybe the Feds had a tape of him talking to Billy. Play it, he would dare them.

"Three cables should be checked Monday on the second car," his voice would play over the wiretap. It was perfectly reasonable for an inspector to talk about cable safety. What he was really saying was, "Three thousand on the away team." If he wanted the points, Glenn would add, "The safety switches are fine." He and Billy created an entire set of code words to cover the possibilities. It was a blast coming up with those things, like being in one of those prison movies where the inmates had to fake out the guards.

Therefore, let the FBI come with their accusations. Let them pinch Billy, drag him in for the rubber-hose treatment, or offer him a free ride if he gives up his book. Deny, deny, deny was what Glenn intended to do, standing on his reputation as an incorruptible employee of the State of Pennsylvania. He knew the State Attorney General's office set up sting operations. A department veteran warned him about that, but Glenn had never been interested in taking handouts from contractors. He did dummy up some certificates for his slumlord pal to get Billy off his back, but that was an aberration. On the job, he was so clean his ass squeaked when he walked. Almost.

Glenn told Jeff Nedd all about his ex-wife, including the times he used her as a punching bag and she didn't report him. He reminisced about cheating on the exam to become an inspector, which he justified because the stupid, elliptical questions had no bearing on anything other than a nerd's ability to take a test. He even mentioned how a contractor tried to bribe him once, which was a fabrication but one that could never be traced because the contractor dropped dead two years ago.

"For all I know," he concluded. "The FBI dug him up from the grave."

For his part, Nedd was attentive, asking for details here and there, but otherwise he kept his mouth shut. Glenn wanted to kick him in the nuts for playing like he was going home if they didn't have an honest-to-God come-to-Jesus moment, but held back because the lawyer showed some respect for a change.

Nedd offered his own analysis of the current situation. "I'm thinking the Arubans may have asked the FBI to come down here to scare you," he said.

"Scare me?" scoffed Glenn. "With what? I'm the one who nearly drowned, too. I'm the one who put her on the beneficiary line and told her to put down her mother. I'm the one who gets locked up in a shithole in paradise. Excuse me for being a little pissed off here, counselor."

"Totally justified, Glenn. Besides, the FBI shows up on a Saturday. I'm guessing it's an agent taking paid vacation before he retires. They want to play that game, they can wait until Monday."

For the first time all day, the lawyer made sense.

Although he was perturbed at having to wait to question Hogan, Chief Calenda understood the prosecutor's fears. Forcing cooperation meant arresting Hogan for a second time without charges, which looked bad in the American media that never went to any length describing the differences in the legal system. Thus, he agreed to Jeff Nedd's arrangement of a friendly exchange at the Caribbean Club set for Monday morning at ten.

"Let him hide," Special Agent Griffith said. "I'll catch some rays on the beach tomorrow, grill him Monday morning, and be on the afternoon flight back to Philadelphia. I'd love to bust this bookie, Billy what's-his-name, before the week is over."

The chief was the senior officer in charge of the investigation, not Griffith. Nonetheless, he allowed the lapse in protocol to slide without comment. To this point, he lacked a solid motive for Hogan. Griffith dropped one in his lap. Private gambling debts were not collected through the court system. Ugly men with brass knuckles came calling. Was Hogan in that deep? It wasn't a stretch to believe he was.

While it may be true that Kathy Barrow inadvertently picked a degenerate gambler for a travel companion, Calenda continued to ponder if she had designs of her own. Her background gave no hint of her finding men like Hogan appealing. It wasn't until later, after he turned down a free dinner with Griffith that the chief gleaned the first trace of something amiss with Barrow.

Agnes came home late, but early enough to keep him from walking the streets of San Nicolaas the way he did most nights of the year. She wasn't in the mood to stop at Zeerover, the local fisherman's wharf, for a beer with her friends. They ate at the kitchen table, him telling her about Agent Griffith, her relating the tale of a moronic Venezuelan pilot who by accident changed frequencies during approach and didn't figure it out for five minutes. Thankfully, disaster had been avoided, convincing Agnes that God must be looking out for some of his hapless creatures.

Then they were in front of the television, taking turns dozing off and complaining about nothing of interest being on. Agnes settled for *Night Watch*, a fateful decision indeed. Together they viewed the segment with Phil Ryan.

"She's got bad taste in men," Agnes commented when the program went to commercial.

While he agreed with the understatement of the evening, the chief stuck on something else, the story Ryan told about the water rescue. It smacked of machismo swagger. Just the same, twice Kathy Barrow had trouble in the water with boyfriends. Had one incident inspired the other? There was one way to find out. He could squeeze the truth out of Phil Ryan.

Unlike so many FBI agents on television, Bernie Griffith was not a glum-looking drone with a bad suit and a short haircut. He was rather stylish, standing at the bar in a linen jacket, sipping a Coke, brushing back a wave of sandy hair. Tromp wondered why the stereotype was perpetuated. Didn't the scriptwriters get out once in a while to see their subjects in action? Of course there were the action-hero types, big-muscled geniuses who alternately cracked heads and computer codes. Griffith didn't appear to be that type either. He could have been anyone on vacation.

Tromp found Griffith in the Holiday Inn lobby where the bar flanked the reception counter. A high-school friend who worked the second shift tipped off *Diario's* star photographer about the FBI's arrival, describing Griffith as "cute and kind of young to be a Fed," language she must have picked up from the same movies that pigeon-holed agents as sedan-driving robots.

Recent experience taught Tromp to make no assumptions. He'd been hoodwinked by McCabe, browbeaten by Wofford, and given a third chance by *Diario's* editor, who had every right to replace him. Would he have expected such treatment from that pantheon of fellow news professionals? No, which is why he approached Bernie Griffith with extreme caution, thinking the agent might be the FBI's Lone Ranger sent to lasso Glenn Hogan.

Naturally, caution did not imply temerity when it came to an eighteen-year-old who'd recently been banished from his dream job beside Clive Mitchell. Tromp boldly stepped into the fray and literally up to Griffith, thrusting out his hand to introduce himself.

"I'm Romy Tromp," he said.

Not anticipating a stranger's approach, a bewildered Griffith looked side to side for the person the young man must have been talking to. Then he caught on, shook hands, and said, "Bernie Griffith."

"My friend works at the check-in desk," Tromp continued. "She told me you're with the FBI."

"Word travels fast on an island."

"I guess you're on the case of the missing American woman."

"That's no secret, but you understand I won't be talking about it."

"I get it," said Tromp, flagging the bartender for a Coke of his own. He wasn't going to pretend to be a drinker, but he needed a reason to stay.

"Is there something I can do for you, Romy?" asked Griffith.

Sticking to the truth for a minute, Tromp answered, "When I was in high school I thought about becoming a cop, but that's a tough job here in Aruba."

"I wouldn't think a small island would have a lot of crime."

"It doesn't, just bar fights and people getting drunk during Carnival and smashing their cars, stuff like that. The hard part is arresting your cousins and friends who want you to give them a break."

This made sense to Griffith who bobbed his head with

sympathy.

"How are you supposed to sit down for a family Sunday barbecue when your aunt is angry that you cuffed her spoiled son for punching a rival who was staring at his girlfriend? Her favorite makes the front page of the newspaper for being a hot head, and you're the bad guy."

Impressed with what he heard, Griffith said, "That's a mature assessment."

"And a good reason to stay on the sidelines. Doesn't mean I wouldn't like to be an investigator." Although this statement was also true, Tromp left out the part about being a newsman. "I heard this Americano they locked up has enough baggage to be kicked off a plane."

Chuckling, Griffith let the comment pass, sipping his Coke for cover.

"What about a job with the FBI?" Tromp asked. "Is there room for someone like me up there?"

"You have to be an American citizen to be an agent."

"What about the people they hired to help with the War on Terror, the ones who spoke Arab languages?"

"You speak Arabic?"

"No," Tromp said. "I speak English, Spanish, Dutch, and Papiamento."

"That's a start."

Enthusiasm turned on full, he rambled, "I'm good with a camera, too. You need me to stay awake all night on a stakeout and snap pictures in the dark, no problem. Think about it. Hogan goes back to the States, he's expecting somebody like you keeping an eye on him. Me? No way. I could get up close without him suspecting a thing."

"If he gets out of here, he'll be lucky if we arrest him before his bookie busts his kneecaps," Griffith said off-handedly.

Tromp, now in possession of the clue he'd been desperately seeking, blathered on as if it meant nothing, "Or maybe I could use my language skills in the narcotics division."

Griffith's reply and most of what he said for the next ten minutes went over Tromp's head. The erstwhile GNN local guide analyzed Hogan's story with a measure of gambling debt thrown in the mix. Depending upon how much Hogan owed, it might be a case of kill Kathy Barrow to collect the insurance money, or be killed by a bookie for not covering his losses.

"You should get yourself into a good college," Griffith was saying.

Catching up with the conversation, Tromp said, "I've been saving my money."

"I'm still paying off my loans," Griffith moaned.

"Thanks for your time," Tromp closed. "It was interesting talking to you."

"Hey, no problem. Good luck."

Tromp walked through the shopping mall that formed the northern corridor under the Holiday Inn. At the end he turned right and passed through the Excelsior Casino on his way outside. The flashing lights, spinning wheels, and rolling dice held no appeal for him, but there were people in every spot, plunking down their money in the hopes of winning more.

While he was not inclined to wager a florin on the turn of a card, Tromp had to make a bet with the information he had. It wasn't money he could put in the bank. It was a time-sensitive, perishable commodity that would expire when anyone else in his trade discovered it. He asked himself who should have it, the network willing to pay the most or the one he thought deserved it? Was there a difference?

17

———

Sunshine on her face would be the next best thing to a hot shower. Kathy had neither for almost a week. She prepared for the day by rinsing off with the hose as close to dawn as she dared. Using a fork as a makeshift comb, she raked her hair into shape, but it was a lost cause. Not wanting to waste time, she wound it into a loose knot, secured it with a strip of fabric, and hoped for the best.

The chef's whites and her flowered dress were neatly folded inside the Bamboo Bazaar bag, the one from the gift shop where she bought the dark dress and sandals on the day Glenn tried to kill her. She carried it under her arm like a tidy parcel, walking across the boatyard as if she belonged there. As the first rays of daylight appeared, no one saw her exit the iron gate and begin the walk to the other side of the airport.

Kathy didn't follow the blue signs to the General Aviation Terminal. She took the ring road, the one on which she and

Glenn had traveled with *Consuela's* crewman from the hotel to Varadero Marina. At one point, she stopped to look down the broad runway that ran perpendicular to the lane. Rounding a lazy corner, she passed a collection of rental car agencies, all with their lights out.

It wasn't until Kathy stepped over the curb bordering the wide sidewalk at the International Departures lobby that she encountered the first person. He was a security guard seated on a bench, his head bobbing as he dozed in the early-morning light. When her shadow drifted by, he bolted upright.

"Bon dia," he said.

"Bon dia," Kathy replied, disguised by her hat and sunglasses, showing him a jaunty smile.

Although her ankle was unwrapped, it gave her no pain, which she attributed to the combination of excitement and adrenaline that occupied her mind. She thought a wrap would give her a characteristic somebody who saw her might remember, and so she left it off and stepped precisely without being obvious. Thankfully, she was in no hurry.

There were five taxis already in line but Kathy ignored them. In the USA Arrivals hall, she helped herself to a sturdy, red and white bag emblazoned with the Little Switzerland logo. A pleasant lady had handed Kathy an identical one days ago when she arrived at this point with Glenn. It was probably still somewhere in Suite 1406. It contained brochures for various activities, restaurants, and shops on the island. Gingerly, she lowered her changes of clothes in with the glossy advertisements thereby concealing another distinctive characteristic.

Nearby, a woman slid freshly baked buns into Cinnabon's

trademark blue boxes. Kathy's mouth began to water from the aroma. Rather than surrender to the urge for one of those sticky delights, she escaped to the bathroom. She knew if she had one, she would gorge herself on a dozen. So it was on to the ladies' room where she inspected her outfit.

Turning left then right, holding the Little Switzerland bag at her side and examining her reflection in the mirror, she was any other tourist come to Aruba. The dark dress was perhaps better suited to evening than morning, but it was island-weight, and therefore acceptable. With her sunglasses on and hat atop her head, she was confident in her similarity to the others who would soon fill the arrivals hall, anxious to begin their vacation. As self-assured as a runway model, she went outside, took a deep breath, and stepped up to the first taxi, pausing a beat to feel the warm sunshine.

Sliding onto the back seat, Kathy affected her best Texas drawl, saying, "How y'all doin' today?"

Sunday mornings Chief Calenda reserved for mass at Saint Teresita's in San Nicolaas, except on those rare occasions when official business interceded. Today, he was in uniform, standing by as Detective Bakker pounded on the door to Room 2730 at the Hyatt. The chief was correct in his assumption that Phil Ryan had not paid for his accommodations, but instead was enjoying them as a gift from the network that broadcast his story about Kathy Barrow.

While they waited for Ryan to get to the door, Bakker gave his boss a look that asked, *Are you sure you want to do this?* Calenda's steady eyes answered affirmatively.

"Hey, whoa, the cops," Ryan said after opening the door.

The chief moved forward like a rhino, not asking permission nor caring who was in the way.

"Sure, yeah, come right in. What can I do for you?" stammered Ryan.

Bakker closed the door and stood by while the chief surveyed the room, deliberately taking his time to raise the tension. His gaze eventually rested on Ryan, who sported pink splotches in areas missed with sunscreen.

"Great beach you have here," Ryan said to break the silence.

"Take a seat," the chief instructed.

Ryan sat, lowering his boxer-clad ass onto the bed, cocking his neck to gawk at the uniformed officers glaring at him.

Calenda started with a name. "Kathy Barrow."

"Sweet girl."

"Woman," the chief corrected him. "You dated her. How long?"

"A month, give or take."

"When?" Bakker put in.

Rotating his head, Ryan answered, "Last summer."

"Look at me when you speak," Calenda said.

Catching on, Ryan sat up straight, and said, "Is this like an official thing? Should I have a lawyer?"

"The phonebook is in the nightstand," the chief told him. "There are plenty listed."

"What's the problem? I'm here to help."

"Then stop screwing around and answer the questions," Bakker said.

"Last summer you dated Kathy Barrow," the chief repeated. "You went to Cape May. You swam in the ocean."

"That's right."

"Except you changed the story for *Night Watch*."

"I told the truth ..."

"Give me your cuffs, Eddie," the chief said holding out his hand.

Bakker reached for the leather pouch on his hip.

"What the hell!" Ryan griped, shifting his eyes to the plastic bracelets coming at him.

"Watch your language! Why'd you lie to the reporter on *Night Watch*?"

"What's the big deal? I ..."

"You lied. You defamed a woman who may be dead to shill for a book you aren't even writing."

"I got some pages done last night," offered Ryan. "They're on the desk over there."

The chief snatched the hotel pad from the desk and summarily tossed it into the trashcan. "You screwed up this case with your lies," he said. "I'm arresting you for obstruction of justice."

"Wait, wait ..." Ryan pleaded, adding a final drawn out, "waaait," that lasted two seconds. "Let's talk about this."

"Tell us what really happened in Cape May."

"Right now!" Bakker shot from his side.

Ryan sucked air, coughed, shook his head, and rattled on with what the chief and Bakker later figured was mostly true.

"Kathy and I went to Cape May. We checked into this bed and breakfast. Chicks love places like that."

There was that word again, *love*. The chief resisted the urge to give him a vocabulary lesson.

"It was a hot day, calm. Down at the beach we have drinks and munch through a bag of Doritos. I ate most of them. She was complaining about how fattening they were."

"Get to the part in the water," prodded Bakker.

"Okay. She goes in up to her waist then flashes her tits at me."

"The chief doesn't like that kind of language!" hollered Bakker.

"Sorry, sorry. She pulled down her suit like this," Ryan said, demonstrating. "I went in after her. You'd do the same thing, wouldn't you?"

The policemen said nothing.

"Anyway, I swam out there like a dog chasing a bone. She swam away. It was fun. By the time I caught up to her, I got a cramp, all of a sudden."

"Do you believe this?" the chief asked Bakker.

Bakker made the mistake of replying with an honest raising of his eyebrows. Still, it had the proper effect on the subject.

"Seriously! My right leg, it was like it fell off. I couldn't make it go. Then my arms went all rubbery. It was scary. Kathy swam over, just in time, too, or I would've drowned."

"She saved you instead of the other way around," the chief stated.

"Yeah," admitted Ryan. "I figured it was food poisoning or something. Once I got to the beach I was out of it for a long time and then I puked all over the sand. Felt like shit … terrible the rest of the day."

"Pathetic," muttered Bakker.

"Come on, man, it wasn't my fault. If it had happened to Kathy, I would have brought her in just like I said on the show yesterday. The lifesaving stroke, the mouth to mouth, I know all that stuff."

"Except you didn't," the chief reminded him.

"Creative license. Writers use it all the time."

Out of the blue, Bakker asked, "What do you think happened to Kathy?"

"I don't know, but that broad is one strong swimmer."

GNN's Sunday lineup included a cheerful, hour-long program dedicated to human-interest stories. A male-female team engaged in happy banter about lost dogs found, high-school sweethearts reunited, and success achieved by the most unlikely of candidates. The music swelled with the beginning of each segment then backed off to single piano notes before rising again with a funky, upbeat vibe that transitioned with ease into the commercials for fuel-efficient cars, high-fiber cereal, and life-enhancing vitamins.

Forty minutes past noon, the feminine half of the team took an unprecedented seat behind an official-looking news desk where she introduced the next feature.

"Welcome back," Kylie Bennett greeted the audience.

The camera shifted left to reveal an inset map of Aruba.

"Many of you have been following the story of missing Pennsylvania woman Kathy Barrow, who disappeared while snorkeling in Aruba with her travel companion, Glenn Hogan. There has been a new development in the story, and GNN brings it to you with a live report from our correspondent, Clive Mitchell."

Bennett's face replaced the inset map while the larger part of the screen was taken by Mitchell standing in front of San Nicolaas Police Headquarters.

"Thank you, Kylie," Mitchell said. "As I reported earlier in the week, Aruban police have uncovered an interesting insurance policy while investigating the disappearance of Kathy Barrow. We have learned there are two payees named in the policy."

"Explain to our viewers what that means, Clive."

"In this case, it means that Ms. Barrow named Glenn Hogan as her beneficiary. Mr. Hogan was her travel companion, and as we discovered from prosecutors and Mr. Hogan's own attorney, he was also romantically involved with Ms. Barrow."

"Who's the second payee?" asked Bennett.

Tilting his head, Mitchell narrowed his eyes, and replied, "Well, if Mr. Hogan were to meet an untimely demise while traveling on this trip to Aruba, then Kathy Barrow would receive a payment of one point five million dollars."

"So, they named each other as beneficiaries. Is that unusual?"

"Investigators are calling it odd. In my discussions with insurance professionals, I've been told it's normal for people to have such policies, but typically they name someone not on the trip as a beneficiary. Josh Russo, a reporter with our Philadelphia affiliate caught up with Kathy Barrow's co-worker and explains how the decision came to be made."

Off went Mitchell, on came Russo, standing on the porch of the shingled home of Margie Taylor.

"You were there when Kathy and Glenn finalized plans for their trip to Aruba."

"I was," Taylor said, rocking on her heels.

"Tell us about that day."

"Glenn came into the pharmacy with some papers. He had a printout of the itinerary, the flight numbers, a hotel confirmation, things like that."

"Did he have any paperwork related to insurance?"

"Yes. There were two forms with lines at the bottom. He said he was naming Kathy as his beneficiary, in the event … uh … if something happened to him." Taylor wiped her nose then pinched her eyes shut.

"Take your time," cooed Russo.

"He said … he said something like … if I die you'll have a million reasons not to forget me."

"That's generous of him," Russo noted.

"I thought so."

"Then what happened?"

"Glenn said she had to name a beneficiary for her policy and suggested her mother. She's in a nursing home."

"I know."

"Well, Kathy said if he was going to name her, she would name him. Whoever thought …" Taylor wept for a few seconds before blubbering, "It seemed so romantic. I told her Glenn was a keeper." The pharmacist bolted into her house and slammed the door.

"How dreadful," lamented Bennett who took center stage for a moment but then returned to the inset, making way for Mitchell in Aruba.

"While the insurance policy is still considered the prime motive for foul play in this case, the question remains whether it was secured as an innocent precaution or if Mr. Hogan had other intentions."

Bennett set up the next point with, "This is old news, isn't it, Clive?"

"With a new angle," Mitchell replied. "Reliable sources have told me there may be a more nefarious reason for Mr. Hogan to have arranged for this policy to be in effect. While known to patronize Atlantic City casinos where he is in debt for twenty-five thousand dollars, it has come to light that Mr. Hogan also places illegal wagers with bookies in Philadelphia."

"Oh, dear."

"We only have to dig through the GNN archives to know that illicit gambling, especially on professional sports, is a huge industry, in the tens of billions of dollars. The people who run these operations are rough characters when it comes to getting their money."

Pensive and dispirited, Bennett said, "Police believe Mr. Hogan's motive for …"

Mitchell finished the thought. "A man in debt to those people may behave in strange ways, irrational ways. It all remains to be seen as the investigation continues. Yesterday, a Special Agent from the FBI's Philadelphia office arrived in Aruba to assist the local authorities."

"I'm sure they'll get to the bottom of this soon. Thank you, Clive."

By the drumming on his door, Glenn knew it wasn't room service out there with his cheeseburger. Besides, he told them he wanted a steak tonight, medium rare, at exactly six o'clock so he could eat it on the balcony while watching the sun go down. He let the hammering go on for three complete sessions then whipped open the door at the precise moment he calculated Jeff Nedd would start the fourth. As always, his timing was perfect. Nedd stumbled into the room ahead of his own swinging arm.

"Keep it down," Glenn chastised the lawyer. "The high rollers are sleeping."

Like all the women in his life, including his mother, Glenn was finished with Nedd. He no longer cared about the heavy-hitter reputation, the connections to the movie companies, or even the possibility that he might get him out of Aruba any quicker than his local associate, Koolman, who probably worked for half the rate and did all the work. Nedd was a bossy prick no different than anyone else except he had a degree on the wall and shouted objections when he felt like it.

From Glenn's perspective, Nedd was a storyteller who made it up as he went along, especially that business about Kathy stealing drugs. For her to walk off with pantyhose from her own drugstore would be like robbing Mother Teresa. She'd never do it. Chicks who stole drugs came in two flavors: junkies and whores, of which he'd seen plenty around the slums where he slapped inspection stickers in rickety lifts bound to drop down the shaft on any given day. Okay, his ex did donate his suits, but the act made her more bitch than thief. As for the rest of them, they stole joy by withholding sex, talking in the middle of a game, and creatively leaving their jewelry behind for another chick to find. Kathy was one of those three, and if he'd stayed with her long enough, he would have found out which. If he had to guess, and he did just to delay dealing with Nedd another second, he'd put her in the last slot: the jealous-possessive type who would conveniently leave an earring under the tissue box beside the bed, the first place she knew another jealous-possessive bitch would look.

"Illegal gambling?"

Nedd posed the question in his surprised voice, which to Glenn sounded exactly like his ex saying, "Your suits?" The high-pitched drag at the end of the last word was like a Learjet taking off. Also like his ex, the lawyer answered his own question.

"The FBI is here to talk to you about illegal gambling."

His wife got a right jab for her insolence. Nedd received a less potent, but equally dismissive, "So what?"

At this point, Nedd must have sensed he was in trouble, because he tucked his tail, talked like a man, and suggested they take a seat on the balcony. Glenn appreciated the show of respect and reciprocated by agreeing.

Outside, Nedd became the storyteller. He reviewed the GNN segment, which both of them had seen. Next the lawyer waxed on about his duty as an attorney. Then he got to the responsibilities of the client.

"Among the most important," Nedd stressed, "are honesty and forthrightness. I'm not here to judge you. I'm here to make sure you are treated fairly under the law."

Glenn resisted the urge to say, *You're here to skim a handful off the top of my jackpot.* After all, if he were some clock-puncher whose girl went to Davy Jones' Locker with nothing but his 401(k) and a few bucks stashed in his underwear drawer, Jeff Nedd would not be in Aruba to save the day. He'd be on one of those news shows, maybe yapping at Judge Nadine herself, about vagaries in the law. More than a million brought the best out in everybody and Glenn decided to make Nedd work for it.

"Jeff," he said. "You're right."

"Thank you, Glenn. Thank you for seeing how this has to work if we're going to succeed."

It was like those Gamblers Anonymous sessions. Everyone used a calm voice, as though they were ordering in a fancy restaurant, slurring French words for snails, but Glenn stayed the course.

"All my gambling is done in legitimate casinos. I have a marker in Atlantic City, where I had some bad days recently due to stress on the job. Like the mistakes I made with my ex-wife, I see where I went wrong. That's why I enrolled in Gamblers Anonymous."

"You didn't mention that during our talk yesterday," Nedd put in. "And what were you doing in the casino here? You told Koolman you won six thousand and five of it was stolen from the safe."

"Hey, I fell off the wagon," Glenn explained. "See what it got me? A win that was taken away. There's a hard lesson. You think I'll forget that one?"

"No," Nedd murmured into his folded hands.

"The FBI is here to put the heat on me. Getting ahead of the story is what you called it. Here's where they're wrong. I make a mistake; I fix it. I pay the interest and some principal on that marker every month. I enrolled in Gamblers Anonymous and haven't missed a meeting at Saint Anthony's ever since. I publicly apologized to my wife. I paid the fine. I did the community service with a smile. The FBI wants to hook me up to a lie detector and ask me what happened to Kathy, I say bring it on. Let's get Clive Mitchell in the room to tape it because the only fool on TV is going to be the Fed they sent to break my balls."

Nedd absorbed the speech without reaction, spreading his hands flat over his knees for a glimpse of his manicure. "Lie detector," he said without looking up.

Glenn gloated with a sullen grin.

Springing to his feet, the lawyer said, "Forget Mitchell. I'll call Zach McCabe right now and set up a press conference for six tonight. That way it'll lead tomorrow's morning news cycle."

"Take it easy," Glenn cautioned. "Who's Zach McCabe?"

"A producer for a network that hands out first-class plane tickets like sticks of gum. GNN is a stingy stepfather in comparison, although Mitchell does have better ratings when he's on with Judge Nadine."

"That settles it then," Glenn said. "Get on tonight and tell the FBI either they send a lie detector down here by four o'clock tomorrow or we're going to do our own and make them look like chumps. Judge Nadine will be spitting nails when I pass that thing with flying colors."

"The FBI will never go for it," Nedd muttered.

"Do we care?" Glenn beamed. "We're ahead of the story."

18
——

Kathy handed the taxi driver a five-dollar tip, saying, "What a beautiful hotel," in the same southern accent she used when getting in at the airport.

"You should see the Caribbean Club."

"Is that right? Well, y'all have a real nice day."

She walked into the Holiday Inn's open-air lobby one more time. Glenn brought her here after dinner on their first night in Aruba. He wanted to check out the casino, which he did, promptly losing five hundred dollars. Kathy remembered thinking he was an idiot for gambling away in half an hour what some people earned in a week. However, to be fair, she also recalled being impressed when his stack of chips totaled over a thousand later that night at the Caribbean Club.

Cruising through the lobby, she smiled beneath her sunglasses, giving the impression of a woman excited to be on vacation. To further the ruse and acquire what she needed to accomplish her goal, she bought sunscreen, a paperback novel, two packs of Peanut M&M's, and a small bottle of red wine with a screw top. The clerk at the gift shop bagged the items and took Glenn's money from Kathy's hand.

Walking on the beach, it didn't take long to realize the wait would drive her crazy if she didn't occupy her time. Her goal was to arrive at the Caribbean Club no earlier than five. To pass the hours, she reminisced about happier days. She recalled the spring-break trip she took during her year at Temple. She and three girlfriends drove to Myrtle Beach, South Carolina. The water had been too cold to swim, but the sun was warm and they achieved their stated intention of encountering real men instead of the beer-chugging boys who circled them on campus. Kathy hadn't gone as far as her girlfriends, but she had been topless in a man's apartment, enjoying some heavy petting in the lead-up to the act, when the session was interrupted by the abrupt arrival of her partner's octogenarian grandfather. A night-fishing trip had been planned, one forgotten in the pursuit of Kathy but not by the old man who insisted his days of landing game fish were not yet over.

After hearing the briefest of details about her friends' couplings, Kathy lied in the most limited way so as not to be the prude. Secretly, she had been glad it ended with an embarrassed hug. Sleeping with some stranger she knew less than a week was beyond stupid. She caught a chill thinking about what might have happened had he been like Glenn instead of just a horny bachelor. She was alone with him, at his place, in his town. He could have been the resident ax murderer.

If ever I have children, Kathy thought, I'll tell them scary stories about kids being boiled in pots when they did stupid things like traipsing off with strangers. Wasn't that the purpose of those fairy tales, to teach lessons disguised as entertainment? It was and she would modernize them to include girls with cellphone batteries gone dead. In college, the answer to every fear was *Dial 911*. That's great except for when a monster is trying to drown you. Furthermore, her son or daughter would get more personal combat training than the standard, *Kick 'em in the Nuts*.

Having been in the hands of just such an animal, she saw how useless the typical advice was. As those dreadful moments began in the water, her reaction had been disbelief. *This isn't happening. This can't be happening.* Next came shock. *Oh, my God! It is happening!* Already Glenn had the upper hand. No cellphone, no foot flung at his groin, no screech for help was going to save her. And what about those friends she was supposed to stay with at all times? In Myrtle Beach they split up, going off with sexy prospects to places each of them had never been nor could locate if a call for help had been made via the cellular-powered do-it-all.

Beyond that, Kathy pushed her luck past the limit by thinking she could handle a man like Glenn, someone with a sketchy history, someone she had sex with as part of a moronic plan to give him a taste of the fear he instilled in everyone around him. Talk about volunteering for disaster!

After stealing the pills from the expired lots she had stopped to think about what she was doing and what the ramifications might be. Like that teenage college freshman she'd been, she talked herself into it using the kind of hubris only somebody too smart for her own good could possess. She had been naïve to think a punch in the face was the worst thing that could happen. A broken nose? I'm quicker than that, she'd answered. Maybe a black eye or a bruised arm. Big deal, I can handle that. What a fool she'd been.

Now, sitting on the beach in the shade of a palapa hut, Kathy pierced the shell of her stupidity for a glimpse of her opponent's cleverness. To get her into a position of extreme vulnerability, Glenn morphed into a charming shadow of his wife-beater image. He hardly sighed with impatience when she dithered over a menu let alone gave a hint he might raise his hand to strike her. All the while, he watched her following his lead to the point where it was too late to have second thoughts.

The insurance policy, an obvious warning, didn't send her running for the door. Like a haughty queen, she signed it. Why? Because she didn't want to be outdone by a loser who smacked his ex-wife for fun. Because she wasn't afraid of the Big Bad Wolf. Yeah, and how did that work out?

Kathy was about to make sure it went exactly as she planned. Until then, she walked to the nearby Paseo Herencia Mall for some window-shopping. Only a handful of tourists milled about, sipping their morning coffee. None paid her any mind. After a stop in the ladies' room, she stuck to the shade, popped M&M's, and read her book while seated under the awning of a café that had yet to open.

Midday, the stores unlocked their doors. She bought herself a pair of petite, tasteful gold earrings at one place and a wine glass in another. Despite her face appearing on GNN in recent days, no one gave the slightest note of recognition. Her new dress, big hat, and sunglasses had rendered her just another visitor enjoying vacation. When the plaza began to fill with tourists, she headed back to the Holiday Inn, pausing at the bus stop to check the schedule.

The reliable source mentioned by Clive Mitchell, none other than Romy Tromp, watched the GNN report in his room. In the end, he decided to call Mitchell directly without making any demands, bold claims, or tearful apologies for walking away. For Tromp, passing along Griffith's unwitting tip was an opportunity to do two things: prove he was a team player and test his bond with Mitchell. He could've called McCabe, got another pen or money or time on the air with Gerald Wakefield, then he could have stuck it to Stan Wofford by mentioning the tip in a snide call right before it went live on the other network.

Spiking the ball on Wofford would have done nothing but prove he was eighteen years old, a fact everyone knew and he was striving to outrun faster than the calendar. Thus, he acted cool, making the call to Mitchell after he got home from talking to Griffith. Instead of a hyperventilating kid, he spoke like a professional colleague.

"Clive," Tromp had said, risking the use of his idol's first name, "I had a conversation with Bernie Griffith of the FBI this evening."

Mitchell responded accordingly, as if he were speaking to an equal. "What did you learn, Romy?"

Griffith hadn't told him much, but he didn't have to. The blanks were few and far between. A man better off in custody than in the hands of his kneecap-busting bookie said it all. The same man had an insurance policy on a missing girlfriend. One and one was two no matter who did the counting.

And yet, Tromp still believed he was missing a chunk of the story. He could name people who saw ghosts, even a couple who claimed to talk to spirits, but Floyd Dunham was not among them. Floyd was neither a drunk nor a crackpot. Floyd was reliable. If he said he saw Kathy Barrow, he saw her.

This possibility occupied Tromp for hours as he gamed out various scenarios in which Barrow was alive. It was a long-term insurance scam. She was escaping the same bookie Hogan was. The mafia was holding her until Glenn paid off. She had a twin sister in on the whole thing. She wasn't Kathy Barrow after all but someone else, which would explain how she could get off the island undetected. He liked the last one best, but it meant the real Kathy Barrow was out of the picture for good or she could show up and ruin the whole affair.

Three aspirins later he was no closer to solving the riddle. Ironically, a better idea occurred to him via Stan Wofford, one as twisted as his Barrow-Hogan schemes. Wofford was furious at McCabe for scooping him with Phil Ryan, so if Tromp wanted to augment his investigation, he need only tail McCabe, who proved he had sources in Philadelphia and beyond. Although a bit juvenile, it would be a pleasure to outwit McCabe by passing along his information to Mitchell.

Encouraged by this development, Tromp set off for the Westin Resort at the south end of Palm Beach, where he knew McCabe and his team occupied half a dozen rooms.

Like Aruba's youngest reporter, Chief Calenda was home thinking hard about Kathy Barrow. Unlike Tromp, the chief worked from Phil Ryan's statements as opposed to a hunch. He reconsidered Floyd's claim to have seen her. He even went through all the crooked ploys he either uncovered himself or heard about in his more than thirty years as a policeman.

None of his theories fit the facts. It was Hogan who had the strongest motive, paying off his bookie with the insurance money. Kathy alive meant he was doomed. Her motive, unless they were missing something, was limited to the payout. The problem with that was nothing in her background pointed to a killer in waiting. Did she have bad habits? Gambling, drugs, or sticky fingers at work? Not according to the FBI, her local police, her landlord, or her co-worker. He admitted to not knowing about Hogan's illicit activities until the FBI uncovered them, reasoning the same may be true about Barrow. Eventually her secrets would be known, if he found a way into them.

Was he supposed to mount an all-out search for a woman who didn't want to be found? Not on his budget. Calenda thought it might be better to give things time to develop. If Floyd had seen Barrow, then she made the mistake of coming in contact with the public once. Surely she would do it again.

"We have a leak," Agnes called from the living room.

Assuming it was the air conditioner drain, the chief entered with his eyes on the wall, expecting to see water seeping down from the condenser.

"Who would have told Clive Mitchell something about Glenn Hogan and a bookie?" Agnes asked, pointing at the television.

"There's only five people I know," Calenda replied with disgust. "You, me, Eddie Bakker, Prosecutor Evert, and Bernie Griffith of the FBI."

"Who do you think it is?"

"Griffith," the chief said. "Americans *love* to talk."

Originally built as the Concorde, the Westin Resort was the first high-rise structure built on Palm Beach. Later there would be others, including the Caribbean Club. For years it stood where Aruba's shoreline turned on a bend of rocks that separated Palm Beach from Eagle Beach. When Tromp arrived just before five, he spoke with his father's friend who worked as a guard in the booth at the parking lot.

"A caravan of Americanos pulled out about fifteen minutes ago."

"Where'd they go?"

"That way, Romy, toward the Holiday Inn."

Tromp spun the wheel and jammed the accelerator.

The Caribbean Club was in the same direction as the Holiday Inn but closer. Tromp flew into guest parking, after spotting McCabe's fleet of vans and SUVs. Instinct told him to give Mitchell notice that something was up. If it turned out to be nothing, he would be a fool in front of Wofford again, if not, he might be a hero.

"Tell me, Romy," Mitchell answered.

"Caribbean Club. McCabe and his crew are inside," responded Tromp.

"Details?"

"On my way in to get 'em."

"What's your gut say?"

"Reaction to your piece about the gambling-debt motive. Press conference. Exclusive to McCabe. Nedd's trying to make peace for not keeping McCabe in the loop on the story you got from me. McCabe assumes Nedd is holding out on him."

"Makes sense. Rolling your way."

The woman who took Glenn's room-service order sounded sweet, which would have been great if he was a newlywed coming up for air and wanting to chow down on champagne-soaked strawberries. But, he was in a bad mood from being cooped up in a place that for all its creature comforts was turning out to be worse than the blockhouse from which Koolman sprung him. It was one thing to be in a hole with no temptation. It was another to be trapped on the wrong side of the fence staring at bikini-clad women, jet skis zipping across the water, and casino lights reflected in the building next door.

Food always raised his spirits and he wanted a porterhouse, medium rare, at exactly six so that when the sun touched the ocean he'd be burping gases from digesting Argentinian Angus or whatever it was called on the menu. He repeated himself three times, emphasizing six o'clock. He considered ordering dinner the most important part of his day and completed the task at two, although he was doubtful of the execution coming off as instructed. Dealing with Nedd took another hour—forty minutes longer than it should have—but now the lawyer had his marching orders.

Nedd insisted on bringing Koolman in for the press briefing to lend credibility to their cause in Aruba. Glenn respected Koolman for getting him out of prison, but saw no reason to pay two people to do one person's work. Of course, he couldn't put it that way to a lawyer who thought like a kid with ten fingers in front of a leaky dike trying to stick them all in at once.

"Who's going to see this?" Glenn asked.

Nedd knew precisely. "Six million Americans."

"And how many Arubans?"

"They get all the major networks here, Glenn, and it will be in their local papers. Having Koolman say a few words will show it's not an us-versus-them thing."

"It's them versus me," Glenn corrected. "They arrested me for making the mistake of bringing a chick to this island. I should have come alone and scored a local girl to warm the other side of my bed."

"Koolman has prepared a petition to have the custody conditions relaxed so you'd be free to move about the island. Now would be a good time to let the public know that."

"What good does it do if I can't go back to the States?"

"One step at a time, Glenn. Already you're out of prison, in a suite at one of the best hotels on the island, and tonight you'll be enjoying a steak dinner."

"On my own dime," Glenn groused.

He relented when it dawned on him that every minute spent talking with Nedd was billable. He stopped the clock with a final order.

"You and Koolman go have your press conference at six. The Eagles play the Rams at seven. Don't come knocking on that door until tomorrow when you're ready with the lie detector."

With Nedd gone, Glenn set up his balcony for optimum viewing. Only a slice of ocean was available due to the proximity of the neighboring hotel. Regardless, straight down was the apron around the pool and there lounged several chicks with legs worth noticing even from the fourteenth floor. If he had his binoculars, the set he took to the Eagles' home games, he'd be scoring those legs. He shoved a chair up against the far railing and set the table a comfortable distance in front of it. The test was to lean back on two legs, prop his feet on the table, and still be looking down at the women. *Certified!* he declared upon making the pieces fit.

In the room later, he watched other football games on TV for a while, evaluating how much he would have won had he been able to call Billy. He was up an imaginary four thousand when the early games finished. Next, he went through the news channels, but only the political shows were on, nothing but geezers in suits talking deficits and debt. He could teach them a thing or two on the topic.

As soon as he cashed that insurance check, Glenn was planning to pay Billy and reset the interest clock. In fact, with a million-dollar bankroll, he could take action himself. Billy would be paying him the juice. He liked the thought of that and was using the hotel stationary to work out the numbers when the sound of female voices in the hallway interrupted his mathematical exercise.

"Shut up you goofy broads!" he hollered. A few more words were said then it went silent. "Thank you!" he added to show he wasn't a bad guy.

Just then a new TV program started indicating the top of the six o'clock hour.

"Son of a …"

Before Glenn could complete the phrase, he heard a knock at his door.

"Right on time."

In a conference room that cost five hundred dollars per hour without refreshments, Jeff Nedd faced Zach McCabe in a standoff neither realized had been created by Romy Tromp.

"What's *he* doing here?" McCabe said, stabbing a finger at Clive Mitchell, who came through the door looking underdressed for any proceeding in such an opulent room.

"I didn't call him," Nedd replied.

"He's psychic?"

"My deal is with you, Zach. It's not my problem if Mitchell gets wind of something because he's bought every desk clerk on Palm Beach."

McCabe grinned a phony smile at Stan Wofford who lugged a tripod behind a camera-laden Bruce. He didn't see the skinny kid he tried to lure away. Had they kicked him off the bus or was he lurking in the duct work? McCabe wasn't sure.

"The network is going to run some of this with the headlines tonight," McCabe informed Nedd.

"That sounds like a teaser for Monday morning."

The conference began ten minutes late, with everyone pretending to get along until Koolman arrived. Nedd spoke first, railing against continued leaks from the prosecution, police, and now the FBI that painted his client in a bad light. He demanded a gag order. He also challenged the FBI to produce a lie-detector expert with equipment to question Glenn on the subject of Kathy Barrow's disappearance.

"My client is willing to put his reputation on the line to demonstrate his innocence. He does this against my advice, but I think we can all agree, an innocent man has nothing to fear from the truth."

Koolman picked up from there explaining his intention to seek the gag order in an emergency hearing tomorrow, as well as a complete relaxation of the custody requirements.

"Glenn Hogan came to Aruba as a tourist. We must treat him fairly, honorably. I will make this request with dedicated passion to preserve the island's reputation as a nation of laws, order, and justice."

McCabe's correspondent bombarded the lawyers with questions, but none were answered. Seeing it was pointless, Mitchell turned away. Right before Bruce switched off his camera's light, Romy Tromp snapped a photo through a gap between the doors at the rear of the room. He had plenty of time to get it to *Diario*, but he knew his editor would be more excited about the one he just took on the fourteenth floor. Exhausted and panting from descending the stairs two at a time, he checked the shot on the camera's display, it showed the room service waitress wheeling a cart through the door of Suite 1406. With the photo, he would send the tag, "Prison Food?" He could see it now, printed above the fold in tomorrow's edition.

As Mitchell arranged, the quartet reunited for dinner at Hostaria Da' Vittorio. The restaurant was nearby and it was easy to agree on Italian food. No sooner had they taken their places than Wofford raised his glass to Tromp.

"Good work today," he said.

"And yesterday," Mitchell added.

"Thanks," Tromp responded. He wasn't certain of Wofford's sincerity but took the man's words as a signal his dues had been paid even if his ticket to debut on GNN had not been punched.

"Let's eat," Bruce urged. "I'd like to get some sleep tonight, so I can stay awake through those hearings tomorrow."

Glenn was interested in sleep, too. He wished for company so he could brag about the flavor of his Argentinian beef. It was broiled to perfection. And the baked potato? Crispy skin the way he liked it. The house even kicked in a free glass of red wine. Delicious stuff. Tomorrow he'd find out what it was and order a bottle. No sharing with Nedd, either. Let the shyster get his own.

"The sun goes down quickly near the equator," Glenn heard Kathy say inside his head.

Recalling the sound of her voice bummed him out. The sunset, the women bending over to gather their stuff by the pool, the meal, everything else was perfect. Why did she have to step in and ruin it? To put her out of mind, he moved the balcony table to one side, giving a clear view to the sea from the bed. That bed also had the best view of the TV, where the Eagles game was just getting started.

His team was on fire. They scored two touchdowns in the first quarter. Then he dozed off and missed a Rams comeback in the second. He could barely keep his eyes open for the half-time update. How the game ended, he didn't know because he was snoring at the ceiling still wearing his clothes.

"Come on, Glenn. Let's get in the water."

In the dream, Kathy's voice was so close he felt her breath on his ear.

"Give me one of those snorkels."

"What? Uh … yeah …"

"Thanks, Glenn. Thanks for bringing me to Aruba."

"Hey, no problem."

"You're such a great guy. Let's take a look at those fish."

Opening his eyes, he saw Kathy standing a few feet away. Like every dream he had, it was dark all around, but he could see the flower on the sexy sundress she wore that day. She lifted it over her head, revealing that one-piece bathing suit. Where did she put the dress? There it is. She dropped it on the ground as she walked away.

"Let's get in the water, Glenn," she repeated, giving her ass a shake.

His vision blurred then cleared after he wiped his eyes. He was a few steps closer to Kathy. She was looking back over her shoulder. Glancing down, he saw his shoes. He couldn't go in the water with his shoes on. He slipped them off, tossed them to the side and felt the soft sand beneath his feet. He wiggled his toes into it. He remembered it being rocky, or was it? Whatever, he knew where the dress was now. He could tell that smug cop to go fetch it like a good boy.

"It's going to get dark soon. The sun goes down quickly near the equator."

From the grave, Kathy ruined his dream. She had to show him how smart she was.

"Let's check out those fish," he said moving closer to her, as the breeze ruffled his hair.

"Have you ever been snorkeling before?" Kathy asked.

"Lots of times," Glenn answered.

"It's like being weightless when you're floating on top of the water."

A know-it-all to the end, Glenn thought. Too bad she didn't have the sexy glasses to go with the brain, then he could have played hot-for-teacher with her instead of cuff-the-cowgirl.

"You sure you know how to swim?" she taunted him.

That was it. He lunged for her. His right hand caught her shoulder, then slipped off, just like that day in the water. He got both hands on her the second time and bore down with all his weight.

"You lousy bitch," he hissed when Kathy broke free.

Weightless in the water now, he reached for her ankle. It passed close by his hand, just out of reach. She faded in the distance, getting away when she was supposed to be under the water. Oh, well. At least he knew what happened, which had him worried about passing the lie detector test.

Only Tromp and Mitchell remained at the bar. Bruce spewed garlic fumes into the SUV while he slept, and Wofford sat outside, using his smartphones to file an expense report.

"What's the drinking age in Aruba?" Mitchell asked his understudy.

"I'm past it," Tromp assured him.

"Two whiskies. Ice. Water on the side," GNN's top correspondent told the bartender.

Johnnie Walker and Grand Old Parr were the two most popular brands of whisky in Aruba. His past experience with Old Parr left Tromp squeamish about drinking it in Mitchell's presence. In the second before the bartender asked which one Mitchell preferred, Tromp jumped in with a suggestion.

"Bourbon," he said, remembering an old John Wayne movie his dad watched whenever it was on.

"Maker's Mark," Mitchell specified, waving for the bartender to bring the drinks.

Like two gentlemen, they savored the smoky flavor in their glasses and exchanged stories. Mitchell kicked off the session with one about dodging a tiger attack while doing a story in Bangladesh. All twenty shots fired by the security team missed the tiger but managed to take out both front tires and the windows of their jeep. Tromp followed up by recounting a spectacular, single-vehicle car crash in which the driver succeeded in jumping the curb at a traffic circle, launching his vehicle twelve feet into the air, and shearing off a fifty-foot-tall palm tree.

"That's some damn good driving," Mitchell reflected.

"He managed to walk to his mother's house and slept like a baby," Tromp answered.

On it went, with just enough drinking to make the sad tales bearable and the funny incidents hilarious. The restaurant emptied behind them, and if the pair of reporters hadn't been entertaining the bartender along with themselves, they would've been told it was closing time an hour ago. It was Stan Wofford who pulled the plug. He'd caught up on his work and was ready to get some sleep. He also had the honor of paying the tab.

"What did you drink?" he said scrolling down the check.

"Nothing but the best, eh, Romy?" Mitchell replied clapping the young man on the back.

The alcohol swirled through his head, but he'd been careful to go easy so as not to get drunk. He sensed Mitchell had drawn an imaginary line for him to see if he would cross it. If he stayed inside the boundary he would pass the test. If not, he'd be calling Floyd for another ride.

Whatever his grade, they walked out together, where Wofford banged on the glass for Bruce to wake up and open the doors. In the breast pocket of his safari shirt, Tromp's cellphone buzzed. He nearly missed the call for laughing at the look on Bruce's face when he jumped awake.

"*Bon nochi,* Reynaldo," Tromp said, a bit of bourbon glee

creeping into the greeting for his cousin's cousin.

The locks popped and Wofford pulled the handle on the driver's door. Before he could slide into the seat, Tromp shoved him out of the way.

"I'll drive!"

19

By dawn on Monday, no one would have known that a man had fallen from the fourteenth floor of the Caribbean Club and landed atop a pool lounger. His body had been removed by the coroner. A team of cleaning experts scrubbed away the sticky fluids and a landscape designer arranged a series of planters to create a nondescript barrier that would remain until a concrete contractor restored the cracked apron, a small job already scheduled for Wednesday.

There were those guests who didn't hear about what happened until breakfast. Sometime before midnight, that guy who had been with the woman who disappeared, the one who was in trouble with the cops and wasn't supposed to leave the hotel, well, he jumped or fell from his balcony. No, really? Unbelievable. A newlywed couple coming back from a late-night stroll along the beach happened upon him, otherwise he might have been there until the morning joggers headed out for a run or the early birds reserved their loungers by the pool.

Waiters, bellmen, and desk clerks said they weren't on duty at the time and didn't know much about it.

"Would you like more orange juice, ma'am?"

"Let me help you with those bags, sir."

"A pleasure to have you staying with us."

As though nothing had happened, these phrases and similar ones ushered the day into existence for vacationers ready to soak up Aruba's bountiful sunshine, balmy waters, and soothing breeze.

Unlike the tourists who had the luxury of sleeping in, Chief Calenda and Eddie Bakker had been up all night gathering facts. For them the case wasn't over and wouldn't be until the coroner completed his examination, hotel employees were interviewed, and security-camera footage was scrutinized. As for Clive Mitchell's crew, and Zach McCabe's for that matter, it was time to wrap up.

No one took this harder than Romy Tromp. Glenn Hogan taking a header from the fourteenth floor wasn't the end of the story; it was another chapter. What happened to Kathy Barrow? People wanted to know. They watched GNN every night to find out. Judge Nadine was going to be furious and not just because Hogan left the planet without facing her across the bench. Surely she wanted to follow the case to the end with the discovery of Kathy Barrow, dead or alive.

Wofford gave Tromp the bad news of their departure right after Mitchell finished his stand-up on the Caribbean Club's stretch of Palm Beach. From the promenade, Bruce zoomed in to show the balcony of Suite 1406, then panned to follow Mitchell as he ambled along the sand informing America of the latest, tragic developments.

"Up there, in Suite 1406," Mitchell began, "the story of Kathy Barrow and Glenn Hogan began ... and last night ... it ended in a second tragedy."

He recapped all the high points of the previous week, from the couple's jaunt aboard the *Consuela* to Barrow's disappearance. He went on to mention Hogan's arrest and release. Then came Barrow's possible sighting before the arrival of the FBI with critical information. His richly textured voice flowed under scenes Bruce had taped for this exact purpose.

"And it may," Mitchell said with emphasis, "just may ... have been the presence of an FBI Special Agent with information Glenn Hogan thought no one would ever discover, that pushed him to the point of doing something drastic."

Doing something drastic remained undefined. Chief Calenda said nothing about Hogan's fall being a suicide or an accident. A murder? Committed by a bookie from Philadelphia come to collect? The answer was the same.

"No comment."

Naturally, there was a statement from Jeff Nedd, Hogan's American lawyer, who spoke with Mitchell ever so briefly as his suitcase was loaded into the trunk of a taxi.

"My client was a man with many issues. I did my best to help him in every way I could. That he met his end in this terrible way is a reminder how we must all heed the warnings of the professionals around us who have our best interests at heart."

Mitchell turned rhetorical for his summary. "With Glenn Hogan's untimely departure," he said, "we're left asking ourselves if we will ever know what happened last week off a nondescript corner of this island, the so-called Rocky Point."

Viewers had three seconds of his shrinking figure as Bruce zoomed out to capture the sweep of palm trees swaying over the beach. Then came the handoff to New York. "For Kathy Barrow's family, I hope so. Reporting live from Aruba, this is Clive Mitchell."

No sooner had Bruce checked the footage than Wofford announced they had three hours to get their gear packed and be at the airport.

"Yeah, but let me tell you my theory about Kathy Barrow," Tromp said. "I think she's still alive. I think Floyd Dunham saw her that night."

"Could be," Mitchell replied.

"We should start at Spanish Lagoon, take a boat along the coast, look for places where she may be hiding."

"Why would she be hiding?" asked Mitchell sounding somewhat indifferent.

"I don't know. Maybe she was afraid of Hogan's bookie or maybe they were in this together and something went wrong."

Mitchell dismissed the idea. "Doesn't make sense."

Suddenly embarrassed by his own lack of nonchalant professionalism, Tromp shut up. Begging wasn't going to get him in front of the camera. He ventured a shrug then helped Bruce coil the audio cable.

"It was great working with you," the cameraman said. "I'd like to come back here and check out the local scene."

"Give me a call," Tromp said. He realized he didn't have business cards to hand out, a critical error. "*Diario* knows where to find me."

"Maybe you'll be on assignment in another country," Bruce told him as he latched the camera case closed.

These encouraging words boosted Tromp's ego but left him frustrated that they were giving up. He'd overheard Wofford talking about viewership. The story drew the highest weekly ratings since the earthquake in Japan. More relevant, it wasn't over. You don't walk off the court when there's time left on the clock. What about the autopsy results? What about Detective Bakker's search of the room? Why not an interview with Prosecutor Evert?

It wasn't until they were at the Renaissance that Tromp accepted his time with GNN was over. As agreed, Wofford totaled the number of days he'd worked with them, confirmed his contact info, and said payment would be sent within thirty days.

"Sorry, I was tough on you," Wofford finished. "This business makes you paranoid. No matter what, stay away from McCabe. He's poison."

Mitchell stepped into the conversation and said, "Give me a ride to the airport, young man."

Any other day, traffic would have delayed his progress down the busiest road on the island. Today, there was hardly a car ahead of Tromp as he rolled south along the water. Mitchell held his tongue, too, which left him wondering if he was providing taxi service or if there was going to be an exchange of sentiments at some point.

The traffic light at the airport was green, denying Tromp one last opportunity to question the man whose career he hoped to have some day. Pulling to a halt in front of the USA Departures hall, Mitchell gripped his shoulder.

"You have good instincts," he said. "Stick close to your Chief of Police."

"Calenda never says anything," Tromp responded.

"Earn his trust the way you earned mine and that will change."

Tromp could not have asked for a better send-off. He thanked Mitchell for giving him a chance and said he would be in touch if there was a break in the case. As they parted ways on the sidewalk, Mitchell gave him one more reason to stay the course.

"When Kathy Barrow shows up, we'll go to you live on the scene. Be prepared."

"Batteries are charged," Tromp assured him.

Because the coroner was the only one who had a full night's rest, his report came first. It contained too much of the obvious to be useful, but Detective Bakker read the preliminary findings anyway, sharing a copy with Chief Calenda. "Cause of Death: massive injuries sustained by Caucasian male, mid-30s, resulting from a fourteen-story fall onto a concrete surface." Photos and medical description of said injuries filled several pages. As for the presence of drugs in Hogan's system, it was too early to tell. The toxicology screen would take a week.

In contrast to the coroner's summary, Bakker's findings were detailed to the minutia of the position in which he found Hogan's shoes. One was beside the bed, the other near the open sliding door to the balcony. Laces on both shoes were still tied.

The detective noted the television was on and tuned to an all-sports channel. The remote control sat on the nightstand beside the bed. Adjacent to the remote was a single blister pack of Ambien, a sleep aid found during their previous search of

Hogan's property. Two of the plastic bubbles where pills had been were empty. Eight remained untouched. Also on the nightstand, a single Valium tablet on a pad of the hotel stationary. Written on the paper, a series of mathematical calculations involving percentages.

Bakker's report mentioned the room's contents, had a diagram of the furniture locations, photographs, an explanation of fingerprint positions, all filling a second binder that had joined the first Bakker used on the day Kathy Barrow went missing. He included photos taken from the balcony looking down at the pool as well as pictures of the buildings visible from the balcony. The second set he could use to determine who might have seen Hogan's fall from the other direction. He doubted it would go that far.

Bakker had been the first ranking officer on the scene. He didn't need to be told to lock down the building. Before his arrival, he began the process using his cellphone, ordering Caribbean Club staff to secure every exterior door and guard both sides of the lobby, allowing no one in or out. From his house in Noord to the hotel, he had driven with all due haste and the trip took less than five minutes thanks to the late-night absence of traffic.

Bakker added this transit time and the three minutes he spent dressing onto his estimate of six to ten since the body had been discovered and he received the call from central dispatch. A timeline was critical to determining cause, be it a crime or an accident, and Bakker was frustrated at not being able to pin this one down because no one knew how long it had been between the moment Glenn Hogan fell and his discovery by the newlyweds. A security guard passed through the area at ten-thirty and didn't see a thing. The next step was to go backward and forward in search of relevant evidence, specifically people who came into contact with the decedent.

One look at the knots of people gossiping in the lobby and Bakker knew his time would be wasted on interviews. There would be twenty-five different accounts, one or two containing some facts, and the rest would be throwaways from gawkers seeking attention like Barrow's ridiculous ex-boyfriend. Hotel staff notoriously told each other every sordid detail about guests but turned amnesiac around police. A loose-lipped maid never graduated to manage a floor team if she ratted out a cheating husband, nor did a bellman become a captain in charge of luggage-luggers if he remembered who he saw with whom getting out of a taxi. Word spread fast about hotels with wagging tongues. The Caribbean Club's manager said so himself.

"To protect the privacy of our special guests, we don't have cameras on that level."

Apparently, if you have the money to stay on the top floor, in a high-roller suite, you can have your hookers, your drugs, your five plates of sausages and chocolate cake without fear of it showing up in divorce court or the tabloids. Then again, you might be robbed or murdered and have no way of knowing who did it. The price of discretion varied according to your proclivities.

Video cameras in common areas sometimes helped, though the pathetic quality of their images often served to confirm their uselessness, which was aggravating given the cheapness of high-definition units. Furthermore, the recording angles tended to favor cash registers, liquor racks, and storage access as the establishment utilized the presence of cameras to keep their staff honest.

These realities created a black hole and slogging grunt work for Bakker. He didn't do it alone. Chief Calenda, despite his rank, took the statement of the newlywed couple who found Hogan on the ground. He spoke with guests, bartenders, cooks, and janitors. The chief, much more than Bakker, believed Kathy Hogan was alive and had somehow been involved in Hogan's fall.

Bleary-eyed, Calenda watched the hotel's security camera footage over and over, going as far back as noon that day until one the following morning when the lockdown ended and everyone was permitted to move about the property. There were plenty of women of Barrow's type: tourists in casual clothes, some dressed for dinner out, a few a little tipsy as they came out of the bar. Any one of them could have been Barrow for their size and shape, but the clarity was poor. Sun-visors, hats, mussed hair, and zinc-coated noses might have been disguises or simply people taking reasonable precautions.

The same defects applied to images of the staff. When news of Hogan's discovery spread through their ranks, the curious rushed for a look, leaving their posts unattended until management wrangled them back to work. A trio went out to sneak cigarettes, the bright light from their matches bloomed on the screen. They tossed half-finished butts into the lot and hurried back to their stations.

The chief asked for copies to be sent to San Nicolaas where he would review the footage again when he was well-rested. He didn't waste time asking the coroner to hurry. He went home, hung his uniform on the rack, and sat on his end of the couch wishing Agnes were there.

Growing drowsy, Calenda ruminated on a discussion he had with Bakker before they split up to continue their efforts. Bakker told him Hogan's room door was locked. No sign of tampering with the lock, the frame, or the handle. The manager opened it, stood back, and ground his teeth over explaining the incident to corporate headquarters. Inside, the TV was on. The bed had been used. The sliding door to the balcony was open, both curtains pulled to the side. Ambien and Valium were on the nightstand. Hogan had admitted to using the drugs, one to help him sleep, the other to dull lower-back pain. Ambien was known to cause sleepwalking.

The chief had rolled his eyes at that one. "You're telling me he was sleepwalking and went off the balcony?"

Bakker had answered. "It's possible according to medical professionals including our coroner."

"Do we have her fingerprints?" had been Calenda's next question.

"A courtesy from Griffith. They were part of Barrow's background check for working at the pharmacy, but it may not be worth looking at them."

The chief knew why. Because Barrow had stayed in the room with Hogan, her fingerprints were sure to be present, proving she had been there, but not when.

Sliding his legs up on the couch and folding his arms behind his head, a position that Agnes had warned him would bring on a wicked stiff neck, Calenda recognized that his belief Kathy Barrow may have precipitated Glenn Hogan's fall did not make it true. Certainly, the ability to collect a million and a half gave her as good a motive to shove him off the balcony as Hogan had to drown her near a spit of land that newsmen coined the *Rocky Point*. Unless there was another reason.

Romy Tromp fell asleep too early on Monday night. Tuesday, he was up before daybreak. On an island whose many visitors slept late, the small hours of the morning offered no action. Regardless, Tromp grabbed his camera bag and headed to the cruise ship terminal in Oranjestad.

It wasn't exciting work, like a car wreck or a championship baseball game, but he took his time documenting the arrival of Royal Caribbean's *Serenade of the Seas*. The rising sun provided the perfect amber overtones on the ship's hull. For contrast, he waited for the tugboats with their black bulwarks to enter the frame. Always considering the commercial possibilities of his work, he thought he might offer the shots to a website dedicated to cruising.

Soon after the ship docked, her passengers flowed into town like a well-organized invasion. Some rented cars or boarded tour buses. Others wandered about the many shops promising the best prices and selection in the Caribbean. In the nearby marina, fishing-boat captains hawked their good luck to passersby. Tromp noticed *Consuela* docked there as well.

"Romy Tromp, the man with the camera!" Captain Hubert greeted him.

"You hoping to take some cruise ship passengers sailing?" Tromp asked.

"If we're blessed."

"If not?"

"The breeze is strong today," Hubert replied. "If I don't get a group that pays, let's have some fun. You can take nice pictures of me looking like the seafaring master I am. My brochure needs an update and great photos would be a good start."

As a warm-up exercise, Tromp took various shots of the boat. Close-ups of the winches and cleats, compass and anchor. He stepped back for wider captures of the name across the stern and the bow. The crew shared a plate of fruit while they waited for the tourists to make their selection.

With the deckhands restless and the prospects not getting any better, Captain Hubert helped Tromp aboard and headed for sea. Up went the sails, catching Aruba's famous winds, sending the boat cantering through the water. They rounded the point near Manchebo, ran past Eagle Beach to show the people what they were missing, and angled in even closer to Palm Beach where fingers pointed out at the sleek hull.

"Best advertising there is," Hubert told Tromp.

The photographer thought he might get seasick. Thankfully, his stomach held. Moving his camera, working the lens, trying different angles, he forgot about the motion. A wave tried to ruin the day by wiping out his Nikon, but he rolled to the center just in time.

"Let's go home," called Hubert from the helm. He then asked Tromp to get some shots of the interior.

When he finished the job, Tromp settled in the galley where he put his head down on the table for a rest. Although her sails were taut with wind, *Consuela* wasn't a sprinter. Returning to Oranjestad would take at least an hour.

"Five lashes for sleeping on the job," Hubert said in his booming sailor way.

Opening his eyes, Tromp thought he'd been asleep only minutes until he felt the gentle rock of the boat, indicating it was tied to a dock.

"Sorry," he said to Hubert who was busy securing some equipment.

"Let me wrap up here, then I'll take you back for your car."

Coming up on deck, Tromp saw he'd slept all the way to Varadero Marina, *Consuela*'s home base.

"Hang out by the van," Hubert told him. "I'll be with you in a minute."

Starting down the planks to the restaurant and parking lot beyond, Tromp saw the bartender wiping down the stools in preparation for his lunchtime trade. Tromp thought back to the last fishing tournament winner he had photographed here. He searched for the boat but didn't find it. Then he heard heavy footfalls thumping off to his right. Captain Hubert was running at full speed.

"Get a hacksaw!" he hollered.

A crewman put his hands up to ask why.

"Get a hacksaw!" repeated Hubert.

Curious about what had the man flustered, Tromp reversed direction.

"There's a dead lady cuffed inside Ernesto's boat."

20

Chief Calenda watched the video on Detective Bakker's monitor. It began with bobbing footage along a wooden dock. Someone in shorts and a red shirt sprinted past the camera carrying a hacksaw before a heavier man pounded after him. They both hopped onto a shabby-looking sailboat at the end of the pier and disappeared inside. The camera caught up to them, tilting sideways as the videographer himself made the leap.

The screen turned dark for a second as the iris adjusted to the changing light of the cabin. A short door swung out of the way, revealing a narrow passage into what was the vessel's galley. Ahead came the sounds of men grunting and cursing.

"¡Por dios!"

"She's alive!"

Detective Bakker paused the tape. "The kid must be left handed," he said, pressing the play button.

While still filming the scene of Captain Hubert and his crewman frantically sawing away, Tromp took his cell in hand to dial 911. The camera's autofocus mechanism captured the phone's screen then readjusted to the action farther ahead.

"Forget the ambulance!"

Just then Captain Hubert shifted his bulk to the left. Kathy Barrow was stretched across the floor wearing a sundress with a big flower, her hands bracketed by pink fur and divided by a stout wooden pole, most likely the base of the boat's mast.

The policemen shook their heads at the screen. The sound of the hacksaw ripping at the chain between the cuffs, Hubert's heavy breathing, his crewman offering to help, all played back in Dolby stereo.

"Look there," the chief said pointing to a corner of the frame.

Bakker froze the image. "Soup can," he told his boss. "I found a total of four opened ones."

"She lived on four cans of soup and a bunch of crackers?" asked Calenda.

"Two Peanut M&M wrappers were also found. Hubert's crew might have thrown more stuff away."

"How did she open the cans?"

"They were the newer kind. Pull tops. The passage between the settee on the right and the cooking area on the left is only a few feet wide. There's plenty of room to snake an arm to the shelves, even with the wrists cuffed."

The chain finally parted and Kathy Barrow's arms fell to her sides. Tossing the saw out of the frame, Hubert picked her up and made for the door. The opening was too small for him to go through with her in his arms. A split second of frustration was replaced with quick thinking. Putting his hands under Barrow's armpits, he lifted her through like a child. The camera followed him all the way.

"What a mess," an off-camera crewman said. "It's going to take all day to clean this up."

Tromp turned the camera for a moment, capturing the crewman as he shook his head at the empty cans and debris surrounding his feet. Again, Bakker stopped the tape.

"The person in the cabin, his name is Rico. He told me the big coffee can there on the floor was used as a latrine, but that it spilled. He said there was human waste on the floor."

"Horrible," commented the chief.

"We have the dress from the hospital and her bathing suit. Excrement stains. Filthy."

The policemen had little evidence from the schooner other than Romy Tromp's video, and it contained only seconds of footage from inside the cabin where Kathy Barrow had been found. Tromp rushed outside to film Captain Hubert scrambling off the boat.

"I'm taking her straight to the hospital!" *Consuela*'s master hollered.

The screen went dark.

Rico and two of his mates brought order to the schooner's interior. Its owner, Ernesto, had been off the island for several weeks, and they were charged with keeping an eye on his boat while he was away. Into trash bags they tossed scattered soup cans, empty water bottles, plastic wrappers, and sundry other smelly and disgusting items. Using mops and rags from *Consuela* they cleaned the floor, the galley surfaces, and the entire cabin, a task well underway when the police arrived.

Experienced sailors who worked for a fastidious captain, they thought they were doing the right thing, all the while obliterating potential evidence. They knew if Ernesto came back and saw how they had allowed his boat to be used, friendships would end.

"Can't blame them," Bakker said of the crew.

"Shipshape is the term," the chief put in. "How did Hubert know to go aboard the schooner?"

"He didn't. Ernesto called from Colombia where he was buying lumber and antiques to restore the boat. It was taking longer than he expected, so he called Hubert to ask the favor of checking on her to make sure there were no leaks or other trouble."

"To check on her," Calenda repeated.

Bakker smirked at the double entendre. "Another *Consuela* deckhand, the one who drives the van, confirms Hogan showed interest in the boat. He walked down the dock to examine it. The deckhand says Hogan seemed to know a lot about boats, and in the conversation the deckhand did mention Ernesto not coming back for a week."

"He didn't tell us this when we were there last week," the chief said.

"When we made our visit, it was his day off."

Calenda placed a notecard on his desk. "How long does it take to drive from the old Esso Club to Varadero?" he asked.

Bakker held up a card of his own. "And from Varadero back?"

Separately, they had driven the round trip to test a theory. Exchanging cards, the policemen compared their almost identical times. If Hogan took Barrow to the schooner prior to five-fifteen, he could have made it back to where fisherman Dennis Rosina found him in the fading light of the afternoon.

"Based on his account of the day, it's possible," Bakker concluded.

"And no one saw them at Varadero?" the chief wondered aloud.

"Most of the area near the parking lot is boat storage," Bakker said. "The workers I talked to said the heavy repairs take place about fifty meters beyond the bar so fumes and dust don't blow over the beer. As for the rest of the boats, they go out early and come back at lunchtime or sunset. In between, there's next to nothing going on around the docks."

"Glenn Hogan knows the goings on of a boatyard to which he'd never been?" posed the chief.

Bakker had an answer, one he gave more as a suggestion than a convincing argument. "He and Barrow returned on *Consuela* about this time the day before she went missing."

"Let's talk to her," the chief said, out of patience.

Kathy Barrow opened her eyes in a room too bright to be the schooner's cabin. One by one she tested her fingers. They all worked. Wiggling her toes, she got the same result. She was alive. If she needed confirmation, a wave of aches and tingling pain flowed down from her neck into her hips all the way to her ankle then rebounded out through her shoulders and to those bony knobs on her wrists. A long groan brought the most pleasant distraction.

A Styrofoam cup sat on the table beside her bed, the straw tempting her. Her throat was scratchy dry, like she'd been screaming for her teammates at a swim meet. She leaned over for the cup and it felt as heavy as a gallon jug. She drew delicious cold water into her mouth, holding it there for a second before swallowing. The cool liquid coated her insides.

By the time she emptied the cup a cheerful nurse came in to check on her.

"The lady come awake," the nurse said. "Feeling better?"

Confused was the more accurate word. Kathy smiled and felt her lips crack.

"The Chief of Police himself want to talk to you," the nurse said. "He asked to be called as soon as you open your eyes. Want me to do that or wait a little longer."

"A little longer," Kathy said, barely recognizing her own voice.

After refilling the water, the nurse left.

Late on Monday afternoon was where Kathy's memory ended. In the morning, she awoke on the schooner, watching through the narrow portholes as the darkness outside dissipated. She didn't know when the boat's owner was due, only that it was supposed to be on Monday. Thus, the wait couldn't be that long.

She hadn't opened the portholes because they had been closed when she first came aboard. The owner might notice something like that. She did crack the vent in the forward cabin, thinking it would provide enough air, but with the door closed at the stern, there was no flow. Had she not already handcuffed herself around the mast, she could have changed the situation, but it was too late.

She hadn't remembered to plan for a lack of fresh air because she'd been busy testing her ability to open a soup can with her hands cuffed. She held the can then mimicked the motion of opening the top and pouring the contents into her mouth. Yes, it could be done. The same was true of the water bottles. In a hurry for the last act of the play to begin, she set the cans and bottles near her body, cuffed herself, and gave the metal bracelets a last, serious tug to make sure they were real.

"Owww!" she'd yelped.

Gradually the temperature rose inside the cabin. She started sweating profusely, then she recognized an early symptom of heatstroke, a lack of sweat. Where was the owner? Why hadn't he come back the way *Consuela*'s crewman had said? She struggled with the cuffs up and down the mast, trying to get as low as possible. In the process, she kicked the coffee can, spreading the stench of her urine. In the rising heat, it mixed with the aroma of stale chicken soup and dust. If anything had been in her stomach she would have puked.

Dizzy, retching, and growing scared, Kathy issued a feeble yell for help. The heavy wood of the hull stopped the sound. She berated herself for tossing the key to the cuffs in the ocean along with her room key. She didn't want to be found with either, but she could have left the key to the cuffs nearby, then tossed it out of reach when she heard footfalls on the deck. If she couldn't get to it, she couldn't be blamed for not setting herself free.

At some point in the sweltering afternoon, she passed out. Exactly what happened after that, she didn't know. However, she recollected in great detail the events of Sunday.

Sooner than she expected, the Chief of Police was in her room. She recognized him from the many times he told GNN, "No comment." He didn't come alone. There was another man with him, wearing civilian clothes and almost tall enough to play professional basketball.

"Welcome back," the tall fellow said. "I'm Detective Bakker. This is Chief Calenda."

What do you say to the police when you wake up from what might have been a coma? Kathy wasn't sure so she tried a question.

"Where's Glenn?"

Without missing a beat, Bakker said, "He's not here. You're safe."

These two facts Kathy already knew, but she wasn't supposed to know them, not if she'd been locked away in an old boat by a crazy man. She held the detective's eyes as long as she dared, then shifted her gaze to the chief. Assurance is what she wanted, a solemn oath that the man who brought her to Aruba intent on drowning her was not going to show up for another try.

"The doctor says you'll be feeling better soon," the chief said. "Unfortunately, we must ask you some questions now."

"I want to see him," Kathy said, summoning the anger she felt during those first moments after she escaped from Glenn in the sea.

"Later," the chief told her.

"He's in jail? Tell me you have him in jail."

"You don't have to worry about Mr. Hogan," Bakker said. "Tell us what happened."

Neither of them held a notepad, which led Kathy to believe they were recording what she said. She did her best not to sound rehearsed because that would come across on tape.

"That cretin brought me to Aruba," she began.

"Start from the moment you checked in at the Caribbean

Club," the chief prodded.

As she was instructed, Kathy described how she and Glenn arrived at the hotel in a car rented at the airport. They walked along the beach and had a nice dinner before Glenn went to the blackjack table. He lost some money at the Holiday Inn, but won it back, and more, at the Caribbean Club's casino.

"Did your companion ever mention gambling debts?" the chief asked.

"No. Why would he? It seems like he wins a lot," Kathy replied.

After a glance at Calenda, Bakker went next. "Who arranged for the private cruise?"

"Glenn did, but I agreed after looking at the *Consuela* on-line. The reviews were mostly five stars."

"Go on."

"The cruise was fine, but Glenn was annoyed. He said we should be sailing instead of motoring. There wasn't much wind. How was the boat supposed to move?"

"With the motor," Bakker suggested.

"Yeah, I know, except Glenn didn't like it. That night we ate another expensive dinner and spent more time at the casino where he won again. I don't know how much. He had a big stack of chips. He gave me one worth a hundred dollars, which I lost in the slot machines. He was nasty about it, too. I should've walked away right there. Slots are for suckers, he said. The hotel rewarded him like a winner by upgrading our room to a suite."

"When did you go snorkeling?" asked the chief.

"The next day." Kathy sipped some water then continued. "In the morning, Glenn said he wanted to go back to the place where we went with the *Consuela*. He said he'd rather drive than waste all that time on a boat. He was super nice and talking about it being just us and I felt guilty about losing his hundred bucks. He left the room for a while and came back with masks and snorkels, brand new, still in the plastic. This is a good guy, I thought, spending the money to make the trip special."

"Did you pay for anything?" inquired Bakker.

"My plane ticket," answered Kathy. "I'm not one of those women who expects the man to pay for everything. I offered to pay for half the room, but Glenn said he had frequent flyer miles, no, sorry, credit card points."

"You drove to the other end of the island together. Did you stop anywhere?"

"No. We went on the main road into the town where the refinery is. He made a wrong turn but got us there eventually."

"You weren't worried about it getting dark?" asked the chief.

"I was. I told him the sun goes down quickly near the equator. I also asked him why we didn't park over by the beach. It looked much nicer over there. He gave me a big kiss and said he wanted to be alone with me. Charming isn't he?"

"How long were you in the water?" questioned Bakker.

"Maybe thirty minutes. I don't know. I was having fun. We got out and Glenn wanted to, uh … make out, I guess you'd call it. We were kissing … and …"

Both impassive, Calenda and Bakker stood by as Kathy started to weep. They let it continue offering no comfort or understanding.

"He told me he had a surprise for me," Kathy said, restarting her narrative. "It had been a pretty awesome couple of days so

I was excited. He went to the car and I heard a *pop* like a champagne cork. Sure enough, he came back with a bottle of Moët."

"Was it cold?" interjected Bakker.

"Hardly," Kathy retorted. "And he didn't have any glasses. He said it was like being shipwrecked in paradise and handed me the bottle. Drinking from the bottle? Really? Oh, well, it wasn't like anyone was watching. I took a big gulp and handed it back to him."

"Did he take a drink?"

"I guess. I wasn't paying attention. I wanted to find out about the surprise. Seriously, I believed he was making a play for me. Maybe he wanted to get engaged or something."

Bakker took hold of the point. "Were you ready for that kind of commitment?"

Thinking, waiting, giving herself a chance to consider how she would have reacted had everything she said to this point been true, Kathy finally said, "No. I want to go back to school and finish my degree."

"You wouldn't be tempted by such a 'charmer' as you called him, who brings champagne to the beach?"

"I guess I would be tempted," she admitted.

"Tell us about the surprise."

She cried again, genuinely because she was thinking about those last several minutes in the fetid heat of the schooner before she passed out. The despair at having made it this far only to commit accidental suicide had been overwhelming.

"We left the beach, then he turned off the main road, and I asked him where we were going. The surprise, the surprise. Don't ruin the surprise. He kept saying it and I giggled. That champagne was getting to me."

The chief took a turn. "Where did you go?"

"We took some smaller roads I thought I remembered from the drive to the *Consuela*'s dock. *Voilà!* The surprise. We pull into the marina there, and he says he's got another boat lined up for a sunset cruise with dinner. I was furious!"

"Why were you furious?"

"Take your girlfriend snorkeling and then tell her the next stop is a sunset cruise with dinner," growled Kathy.

"Did you tell him you were angry?"

"Of course not! I told him I wasn't dressed, needed to do my hair, wanted to freshen up. He said this was part of the shipwreck adventure surprise or something silly like that. We're pirates! Kid's stuff."

Bakker jumped in with, "Kid's stuff from the charmer."

"I should have seen it coming, right? A faker. A guy who pretended to be like some stud in a movie, when in reality he was just an asshole. I hope he's rotting in jail right now."

"Did you have an argument?"

"Not really. I tried to beg off but he told me to come check out the boat. It's cool, just have a look he said, everyone's barefoot, and nobody cares how you're dressed. Go with the flow."

"And you did?"

"I did, but as we got out of the car I felt kind of woozy. My legs were wobbly. I didn't think I drank that much champagne, and even if I did, it wasn't like I'd had a bottle of Jack Daniel's or something. Then I stumbled along the dock. He put his arm around me and said not to embarrass him on the boat."

"What time was this?"

"I don't know," Kathy replied.

"Were there other people on the pier?"

"Not that I remember."

"Then what?"

"I knew something was wrong. I was having trouble walking and couldn't speak. My lips were like rubber. Then I woke up soaking wet."

"Wet?" asked Bakker.

"Yes. He must have tossed water on my face to bring me back. I was handcuffed with those pink furry things of his. He tried to put them on me in the hotel, but I wouldn't go for it. Another warning sign, eh?"

"Where were you?"

"On a boat is all I can tell you. It was kind of like the *Consuela* but old and musty and dirty. I thought about the champagne and that there's no way I was drunk enough to pass out. Then I remembered Glenn takes Valium for a bad back. He also took an Ambien the first night we were in the hotel. I was trying to remember what Margie, the pharmacist I work with, said about those drugs, if they could, you know, knock you out. Then I heard some noise and in walked Glenn. He was laughing at me."

"Laughing?"

"Yeah, laughing like he'd been told the funniest joke of his life. I begged him to let me go, to tell me why he had me cuffed. Pirates and wenches, he said. I was crying and begging and he slapped me. I couldn't believe what was happening."

The chief spoke again. "Did he give you any idea why he was doing this?"

"He said to keep my mouth shut, that some men were coming for me. I asked him who, what was this all about, what did I do to deserve it. He slapped me again and put cans of soup by my feet and an empty coffee can and some other stuff to eat until these men showed up. He was walking out the door and I was screaming. He came back, slapped me hard and said he had someone waiting outside and if I didn't shut up, they'd come in and rape me."

"Did you see another person?" This question from Bakker.

"Not that night. The next day I saw people walking past the boat, just their legs as they passed by the portholes."

"Did you call out for help?"

"Plenty of times but not until what had to be a few days later. I'm not sure when it was."

The chief said, "But there was a man out there who would harm you."

"It was getting to the point where I didn't care. It was so hot in that cabin and with my hands cuffed I struggled to get the soup cans open. I spilled more than I ate. The water was running low, too."

Those things Kathy had done, ruining her dress and creating that awful mess.

"What's the last thing you remember?" was Bakker's final question.

"Thinking what a fool I'd been to trust a guy like Glenn."

21

Of the many lies Kathy told Tuesday afternoon, her last statement had been true. She'd been stupid to believe Glenn was nothing more than an abusive divorcé. Worse, she let her own silly ambitions blind her to the warning signs. It wasn't the obvious things such as the restraining order. It was the subtle ones. A trip to Aruba for a woman he had been dating only three months. Pay your own airfare to keep it friendly, but enticed by a free hotel room thanks to his credit card points. Frisky sex with handcuffs and the video camera aimed at the bed. He hadn't been pushy about either one, but there they were, serving his purposes without her knowing. The last straw should have been going in the water far away from everyone else, behind an old building, across rocks and coral less inviting than a stretch of broken glass. She did that one to herself. Any decent boyfriend would have said, "Come on, the sand is beautiful over there." He opened the door to her demise by letting her set it all up for him. And she walked right in.

She also walked out. Maybe it was an angel looking over her shoulder or the devil inside. Perhaps a combination of both showed her the way. She wanted to believe so because lying in a hospital bed not knowing whether or not the cops accepted her story, Kathy wondered if she'd done the right thing.

Late Sunday afternoon, bored with the novel she'd been reading to pass the time, and out of M&M's, she left her spot on the beach and strolled to the Caribbean Club. On her arm hung the red and white Little Switzerland bag. She was still wearing the dark dress she bought at the Bamboo Bazaar the day she escaped from Glenn. The flowered dress, her bathing suit, and the chef's whites were inside the bag with the rest of the things she'd need, some of which had been supplied by stores at the mall that morning.

Her first idea was to change in the bathroom, putting on the chef's whites, but seeing a security guard and too many hotel employees in the lobby frightened her. If she were called out as not belonging to the staff, the guard was there to haul her in. She almost gave up. More fear pushed her onward, the fear that she couldn't explain a week away with anything better than a story about escaping from a bastard who tried to drown her and then hiding out for some silly reason until finally breaking down and coming forward.

No one was paying attention to her as she ambled through the lobby with her hat cocked to the side and sunglasses perched on her nose. Most of the women were similarly attired. Kathy thought of herself as one of them, another tourist enjoying a vacation in the sun. Directly to the elevator she went, stepped inside, and pushed fourteen. The doors closed.

Stepping off on the top floor, she saw the clock above a bench indicated it was quarter past five. Knowing from news reports that Glenn was confined to the suite they had shared, food had to be delivered via room service. In the times they'd eaten together, it had always been before seven. Again she needed a place to wait.

First, she walked the length of the hall until she discovered the service elevator. It was on the inland side of the building tucked into an alcove with an icemaker. Unwilling to miss her one chance to intercept Glenn's dinner, she sat down on the floor.

Nothing transpired for so long that Kathy worried she was in the wrong place. Maybe the service elevator was broken and they were using the regular one. She hurried down the hall but found no activity on that end either. Perhaps guests were napping or getting ready for dinner. She returned to the alcove to hide and wait.

Just before six she took the wine glass from her Little Switzerland bag and the screw-top, half-bottle of red. She filled the glass, recapped the bottle, and put it away. Hands a little shaky, she listened momentarily for anyone coming before taking out the wad of plastic wrap containing the crushed Ambien and Valium. The powder dissolved into the wine after a stir with her finger.

A hum preceded a puff of air from the service elevator doors. Kathy stuffed the Little Switzerland bag and its contents under the icemaker, making sure it was out of sight. Next, she carried the glass of wine into the hallway and stood with her back to the first suite. When the room service waitress came out of the alcove, Kathy took a step like someone just leaving her room. Courteously, she allowed the waitress to pass with her cart, which slowed and then stopped next to the door at 1406.

"Excuse me," Kathy called, louder than she intended. "Excuse me!"

The waitress turned and Kathy quick-stepped up to her, looking over her shades, smiling a big mouthful of teeth. In one hand she clutched the wine glass behind her back; her other hand pinched her earlobe.

"I just dropped an earring," she said with the Texas drawl on full blast. "Can you help me find it, please? My husband will be powerfully angry if I lose it."

The waitress said, "What does it look like?"

Kathy lowered her hand from her ear and opened it to reveal a small gold hoop, one half of the pair she bought at the Paseo Herencia Mall earlier in the day. "It fell right around there, by the door," she said, pointing down the hall.

As soon as the waitress moved forward, Kathy set the glass of wine onto the cart. Then she got down on her knees to aid the search for the earring.

"Are you sure it was in this area?" the waitress asked.

"Oh, here it is!" Kathy said popping up and pushing back her sunglasses. "Thank you so much. Really. Thank you."

"De nada," the waitress said and knocked on Glenn's door.

Just before the cart wheeled into the room, Kathy looked back over her shoulder and caught a glimpse of Glenn's profile. Beyond him, at the end of the hall, she also saw the doorway to the stairwell close.

Thinking somebody might have seen her, Kathy lost her nerve. She bolted to the elevator and repeatedly pressed the down button. She sat on the bench below the clock, jumped up, pushed the button again.

"Stop it," she chastised herself in a brutal whisper. "Stop it."

No one saw you and if they did, what could they tell the police? There was a woman in sunglasses. Wearing a dark, blowsy outfit and a hat. So what?

Regaining control, she went back to the alcove by the service elevator and sat down, pulling the Little Switzerland bag into her lap. The smell of Glenn's porterhouse lingered in the space, knotting her stomach. *Almost there,* she reminded herself, *and you can have a steak of your own.* She thought about the glass of wine, which hadn't been part of his order. Would he notice it and suspect something? Doubtful. Glenn liked free things.

"Money for nothing," he said to her at the casino when he handed over the single hundred-dollar chip.

She had taken it as a dig. Maybe it was his philosophy of life.

To her surprise, the service elevator wasn't used for as long as Kathy remained there, which had to have been more than an hour. People walked through the halls, talking about where they were going for the night. Figuring plenty of time had passed for the drugs to take effect, she took out her room key and went to Glenn's door.

Ambien was a powerful sleep aid and when mixed with Valium and alcohol, the combination was enough to subdue a bull, which is why Kathy didn't bother to knock before entering. Nonetheless, she used caution stepping into the living room of the suite. Once inside, she padded to the bedroom with only a glance at the bathroom on the way. That huge shower! Oh, what she wouldn't give to turn on all the jets and just soak under a waterfall of near-boiling goodness!

Later.

On the bed, fully dressed and with the remote on his stomach, Glenn snored like a hibernating bear. Kathy set down her bag without caring about how much noise it made. No reaction. She tapped the bed near him. No reaction. Using a tissue from the box on the nightstand, she dared to lift the remote from atop his shirt. No reaction.

It was time to change.

Back in the living room she stepped out of her clothes, pulled on her bathing suit and topped it with her flowered dress. She left everything positioned in the smallest space possible so nothing would be forgotten when she departed, especially the earrings.

For the last time, she waited.

Pushing the buttons on the remote with a tissue-wrapped index finger, she watched a movie, then part of the early news at ten-thirty. When GNN's top-of-the-hour update came on at eleven, she saw nothing about herself.

"Time to make a headline," she announced and changed the channel to Glenn's favorite sports network.

After spreading the curtains, Kathy gathered a handful of her sundress and kept it between her and the handle on the sliding door to the balcony. She opened the door, turned to the bed, and called Glenn's name.

He responded with a snore.

Shaking his shoulder got him to mumble and roll over.

"Come on, Glenn. Let's get in the water," she said with her lips to his ear.

His eyelids creaked a few millimeters.

"Give me one of those snorkels."

"What? Uh ... yeah ..."

"Thanks, Glenn. Thanks for bringing me to Aruba."

"Hey, no problem," he said, groggy, rubbing his face.

"You're such a great guy. Let's take a look at those fish."

His eyes were strangely focused as he sat up and stared across the room. He fixated on the flower printed on her dress.

Kathy lifted it over her head, revealing her one-piece bathing suit. "Let's get in the water, Glenn," she cooed, turning slowly, poking her butt at him.

On his feet, he lumbered forward. Something distracted him. His shoes. After yanking them off with clumsy effort, he massaged his toes in the plush carpeting.

"It's going to get dark soon," Kathy said. "The sun goes down quickly near the equator."

"Let's check out those fish," he said so close she felt spittle strike her skin.

"Have you ever been snorkeling before?" she teased.

"Lots of times," Glenn slurred, reaching for her in slow motion.

"It's like being weightless when you're floating on top of the water."

Like a robot whose battery went dead, he stopped a foot from her.

Kathy taunted him, "You sure you know how to swim?"

He squinted briefly then sprung at her, grabbing her shoulder just as he did in the water. She felt the power of his fingers digging in, and bent down before slipping away. Against the edge of the sliding door, she couldn't go any farther. His second attempt put both hands on her shoulders. Backing into him with all her strength, she felt the pressure of his weight as he leaned forward to balance against her.

Had the drugs not sapped his strength, Glenn might have crushed Kathy into a pile of bones on the balcony. He was a strong man, eighty pounds heavier than her and a regular at the gym, but at the moment he was polluted with a double dose of sleep aid and muscle relaxant.

Kathy reached for the balcony railing. It was too far. Practically carrying Glenn on her back, she inched sideways until her hand felt metal. Pulling hard, she got close enough. Then, with a single snap of her shoulders and a shove of her ass, she was free. Spinning, she now stood face to face with Glenn who was backpedaling toward the edge as if he had a mile of beach behind him.

"You lousy bitch," he accused her. As he crashed into the railing, his head fell back with the momentum of his body.

The moment he teetered stuck in her mind as she took a sip of water from the hospital's Styrofoam cup. By the expression on his face he never knew what was happening. He was trying to kill her again. Even as his stocking feet slipped on the tiled balcony and he tumbled into space, he reached out to take her with him.

Kathy wasted no time looking down from the balcony. Snatching the now-empty wine glass from the cart, she changed back into the dark dress, stuffed the sundress into the Little Switzerland bag, and left the room pausing only a second to make sure nothing had been left behind. Hat and sunglasses in place, she headed straight to the elevator.

Descending to the lobby there was a single stop, on the ninth floor. A boy, absorbed in a hand-held video game, got in with Kathy. When the doors opened on the lobby, he bumped into her on the way out.

"Argh!" he complained. "Now I have to start over."

"Too bad," Kathy said under her breath.

On the boulevard fronting the hotels she walked to the Paseo Herencia Mall. There she entered the ladies' room and put the chef's whites on over her bathing suit. In the handicapped stall, she ripped the black dress to pieces and disposed of the strips of fabric in the bathroom's trashcan. When Kathy returned to the plaza, she appeared to be an exhausted kitchen employee in sunglasses. Her hair was a tangled mess, she wore no makeup, and the whites were splotched with all the food groups. A crowd of people exited the movie theater, giving her cover to move back across the boulevard to the bus stop.

Had she missed the last bus? It took her twenty minutes to find out, during which no one, tourist or local, gave her a second look. She stood to the side, tired, bored, anxious to get home after a long day at work. Once on the bus, she took a seat near the back, leaned her head against the window and pretended to sleep, keeping the Little Switzerland bag on her lap.

The bus schedule she checked earlier in the day showed the route she'd chosen went the length of the island, all the way to San Nicolaas. She got off halfway, at the airport, by herself.

The walk to Varadero took another hour because she had things to lose. The straw hat she cast into the weeds. Along the road, she ripped apart the chef's jacket. A tattered sleeve fell here, a torn panel there, rags for anyone who cared to look. With the pants she did the same, but not until she was at the marina beside the restaurant's dumpster. In they went, after a drag through the dirt and oil by one of the engines that sat with some other junk. Her new earrings went into the water, two quick plops in opposite directions. After unlocking the handcuffs, she flicked the key and the one to Suite 1406 in the same direction as the earrings.

At last she was aboard the schooner, in her swimsuit, which suffered ruptures of its own courtesy of the struggle with Glenn. Fortunately, the flowered sundress was intact. A trophy it was going to be, something she intended to wear as a poignant reminder of the stunt she'd pulled. If she got away with it.

The final task was to hide what remained of Glenn's casino winnings. Originally, she was going to bury the bills under a rock, but instead decided to donate them to the schooner's rehabilitation fund. She rolled the cash into a tight wad and stuffed it into an empty can, then tucked it in with all the others in one of the stern cabins. Eventually the schooner's owner would find it, and what would he say? *I wondered where I left that money!*

Securing the cuffs, locking herself to the base of the mast, Kathy thought it was all worth it. Then the schooner's owner failed to show up. It started to get hot. She freaked out. She wished she'd married that boy who took her to the senior prom and never looked back at the way her father treated her.

She passed out thinking that Glenn, even dead, would have the last laugh after all. And yet, she survived. She was now in the hospital with an IV replenishing her fluids and had given the cops a story that made enough sense to be believed.

Whatever the police decided to do with her, Kathy knew she'd done the right thing.

Tromp got his first exclusive from Chief Calenda on Tuesday night. In itself this was an incredible achievement. Clive

Mitchell had been right; Tromp earned the chief's confidence by providing him with the videotape he'd taken of Kathy Barrow's discovery before he released it to GNN. Had that been where it ended, he would've celebrated climbing another rung of the ladder and been content to do some bragging to his pals. But there was more. After Tromp interviewed the chief, he asked an off-the-record question.

Tromp had a specific reason for posing this question, one related to the photo he took of what turned out to be Glenn Hogan's last meal. In the dim hallway, there was Hogan's face protruding from the doorway, the food cart about to be pushed in, and the waitress standing there to do her job. In the distance walked another woman, frozen in mid-stride, her face partly turned as if she had just glanced over her shoulder. Tromp used all his tricks to enhance the image but the brightness of the objects in the foreground and the pale light of the hall foiled his efforts. Another problem was the angle of the face, about a quarter visible, maybe less, not enough to get a proper read on the eye and nose.

When he took the picture, he'd been concentrating on the room service cart going in to Glenn Hogan's room. He didn't know someone else was in the frame until he studied the photo closely before sending it off to his editor at *Diario*. Was it Kathy Barrow? Tromp thought so, but couldn't produce a clear rendition to prove it.

Thus, he asked the chief appropriate questions on camera and got logical answers spoken by a man who was no fool. Sleeping pills and muscle relaxants had been found in Hogan's room. They were legal, but he may have overdosed or used them in a dangerous combination. The coroner's toxicology report would ultimately confirm this one way or the other. Yes, the coroner and other doctors have asserted that sleepwalking is a potential side effect of these drugs. As for Hogan's gambling debts, the chief confirmed he had spoken about them with the FBI and said they were a potential motive for killing Kathy Barrow to collect an insurance payment. Agent Griffith was going to contact him when his investigation in the United States showed more progress. At any rate, the same debt may have been a reason for Mr. Hogan to commit suicide. Or, under the influence of the drugs, he might have fallen accidentally to his death. It is possible that none of these scenarios may ever be proved conclusively.

What about Kathy Barrow's claim that she had been held captive in a plot to be sold to human traffickers? Again, the chief referred to the evidence, that she had been found in a shocking condition, suffering from heat exhaustion and dehydration. She had not stated specifically that she was going to be sold in this manner and the chief insisted on sticking to the facts. Barrow said that some men were supposed to come for her. She knew nothing more about them or even if they existed. At this point, Tromp speculated that Hogan might have planned to return to find her body, take it to sea, and make a claim. The chief refused to comment on speculation. He did say that Ms. Barrow would be recovering at a private residence to protect her from the media until such time as she wanted to speak in public.

The camera off and in his bag, Tromp asked his final question, "Do you think that's what happened, Chief? That Hogan cuffed her in that boat and was going to sell her off or leave her for dead, or was it something else?"

"It doesn't matter what I believe, Romy," the chief answered. "The only thing that matters, is what I can prove."

22

"Clive Mitchell! It's a pleasure to have you joining us in the studio."

Judge Nadine finished gushing over Mitchell then turned her trademark scowl directly toward the camera.

"Tonight we have a shocking, absolutely shocking, conclusion to the disappearance of Kathy Barrow. Clive, bring us up to date."

"Your honor, on Monday I left the island thinking this story was going to be another sad entry into the log of human tragedy, but we have good news to report, a tale of a twisted man and of a woman who never lost hope. Let's go to our correspondent for the latest."

"This is Romy Tromp reporting live from Aruba. Clive, you will remember we were together just last week at the Varadero Marina. Well, not fifty meters from where we stood was a battered old schooner, ignored by everyone because only the owner believed she was worthy of restoration. It was in that boat that Kathy Barrow nearly met her fate. Through good fortune and with the help of local sailors, she's alive to tell her story. Here's my interview with her, completed just an hour ago."

ACKNOWLEDGMENTS

The events of 2011 introduced me to many first-rate media professionals. I am grateful to have spent time with them, however brief, learning about their lives in front of and behind the camera. In this regard, I thank Martin Savidge, Don Wood, Jeff Rossen, Jonathan Mossek, Bruce Bernstein, Matt Gutman, Josh Weiner, Jerry Simonson, and Tristan Smith. Also, special thanks to my editor, Susan, and to my wife, Heather, who read the first draft so wide-eyed that I knew I'd done good. And lastly, Mr. Vernon Fletcher is not to be forgotten for his wary countenance.

ABOUT THE AUTHOR

Daniel Putkowski, a graduate of New York University's Tisch School of the Arts, divides his time between Aruba and Philadelphia. Best known for his 2008 bestseller, *An Island Away,* he blogs regularly about travel, food, and the writing life at *The Bent Page. Dark Currents* is his fifth novel.

DanielPutkowski.com

facebook.com/DanielPutkowski

@dputkowski

Read all of Daniel Putkowski's novels on your
Kindle, iPhone, Android, iPad, Mac, & PC

DOWNLOAD FREE APPS AT **amazon**.com
and you're done.